I0671203

JAY TRIPP

The Bow II: Forbidden Romance

Print & Publishing Services
FROM MANUSCRIPT TO PUBLICATION

My Brother, Rev. Donovan K. Maxwell, Jr.

I never anticipated how losing you would create such a void.

I weaved some of your experiences in this story.
You have been immortalized...
Blu Phi
1990 - 2020

Sooner or later, we must all accept the fact that in a relationship, the only person you are dealing with is yourself. Your partner does nothing more than reveal your stuff to you. Your fear! Your anger! Your pattern! Your craziness! As long as you insist on pointing the finger out there, at them, you will continue to miss out on the divine opportunity to clear your stuff.

— Iyanla Vanzant

Preface

"Baby, I've missed you so much. How was your drive?"

"It was okay. Tyler and I switched it up. It was long, but we made it. I'm just tired," I replied.

"Awe, I wish I was there to give you a massage. You deserve one," Orlando said.

"Yeah," I said looking at Tyler who sat looking straight ahead because he knew was about to come. Somehow, I could see a smile of satisfaction on his face. He was enjoying this.

"What's wrong?" Orlando asked.

"Nothing is wrong. I told you I am tired," I lied. Actually I was tired, but I dreaded having to tell Orlando the truth.

"Hmm…nah, it seems like there is something else wrong," Orlando said.

stretched

"I'm good. It's just been a long and eventful day," I said as I kicked out my legs with a little stretching sound.

"Okay, well tell me about it."

"There is nothing to tell," I replied.

Why was I being so evasive? Of course there was something to tell. A whole lot to tell. First, Tyler is gay just as Orlando predicted. Also like he predicted, he pursued me right afterwards. I needed to quit playing and tell Orlando the truth.

"You know I do this for a living right? I can hear it in your voice," he said.

He was right. I couldn't fool him and I shouldn't have wanted to fool him either. Orlando hadn't given me any reason to believe he deserved to be lied to. I won't lie to him so here goes...

"Okay, you are right Orlando. I really don't know how to tell you this. I guess I should just say it. You were right about Tyler. He came out to me, before our last date. I just didn't tell you about it. I considered it confidential. However, last night, he confessed his love for me and well, I mean... you know how I feel about him. I think I want to explore things with Tyler." The line was quiet.

"So, you are telling me...what exactly?" Orlando replied.

I see he is not going to make this easy for me. I should've known a damn therapist would respond that way. I looked out the window at the tree tops skirting by as we drove. I wanted to be one of them—stoic and not having to deal with the conversation at hand.

"I'm saying...in order for me to explore things with Tyler, I will have to cut things off with you," I said.

"You know something...this is my own fault. I knew you and that boy had something going on subconsciously, and like a fool, I still pursued you. But, let me correct you on something. I didn't know a damn thing about you wanting to be with Tyler. Yeah, I may have had my opinion about it, but you tried to be so fucking coy about it. It's all good though. You guys should enjoy your lives together," Orlando said.

"Orlando, don't be upset. You were right, and I should have listened to you," I replied.

"I'm good," he responded. His tone became nonchalant. I could tell he was trying to be cool about it.

"No you are not. You are doing that same shit you did yesterday, shutting down and stuff," I said, trying to keep my voice at a low level. Tyler looked over at me. He knew things were exploding.

"I mean, at this point sir, you don't owe me any explanations, and I don't owe you any either. You have stated what you want. He's there with you now, so go get what it is that you want. Problem solved!"

"Can you be an adult about this, please?" I asked.

"What's with you? Adults get fucking hurt and pissed about shit. They get mad, they curse, they scream, they honk fucking horns in traffic. That's all adult shit. So stop telling me to be an adult. None of that has shit to do with the fact that you have led me on. But like I said, it's my fault. I should have known better than to let my guard down like this anyway after four fucking days. Yeah, it's my fault." I heard things slamming in the background. He was clearly upset. I didn't know if he was at his office, or home, or what.

"I don't want you to think that I am blaming you for all of this nor do I want you to pretend like you don't have feelings about it all. I want us to be able to remain friends if that's possible," I said.

"Friends? Hell no! I can't be your friend. Not after this. Not after I started developing feelings for you. No. As a matter of fact, we should end it here," he said.

"So, what about the internship?" I asked.

"Consider that offer rescinded. Do you honestly think that

we can work with each other after this? You are tripping if you think that."

"Okay, well I won't press that any further. I mean, you have every right to change your mind on that," I said.

"You damn right I do. Look, I got to go. It was nice knowing you the short period I have known you. You can move forward with Tyler. I hope you guys have a nice life." Wow, Orlando is brutal when he has been hurt. That's a typical scorpion.

"I'm sorry, Orlando. I hope that one day we can be friends," I replied.

"Yeah don't wait for that. Talk to you later sometime." The call ended. I genuinely felt bad. Orlando is such a great guy. I feel like I have hurt him for no good reason. But I love Tyler and Tyler is who I want. I just hoped that I was making the best decision. Orlando is so handsome, so cultured, so wise and such a nurturer. Tyler can be all of those things too, but I am running a risk with him because he was DL and in my opinion, he still is to some degree. Will I be able to have the type of relationship with Tyler that I probably could have with Orlando? Only time will tell. I dare not share those thoughts with him as he looked over to me and grabbed my hand.

"You okay, love?" He asked.

Acknowledgement

Simply, thank you to fans of *The Bow*.
  Your love for Brandon keeps him alive.

Part One: There's A Stranger in my House

I'm not sure who you are,
Don't see your shadow around when you walk.
You leave with no kisses, goodbye with no words
If these walls could talk they would have nothing to
tell.

One

Chapter 1

~ ∽੭੦੦੦∾ ~

Brandon: 5 Years After the Storm…

C ars in Atlanta have turtle legs for tires. Even after 5 years, I still could not get used to Atlanta's God-awful traffic. It's for the birds. I would wake up about 6am every morning, put in 30 mins of gym, shower, grab my breakfast to go, and head to the office. I really didn't think I would be in a news room starting out. The documentary Tyler and I did had me thinking of other things, but life happens. "Gooooooo! Damn, don't you see the light is green. Drivvvvveeee!" I tapped incessantly on the horn, almost to the point of throwing up my finger. These people can't drive worth a shit. I was just trying to get to the station so I can prep for the noonday broadcast. I had field assignments to work on.

My phone began to buzz in my lap. I pressed the phone button on the steering wheel.

"This is Brandon."

"Honey, you left your breakfast on the table," Tyler said. He sounded bright-eyed and bushy-tailed. It seemed he was knocked out sleep when I left.

"Shit! Okay, love, thank you. Umm, just put it back in the fridge. I'll just have to wing it this morning. I don't have time to turn back," I said.

"Okay, will do."

"What are you doing up so early by the way? You don't normally hop up right after I leave."

"I have some errands to run before I go to work," Tyler replied. He worked at CNN. He scored big to be able to land such a great job. He was right where he desired to be, trying to be a baby Don Lemon. I asked him had he had the chance to run into Don Lemon. He said no, but he's waiting on the day. He was a field correspondent, like I was. I was working the local TV station in Atlanta. He got to run to national political stories while I had to run to the gas station that the latest victim was robbed at. Such a joy. Blah. He stayed on the road a lot too. That worked for me at first because although I loved Tyler so much, sometimes I just didn't want to be bothered with, and I'd rather be left alone. With him away, I could get some me-time in. Be careful what you ask for though. Eventually, it got to the point where the away time had become more frequent than I cared for and I was really starting to miss having him around.

"Oh okay. Have a great day today. I love you," he said.

"I love you too," he said as he hung up the phone in a rush.

I wondered what type of errand was he running off too. At any rate, I figured I'd better stop by Chick-fil-A and grab a chicken biscuit or something before I got to work. I expected the line to be as long as the Mississippi when I got there. They always seemed to get it moving fast though. Actually, I would usually just order on the app and walk inside and pick it up from the counter. That was always quicker anyway. I would order the egg white grill. That's a good sandwich. Then, I like to put a shitload of grape jelly on it and order a side of hash browns with a very large lite lemonade. I wasn't much of a coffee drinker. By the time I made it to the Chick-fil-A on Peachtree Road, the traffic was maddening. It was a miracle I was able to get in there. The inside was packed as expected.

Chick-fil-A is the perfect place to people watch especially in midtown Atlanta. I love to people watch. My inquisitive mind goes places when I see everyday people in their routine. You see business people, hospital workers, truck drivers, just all types of people. Me being so introspective, I'd often sit and wonder what their day was going to be like for them. Would they laugh that day? Would they be frustrated? Or, I'd wonder to myself, 'Is he an executive, or perhaps maybe she is the director of HR at her job.' That's the journalist in me—nosy as hell. We are not at all nosy. We just want to get to the truth of things, that's all. Chick-fil-A was taking a while that day. It happens. They are not always on point, but they usually are so on point, I didn't mind the few times that they weren't.

I scrolled through my phone at the headlines. 'President Trump Expected to be Impeached in a Landslide House Vote Today' is what the first headline read. I was happy to see that. After 3 years of his chaos, it was about time he was held accountable for something. That came just in time for the presidential election that was coming the next year. These were the type of stories Tyler followed. I'm not a political buff like he is, but I wouldn't have minded covering stories that actually mattered to me the way he was able to. I continued to read articles as I stood in the background and waited for my food.

"My, my, my, well look at what the Chick-fil-A cow drug in," I heard this sultry voice say behind me. I turned around and to my surprise it was Orlando. I hadn't seen or spoken to him since our heated phone conversation. I was actually shocked to see him.

"Oh, hey stranger. How are you?" I said trying to sound inviting but not too much. I pretended to focus more on the pick-up area for my food to arrive as he started to talk.

"I'm well. What are you doing here? Wow you have grown!" He looked me up and down and focused dead on my lower half. I'm sure by grown he meant, my chest was big, biceps bulging and this ass was fatter. The gym was to blame for this body that Orlando was taking in with his eyes.

"I'm just grabbing some breakfast before work. I'm running a little late." Orlando was still fine as ever. He had grown his hair out some. His skin was glowing. Shit, is he a God? He had to be one of those Greek Mythology motherfuckers like Adonis or someone. I still don't understand how one man can pack so much handsomeness in one body.

"Yeah, I better get my ass on out of here before I get into trouble," I thought to myself. Clearly I was still attracted to him in more ways than one. I thought I'd be able to escape all of his goodness if I could keep the conversation short. I'd find out later how stupid I was to believe that.

"Well don't be late sir. You know that's not cute. We must catch up. Let's do dinner soon." He hands me his card. It was his therapy practice card with a nice photo of him. "Hit me up, okay?" He said as he turned his head to the sound of, "McIntyre! Order ready, McIntyre."

"Ok, yeah it's good to see you."

"I concur, text me later, okay."

"Alright, I will," I said as I watched his ass walk away. He is so sexy. Had I just lied or was I really planning on texting him? We didn't exactly end on good terms. I mean…the high-yellow bastard refused to give me my intern and the names he called me, oh my. Perhaps that was all water under the bridge, but the last thing I needed was an old flame coming back into my world when I was already feeling lonely. I put his card away and inched up closer to the counter as my name was being called next. I saw the same look of emptiness on several faces as they too stood and waited for their routine breakfast.

Even though I was leaving, my people watching continued. I wondered as I left towards the door with an "excuse me" me here and a "coming through" there, were they headed off to an unfulfilling job for the next 8 hours like I was too. And I wondered did they have someone warm in their beds every night like I didn't.

* * *

"We are live right outside of the Quick Trip on Chamblee-Tucker Rd. where a young lady was carjacked in broad daylight. Don't go anywhere, details to come."

"And that'll do it. Good segment," Jamie said.

"It's too hot out here for this shit. I'm so glad it's Friday," I said.

"I know Brandon, but somebody has to work these stories. Everybody starts this way," he said.

"I guess. I just wish we could go one day without somebody getting robbed, shot or killed out here. I honestly would rather be downtown covering the Mayor," I said. I walked away towards the vehicle and loaded up the equipment. I could hear the twisting of gravel underneath a pair of Vans right behind me.

"Well, you should put that bug in someone's ear about what you want to do. I mean, hell, it beats sitting out here complaining about things." I pretended for a moment like I did not hear him. My head was stuck in the trunk. But, even though I heard him, I guess Jamie had a point. I couldn't pretend like he was not right. I lifted my head and looked at him for a moment as if I didn't understand what he meant.

"So you like being out here capturing these dull, repetitive stories?" I asked him.

"I mean…it puts food on the table. I'm not picky. I can tell you want to have an impact like your documentary did. But I am a camera man. I just take shots."

"You can have an impact as a camera man," I said.

"How so?"

"You can elect to work on other projects. Be a storm chaser or some shit."

"I'm not about to go chasing no fucking storms. Not all white people chase storms sir," he retorted.

We both laughed. Jamie had been my camera guy for a few

months now. He started with us fresh out of school. Dude is talented as hell. Somehow, he and I clicked well. He was easy to talk to and for his age, since he's a number of years younger than me, he seemed to be rather wise sometimes. He was about my height with nice milky smooth skin. All of his hair was ginger, even his beard which he seemed to always keep trimmed so neatly. He was quite a catch. We have a long-standing relationship, but we've only recently begun to really get to know each other. I'm so used to shelling up like a turtle around new people, especially other guys, and especially if I don't know if they are gay or not.

It's a weird conundrum how that is for me. I'm sure other gays can relate to that actually. The way my childhood went with struggling to be okay with being gay, I never learned how to adapt to straight guys in any type of way. I always saw them as intimidating or I'd become very attracted to their masculinity. I guess you can say that followed me to adulthood. As much time as Jamie and I spent together, I had to be comfortable with him. I eventually got there, but sometimes I would feel like there was more to him that I didn't know. He knew I was gay, but I didn't know much about what he desired. I'd never seen or heard him talk about a girlfriend much or maybe he did and I wasn't paying attention. I was so busy hating my job most times, I didn't have time to focus on that anyway. Eventually, I did find out about his girlfriend or lack thereof I should say.

"I am glad this will be the last story for the day though," I said.

"So let me ask you something. If you wanted to continue to do something that was similar to *The Bow* documentary, then why not do that? I mean, filming a documentary doesn't take a whole lot of resources. You just need a couple of cameras and a good crew, maybe even just one camera man," Jamie suggested with a smile. It seemed more like an offer.

"I don't have the money for that. I don't know if I could do that, and if I did. I would want to talk about sex education among my community, the LGBTQ community."

"Doesn't your boyfriend work for CNN? He can help you finance the project and you are looking at a pretty good camera man. I'd be willing to help you film this thing, man," Jamie said as he walked to his side of the car.

Jamie was always so thoughtful with his suggestions and solutions. I closed the trunk and got into the car as well.

"I don't know. I haven't thought to ask Tyler for help. I know that he would be willing to help finance it."

"Good, then you should go ask him and get back to me with what he says. I'm ready when you are. I'm just tired of hearing you complain about working these stories out here. I can tell that your heart is elsewhere. I saw *The Bow After the Storm* and it was pretty damn good for you guys having been college kids at the time. Now, you have a few of years of professional interviewing experience. You can do this," he said.

"Thank you, Jamie. You are right. I don't know how I've allowed myself to get in a slump like this. I've lost track of my ambition and I plan to change that."

"Great, keep me posted." We were almost back at the station and my thoughts were on doing another documentary. I thought about how I was to do such a thing and would it be a conflict with the station. I felt the excitement of the possibility of finally being able to of focus on something other than Tyler.

I didn't even realize that I was in a slump. I mean I did know that I felt down a lot. I can't say that I was all that happy during that time. Tyler was never home, and I would spend all my time prepping for bullshit stories. I wanted to love and be happy about it. I was in one of the best cities in the country for young professionals and my life sucked! I had a lot to think about. I pondered if I should go forth and start another documentary. I figured it'd be just the thing I needed to revive my spirit. At the station, I sat in my cubicle. Photos of my parents stared at me from the corner. Seeing them made me miss home so I decided to go home to Mobile for the weekend. I needed to be around my family. Tyler was going to be flying out on location in L.A. that weekend. It just made sense that I got away too. It'd be our last night together today, so I was hoping that Tyler and I could spend some time together. Perhaps drive to the airport together in the morning and part ways with a kiss like in the movies. Honestly, he could go with me. His assignment didn't start until Sunday, but I got a feeling Tyler want's to party a little or something in Los Angeles.

Once I got back to our Apartment after work was done, I booked a flight for first thing in the morning to head to Mobile. Our apartment was laid out nicely, but it wasn't very big though which is typical for a midtown high-rise. The entrance opens into a kitchen with a large Island, white granite countertops, and gray washed wood flooring and cabinetry to match. This all overlooked into our living room which we have a sectional that faces the balcony. My desk was the buffer between the kitchen and the living area. When I came, I typically dump my messenger bag on the island and lay my Apple Watch on the desk. That's my routine.

I emptied my pockets and there was Orlando's card. 555.998.8777. I think his number is still the same from

5 years ago. He is so well kept. I stared at his photo for a little while. He had on a silver, form-fitting suit with a pink shirt, pink socks and the shiniest Burberry shoes I'd ever seen. I sighed as I looked around the one bedroom apartment I shared with Tyler who was never there. We had it designed in a contemporary fashion. It wasn't so boyish like how our dorm room was. I think Tyler and I spent all of two years total time together in that apartment. The rest of the time was him on the road somewhere. Why oh why did I decide to date a journalist? As I was pulling out my laptop from my bag, my phone sang out a notification. I walked over to my desk where I had set it down and picked it up.

It's going to be a late night at the center, a text from Tyler read. I rolled my eyes, sat the phone face down and didn't respond. This was usual. I think I stopped responding some time ago when these type of messages would pop up. Once, he sent a similar text and it was already close to midnight. That night, he should've gotten cussed out but somehow I ignored how I felt about it like I normally do. At least, he is early this time. I'd usually feel him climb into bed well after I'd fallen asleep. He would wrap his arms around me. It felt good honestly. I still loved him even when he was not around. I considered if I should talk to him more about being left alone so much, but I didn't want to bother him with things like that. The last thing I wanted to be was a nagging boyfriend. It had been five years into the relationship and Tyler had been good to me. We were both nearing thirty and doing okay for the most part. So, I pretended like I didn't see things, like the late night texts or the errand he had to run this morning. I would just pretend. Tyler had never really given me a reason to believe that he would cheat on me at that time. Maybe he had and I had just not cared to see it. Anyway, our anniversary was coming up and we were going to go some place exotic to celebrate five years. I was in need of that, but in the meantime, to Alabama I would go.

It was turning out to be another lonely Friday for me. After a couple hours of reading Stephen King's *It*, the Sun had left its footprints across the sky and the apartment was dull and dim with the weak shine of our night lights plugged in throughout the apartment. There was an eery silence. Typically in that type of space, my thoughts become loud and they freak me out. I came out of our bedroom and walked over to my desk to grab my laptop. I saw Orlando's face peering up at me from underneath the laptop. The laptop was sitting covering his business card except his head and his smile. He was peering at me and trying to hide at the same time. I picked up his card and stared a while. Then I remembered back to the times when he and I were getting to know each other. I remembered back to his condo up in Buckhead where we made out in front of his fireplace. Then I remembered that his condo is actually not too far from where Tyler and I were living. We were in Midtown and Buckhead was only a fifteen minute drive away. I think for a moment I felt compelled to see if he was available. It was in those moments when feeling lonely can cause one to entertain the wildest things just to feel a bit of comfort. I shook my head to clear my thoughts of the inherent lack of fulfillment that was plaguing me. I put his card away in my wallet and moved on to the sofa with my laptop in my hand.

As I sat down, I heard the sound of the deadbolt twist. It was a very tired Tyler walking in. He came in loaded with his things from work. He threw a dry hello to me and went onward to the bathroom. That was something I had gotten very used to. Tyler wasn't a man of many words when he was overworked or in a mood. You'd think that would not be true as much as he and I used to chatter with each other, but in experiencing Tyler as a lover of five years by that time, I'd come to discover a whole lot of other things about him that I had not realized were there. I continued to peck onto my computer. He'll surface sooner or later and we'll exchange dry hugs and kisses and then retreat to our own minds.

His routine this time seemed a little different though. After he showered, he went into the bedroom and didn't come out. He'd normally at least come and give me a hug and a kiss, even if it was dry. I got up and went into the bedroom to check on him. He had climbed into bed. I went to his side of the bed and sat down on the edge.

"Are you okay, honey?" I asked. I rubbed my hand near his forehead.

"It's been a long one for me, but yeah I'm good," he said.

"Okay, is there anything I can get for you. I'm sorry you had a hard day. Did you eat?"

"I'm not really hungry, but thank you," he replied. He seemed to look past me as he responded. Something was going on with Tyler. I know people have bad days but it seemed like something was on his mind that he wasn't talking about.

"Okay love, well let me know if you need anything. Oh, by the way, I'll be heading out in the morning to the airport. I'm going to go home tomorrow to visit my parents."

"Are they okay?" He asked.

"Yeah, they are good. I just need to get away for the weekend since you'll be gone as well. What time is your flight, we may be able to go to the airport together?" I asked.

"I have a 6am departure," he said.

"Oh okay mine departs at 7. I'll ride with you to the airport if you don't mind," I said.

"That's fine with me," He replied.

"Okay babe. Well I'll let you get some rest," I said. I kissed him on the forehead and dimmed the lamps. I went and sat on the sofa as my mind pondered what could be bothering him. Tyler was always tough to figure out, but there was clearly something more than a hard work day. It was 9pm. I decided to call it a night myself since I had to get up early for my flight. I went back into the bedroom, climbed into bed and spooned behind Tyler as we both fell asleep.

Two

Chapter 2

Down in Mobile at my parent's house, we sat around the breakfast table as my dad paraded around with his 'kiss the chef' apron on, a pile of pancakes in one hand and a pile of sausage patties in the other hand.

"How's the job going, Brandon?" my Mom asked. She sat so poised with both hands clasped around her coffee mug. Tatianna was away at Spelman College in Atlanta. She'd kill me if she knew I came home without her.

"It's going."

"Oh that's all?" My Dad asked. "You mean to tell me after $55,678 on a bachelors and an MBA all your career is doing is going?" He concluded. He sat down with us to have breakfast.

"Dad, don't start." I was no in the mood for a lecture. I looked like I didn't want to be bothered with the conversation. I reached for a plate as if he didn't say anything at all.

"What did I say that was so wrong? I mean, son, you

apparently are not happy. I'd just hate to see all of your effort, ahem, and our money go to waste. Tyler seems to be doing quite well for himself. I've caught him on CNN in the evening here and there. That boy is sharp as a tack, I tell ya." He got up from the table to refill his coffee.

"Should I have Tyler start being the one to visit you guys from now on?" I asked sarcastically. I was in no mood to hear my Dad bragging about Tyler. He seemed to have had some type of bromance with Tyler ever since he first met him. And to think, I was afraid he would be all shitty acting to meet a boyfriend of mine for the first time. Boy was I wrong. Those fools sat down in that man cave all day and night watching football and drinking Budweiser. They both are Saints fans. That's all that was needed to get a bond started, and with Tyler being a frat guy, it was nothing for him to have the type of connection he managed to make with my dad. My dad even got Tyler into drinking bourbon and smoking cigars. Tyler always did know how to click with straight men. He's such a boy. I think I was happier about my parents really being so open about welcoming my life, especially after they had told me before that they didn't want to see any of my boyfriends coming around. I was grateful for growth. To think, they put me out for being gay in high school, and look at how God changed it. I was so, so thankful but it irritated me how they would fawn all over Tyler.

"You must still have some jetlag. Your attitude is on ten today, baby," my Mom replied as she reached for a pancake.

"I apologize. Yes, life hasn't been all too happy for me lately. Tyler is always at work and I'm always having to do these boring stories. It's just not how I thought things would turn out for me. I'm almost thirty. Something has to change, I just know it." My dad was coming back from the coffee pot. He stood by my chair and put his hand on my shoulder.

"Well a man has to work, Brandon. Your Mom didn't complain when I had to go off to Iraq," he said.

"How do you know she didn't complain? Maybe she didn't complain to you, that doesn't mean she didn't though."

"I'm sure of it." He walked over to her side of the table and rubbed her shoulder. "Your Mom was very supportive of me and my work. You should be the same with Tyler. I know gay relationships are different from straight ones, but I am sure things like this work the same in both. Don't you agree, honey?" He asked then he sat back down in his seat. Our breakfast nook sat next to a bay window which overlooked the backyard. The sun beaming through the widows was warming up the room, seemingly trying to help break my cold demeanor.

"Brandon, your father is right. Tyler is just out building a future for you two. Why don't you let his ambition fuel some ambitions of your own?"

I rolled my eyes. I did not want to hear reasoning and points of views that excused Tyler's frequent absences. I heard what my parents were saying, but I was the one that had to feel the loneliness. "I guess I hear what you guys are saying. You're right. I just need to focus on my career a little bit more and take control of it. Disappointment can't be determined by anything that's happening or not happening in my life unless I allow it," I said.

"That's a good way to look at it, son," My Dad said. I loved that my relationship with my family had become so great. It was definitely a work in progress, but thank God we got to a place where we could show each other the love that we really do have for one another.

I always found myself in spaces where I would leave conversations with something new to think about as it concerned my life. This conversation with them reminded me a lot of the conversation I had with Jamie just the day prior. My parents had me thinking about pursuing my dreams instead of feeling bitter about Tyler pursuing his. Was I really lonely because Tyler wasn't around like I was so used to or was I just not fulfilled because of not following my dreams? I needed to talk to Tyler. It was time I made some decisions for myself because I'd become tired of feeling trapped.

* * *

While in Mobile, I decided to link up with Alec. He had remained my best friend since middle school. He and his family helped me out a great deal when my folks put me out. Alec stayed in Mobile. I always tried to get him to come up to Atlanta, but he didn't want to. He liked living in Mobile. He's a minister in a small ministry around here. He feels like this is where God has called him to be. We decided we would hang out once he got off work. He was a manager at the Walmart. I caught an Uber to his job. I hated Walmart. They would never have any lines open and that particular one smelled like cows.

"Hey buddy, give me a couple of minutes. I got to put up this pallet jack and I'll be ready," Alec Said. He scurried away dragging some banging and clanging piece of metal on wheels behind him which I suppose is the pallet jack, whatever that's used for.

"I need a CSM to register three," blared over the intercom. I always felt so icky going into Walmart. It felt like I did not want anyone to touch me. I walked around with my arms flat to my sides and my hands in my pockets. I found myself on the book aisle to check out what good books were out. Then I saw one that particularly stood out to me. It was called *Reposition Yourself.* I flipped it to the back and saw, "Follow great insights on how to implement change and get the best out of life." I instantly felt drawn in, so I decided to get it. Now to stand in one of the 2 out of 35 registers that are open to check out. I was standing at the end of one of the long lines when Alec walked up.

"What are you buying?"

"This book I saw. It looks like it'll be pretty good."

"Oh okay, well meet me outside at the car. I'm parked over by the Garden Center."

"Alright." I waited in line about 20 minutes. "This is ridiculous," I said to myself. I finally got out of the store and made it to the car. "Alec, why in the hell don't y'all open any registers in that damn store? I was in line for 20 minutes waiting on 'Glenda' and her stank attitude, with her slow-ringing ass. I can't deal." I reached back to pull out the seat belt and shook my head.

"Don't be putting down my store. You shouldn't have gotten your ass in line. What book did you buy anyway? It must be pretty damn good for you to stand in line 20 minutes for it."

"It's called *Reposition Yourself* by TD Jakes."

Alec rolled his eyes and sucked his teeth, "Oh Jakes done got you too. I swear that man puts out a new book every month."

"Well, he is an author. That's what they do."

"He just regurgitates the same stuff over and over again, in my opinion."

"He doesn't. Have you even read any of his stuff?"

"Nope, don't have to. The titles alone seem like repeat shit."

"I forgot you are a conspiracy theorist. Crazy ass," I laughed.

"I'm not a conspiracy theorist. But you best believe, the government is out here creating hurricanes and putting Jakes up to these damn books."

I love my friend, but sometimes he was really out there with his thoughts. He stays in church too much and this religion stuff had his mind fried like an egg. He's a bit of a Hotep. We had arrived to Applebee's, our favorite hang-out spot back in the day. We went inside and were seated by the hostess. As we followed her, I spotted a cute guy doing the bartending.

"Your waiter will be with you shortly," she said as she walked away.

"Wow we haven't been here in a hot minute," Alec said.

"Nah, we haven't," I replied as I looked at the menu. Alec sat and watched me. I could tell his mind was going and a question was about to come out. Before he could, I tried to divert his mind. "So, that bartender is kinda hot?"

"Who? You talking about Greg? He aight. Don't be trying to distract me. Now, why you reading that book? What's going on with you? You know you can't hide anything from the prophet."

"There is nothing going on with me. I'm good. I think it's a good read. Besides, you know I like to read."

"Hmmm, that shit might work for Tyler but I've known you your whole damn life just about. Something is up with you. But that's alright. I'm going to get it out of you. Hmm huh. Speaking of Tyler, where is he at right now?"

21

"L.A.," I said with a dry tone.

"Oh, you don't seem like you're okay with that. Why didn't you go with him?"

"He's there for work."

"Work? Hmm," he said with a side eye. He grabbed his menu to find something to order.

"What?"

"He sure does stay on the road a lot. I mean damn if y'all were trying to make a baby, you'd never get it. Chile I crack myself up," Alec laughed and fanned himself with a napkin.

"That's not funny. Ain't no babies coming to our house. No way!" I said looking into the menu.

"You right, cause y'all not around each other long enough to make one."

"Anyway," I replied.

"For real though, Brandon. What's wrong? I can see it in your eyes and you know the Holy Ghost is over here telling me all of your tea," Alec said.

"Well if He is spilling tea, then you don't need me to tell you," I chimed back. Here goes Mr. Clairvoyant.

"So there *is* something wrong. Listen, why you playing? You know you can talk to me about everything. We used to always talk about everything. What happened?"

"Hey guys, what can I get for you?" We were interrupted by the waitress. I think I was actually happy about that. Alec had a way of reflecting a mirror on you, and I don't know if that was because he's psychic or what. I just know I wasn't ready to see my shit. We placed our food orders. When she walked away, I stared off as if I was engaging the game on the bar TVs.

"Sir? There is a question on the table. Why you don't share

with me like you used to?"

"Alec, that was years ago and we were both in the closet so we could talk about certain things like that. That's not quite the same anymore. I'm out. You are not. As a matter of fact, you are celibate and you spend so much of your time in the church. I honestly don't feel like you can relate to me like that anymore."

"Is that right? So, you feel like because I don't do what you do that I can't talk to you about your problems?"

"No it's not that. I know you are trying to do the straight and narrow, and I just don't want to tempt you with any gay conversations."

"You think I can't handle talking to you about your frustrations with Tyler. You think that's going to make me go out and get some dick immediately after our dinner tonight?" Alec replied.

I can tell Alec was serious with his line of questioning. He looked me straight in the face. I sighed and looked down. Ugh, preachers.

"So what you want to know?" I asked reluctantly.

"It's not about what I want to know. It's about what you need to get off your chest, or perhaps what you need some clarity on, like your career for example."

"Why are you talking about my career?" I asked with my eyes peering over my glasses.

"Because you are not happy in it. You are burned out. And the thing is…you're not really burned out, you just have not been operating in your true direction. All of this discomfort you are feeling is just your real purpose trying to meet up with you. The problem is that you don't believe in yourself enough to do it. You've depended on Tyler to lead you for so long now. And, this is why you have feelings of resentment towards him. Tyler is out there building his career just the way he saw it to be. That career is starting to not center or involve you anymore, and now you feel lost. See, it was all good and fine when CNN had him in Atlanta at the CNN Center writing for the internet, but when he got that field correspondent opportunity, he begin to move swiftly towards his purpose, seemingly leaving you behind. You sir, are in transition. That's all this is. Annnnnd you need to stop using that relationship to fill your voids. Are you still seeing your therapist?" He asked.

I knew Alec was sort of like a psychic or something and I've even seen him in action in church before, but he had never spoken to me through his gift of knowledge before. He was 100% right about what he said. I was resenting Tyler about his career. He was living his dream, and it felt like I was lagging behind him, and I hated it. I think the loneliness made it easy to feel some type of way towards him. "No, I haven't been to him in a number of years now, but yeah, you are very right, Alec."

"I know I am. I know what I was hearing since you came into my presence. You don't realize just how heavily you are wearing this energy on you. Everyone can see it. Your boss sees it. She just hasn't said anything to you yet, but she will soon. She is going to ask you if you are happy with your workload," he said.

"What should I say to her?"

"Just be honest. I can see it going well. You'll be surprised. The truth will literally set you free in this situation. Your heart is not in what you do anymore. Don't stress about it. Change is about to come."

"Wow, thank you, Alec."

"No, thank God. He knows the thoughts and plans for you better than I do. I'm just sharing with you what He's sharing with me about you," he said. He reached out to take the plates from our server. By this time, the food had arrived. I ordered hot wings, my favorite comfort food. He ordered a steak.

"Okay, so about Tyler. Sometimes I wonder if he still loves me the way he used to," I said.

"He loves you," he said so nonchalantly as he bit into his steak.

"I know he does, but sometimes I don't feel it from him. He doesn't do the little sweet things he used to do."

"You guys have been together for what, six years or so?"

"Nah, five years. Our anniversary is coming up," I said.

"Sometimes relationships will slow down around this time. It's normal, y'all just got to make sure you keep the spark going. How's the sex life going?"

"That's pretty good. Tyler has always been a beast in the bed, so I can actually say I don't have any complaints there."

"Well alright then. As long as he gives you some good D every now and again, then don't be worrying about him like that. You trying to have the Little House on the Prairie type of life honey, and you just need to focus on you a little bit more. Like I already told you, that's really what your issue is. You are feeling incomplete and you have been using Tyler to feel those voids. Baby, if you aren't careful, you'll find yourself out there filling that void with a man that ain't him," he said.

"Now, you know I wouldn't do that."

"Chile, you don't know what you'll do until you are put in that situation. I'm just saying. Let the right piece of penis come up on you complimenting you, paying you attention, saying little jokes to make you laugh, you'll find yourself secretly texting and secretly having dinners," he said.

"I guess," I said.

"Don't guess, know. The prophet sees, chile, and it'll all be because you don't realize that you need to work on yourself a little bit more. Listen, life is an ever-changing process of growth and experiences. If you don't learn to grow with it, you'll find yourself lost as shit," he said.

"I know, I know. I'm going to get back to the basics of me. I was telling my colleague yesterday that I would like to do another documentary."

"I think you should do that. It'll get your mind off of things a little bit. Actually, I can see you getting into YouTube. Have you ever considered that?"

"YouTube? In what way?"

"You know, like start a YouTube channel. I'm sure you can find plenty to talk about. You know you talk a whole lot anyway, ole talking ass," Alec laughed and bit into his steak.

"You just be taking digs at me. I don't talk a lot." Alec stopped in mid-chew and looked at me with aggravation.

"Ummm, yeah you do. Ole wordy ass."

"I don't know if I can do a YouTube channel. I would have to dumb down the personality of the channel to not affect the brand of any station I work for or could potentially work for. That's the only thing that I could see being a problem."

"It will all come to you how it's supposed to be, but I do see you doing something similar to that. Just allow your spirit to be open to the possibilities," Alec said.

"I'll do that. In the meantime, I think I'll meet with my director and let her know that I need a change in the stories they send me out to follow. I can't do that too much longer.

And my colleague got me to thinking I should do another documentary. I'm really giving that some thought. What do you think about that...I mean what do you *see* about that?"

"Don't mock me," he rolled his eyes. "I think you should go for it, and I think whatever you are going to do it on is going to end up branding you for a little while so you had better put your all into it. This is really how this YouTube presence will begin for you," he said.

"I can see that. Thank you for your insight. When I get back to Atlanta, I'm going to start doing some brainstorming. Wow, this really helps. Thank you. I feel excited already about it," I said.

"Well good for you." Alec took a sip of his tea.

"So enough about me, what's going on with you honey? You still scared of the penis, thinking you going to go to hell because of it?" I asked with a joke. Alec gasped with his hand over his chest as to grasp invisible pearls.

"Yessss! And dick will send you straight to hell if you ain't careful honey. HIV, syphilis, all that shit is hell. Hmmm huh. I'm good just as I am." He takes a sip of his drink.

"I know all of that. That's actually what I plan to do some coverage on when I can. But I'm not done with you, sir. So what's going on? No dates, no nothing. So you just dry and tight right now, huh?"

"I haven't had sex in five years."

"So when you say, 'sex', are you talking about intercourse or no sexual contact at all?"

"Mostly no contact period," he replied.

"How do you manage? I'd been done jumped off a bridge by now."

"It's all in the mind, and besides, I want what you and Tyler have. Something consistent and stable. Someone that I can be in a partnership with. Sex is so overrated now. It's just an action to me."

"So is that why you are celibate?"

"Yes."

"Oh, I thought it had to do with the church. Thought you were trying to do that pretend shit that a lot of these ministers do when they are gay and preaching," I said.

"No, has nothing to do with the church. I'm okay with who I am and what I like. I keep it respectful and classy. I also don't feel like my sexuality is anyone's business. It also doesn't have to define, qualify or disqualify my anointing. Being celibate for me is a personal journey. Being gay is already convoluted enough by itself; I don't need sex to make that even more cloudy. Honestly, being celibate has allowed me to find some clarity on a lot of things in my life. I get horny sometimes and I get weak, but I have learned to master those moments. Now, I don't think about sex, and I don't have urges. I am able to see so clearly in the higher dimensions as a result."

"What have you learned about sex and how it affects us in your experience being celibate?" I asked.

"You sound like you are interviewing me," he laughed.

"Well you know me. I'm not though. I am genuinely curious about that. I think I would like to see how much of my world has become clouded due to sex."

"I'll put it like this: I've learned that sex is way more spiritual than we think, and when I say 'spiritual', I'm not talking about churchy spirituality. I'm referring to the energy realms of our existence."

"Energy realms?" I asked with a lost look on my face. Like I said, Alec was a bit kooky. He wasn't like that when we were kids, but I would listen to him because usually he would drive home really profound points.

"Yes, we all exist in some sort of energy field and there are different levels. You need to read more about Hinduism. But anyway, to answer your question, sex affects us in profound ways which is why it's very important to one, not have multiple sexual partners and two, to be very mindful of who you engage with sexually. Now, as it concerns you, hmmm, I don't think that should affect you. So in other words, the fact that you are not celibate doesn't have anything to do with the sense of cloudiness you are experiencing with your life right now. You have one sexual partner and you both should be monogamous I hope."

"You hope?" I replied.

"Yes, I mean, people lie. I don't know what you and Tyler do. I don't know if you and he are faithful to each other. I'd like to believe that you two are. If you are, then sex between you too is honorable and the energy you two share during sex is cyclical and it lends to you guys building each other up collectively. Now if one is cheating, then the energy is no longer cyclical, especially if the cheating partner, whether its one or the other or both, are cheating with several people. Now you dealing with a chemistry of various energy vibrations and then you wonder why yall are having a hard time agreeing on what TV show to watch. None of what I am saying is scientific but hey, you asked me a question. Those are my thoughts on it. I think sex clouds things when it's not being engaged in responsibly and when two people don't share the same type of energy or chemistry or whatever you want to call that," Alec said.

"I never heard of that and I'm surprised you've deviated

from your Christian ways to adopt Hinduism. Why did you decide to become celibate? Was it because you could not find anyone that you felt had the same type of energy you have?" I asked.

"Well, first, my being a Christian has nothing to do with understanding the tenets of other religions. I mean, they all have basic truths which can be shared across all of them. Christ says you reap what you sow, Hinduism says everything has cause and effect-energy begets energy. You see?"

"Yeah I guess so, but you didn't answer if you feel like you have a hard time finding someone on your level sexually." I said.

"Hmmm, yes and no. I have always understood quite well that I vibrate on a high energy level. I mean, I'm prophetic for god's sake. I know my spiritual playing field. I know for me, sex is powerful. It is more than sex. Sex for a person like me is activating."

"Activating?"

"Yes. You have to remember that we all came from God which is love, which is nothing but an energy force. So we all harness some of God's energy in some way. Some of us, that energy is tainted or darkened. But at any rate, those of us who operate in high levels of energy, God's energy, or what the Church calls, "the holy ghost", will exert a lot of power when engaging in sex, especially when the release happens. So for me, I always understood that I held the ability to establish deep soul ties with people as a result of my high vibration. I allowed that to always help me be mindful of who I engage in sex with and this is the reason why most of my sexual encounters were mostly light and never really ended with intercourse. So for me, I was already accustomed to not having sex often. Becoming celibate just meant tying some level of commitment and meaning to not having intercourse which ultimately forced me to stop masturbating, to stop engaging in anything that was sexual as a way to keep my mind strong on the commitment. "

"Wow, this is intriguing. I have a new level of respect for you and really anyone who says they are celibate. It's like being celibate is a spiritual journey and not so much about not having sex but about respecting the power that comes through sex."

"Exactly," he replied.

"I think I'll do some research on all of this."

"You may want to start with the study of Kama Sutra. Kama Sutra is an ancient Hindu text that explores the way we connect through sex."

"Ok, cool. I'll do that. I bet Tyler already knows some stuff about it," I said.

"He probably does. I'm sorry I went off into that tangent. You know that type of talk get's my wheels going. Anyway, to finish your question from earlier. I do have someone that I have been communicating with, and guess where he lives?"

"Ummm, you sneaky devil. Where does he live?" I asked.

"Atlanta!"

"What, huh? Wow, and you have kept this a secret. How long have you guys been talking?"

"Damn where is that lady with our check so we can get out of here," Alec said. I guess he was trying to deflect.

"Umm you heard me sir. Come with the tea. Spill it," I said. Alec looked bashful. For the first time during this whole evening, it seemed like he was vulnerable and unsafe. I could tell by the way he was fiddling with the straw paper that he was experiencing something new, and maybe he didn't know how to process it.

"It's been about six months. He is such a sweetheart. I think I love him," Alec said.

"Aw this is so cute. Wow. So, tell me more about him. What's his name? What does he do? Come on with it," I said.

"Well, he's a minister. He's a bit older than me. He has his shit together and he is fine, super fine. We met off Facebook. We are both a part of an HIV Advocacy group. He's a shiny guy," Alec laughed.

"What do you mean shiny? Why have you never brought him up to me?" I asked.

"Because, I didn't want to jinx anything, and what I mean by shiny is that he got money. He's educated and he is doing pretty well for himself. This guy really does seem too good to be true. I already have trust issues, and then he is from Atlanta. They say never date a guy from Atlanta because they are whorish to the nth degree. Some reason, I don't think about that. His charm is unbelievable. He had me at hello. His first words to me were, 'Why has someone so beautiful slipped passed me all of this time. Forgive me for not gracing you with a hello before now. Chile I almost had an orgasm on the spot," he said.

"Chile, so a man runs you a line and you melt out of your panties?" I laughed.

"Lol no, not at all. You know me better than that, but what he said was really sweet. Our first phone call was amazing. We talked for hours and hours on end. He is so profound and so cultured. He loves to tell me, 'Knowing about cultures make me cultured, nothing else.' He has a bit of a smart mouth too, but I love it," Alec said.

"A smart ass for your little smart ass. That ought to be a match made in heaven," I said.

"I guess so until one of us gets tired of it and then it turns into an argument," Alec laughed.

"Well, it sounds like you are building out something really nice. I'm happy for you!"

"Thank you, sweetie. I'm taking it slowly though," Alec said.

"So, what does he feel about your celibacy?" I asked.

"He respects it. I don't expect him to be celibate with me though."

"Wait, so you're saying that you are okay with him having sex with other people?"

"Yes...I mean...no, I'm not saying that but I recognize the dynamics here. He is miles and miles away. He is a young man still and I'm sure he has sexual urges. So, actually, I just tell him I don't want to know what he does, but it is my expectation that once we are together frequently or living together or in the same area, then I expect to be the only one. Of course, I would break my celibacy at that point too," Alec said as he sipped his tea.

"Well that makes me want to know then, where do you rank on his list. What if there is another "you" in DC or right in Atlanta?" I asked.

"There isn't. I know, I know. I sound gullible, but for some reason, I believe him when he says that I am the only one. He is open and honest with me. He tells me he doesn't have sex with anyone, but he will have an occasional masturbation session with someone or oral. I try not to think about that. Actually, there is no trying. I don't think about it. I really don't consider it because it doesn't bother me. I'm not pressed like that," Alec said with his eyes avoiding me.

I was not quite understanding why Alec was so trusting with this guy. It just didn't make good sense to me. I guess that is the challenge of having a long-distance relationship where the partner you are with is so far away that you can't see each other but for months and months at a time. If it worked for them then I guess it was cool. I never understand the concept of an open relationship, but I guess plenty people out there do.

"Well, honey, I wish you the best and I hope that in time you two can be near each other and begin to build the relationship out," I said.

"We will see. I know he's not going to move out of Atlanta. He has too much going on there like his business for one. I don't see him uprooting. I guess it'll be poor little ole me making the move there," he said.

My eyes lit up. "Really? Yesss! Awe that would be so great! We could hang out and double date and all of that good stuff. I can't wait!" I said with excitement.

"Well don't get your hopes up so quickly. We've only been together for six months and I'm not moving nowhere for no man after six months."

"I know, but the idea is still exciting."

"Well come on, Chile, let's go back to my place to finish this conversation," Alec said.

Alec and I hung out for the rest of the night and we continued to catch up on old times. It was refreshing to see him dating. He was not one to trust people in that way. I hoped what he had going on with this new guy worked out for him. I didn't want to see it fall apart. He was already skiddish when it came to dating.

Three

Chapter 3

T he night was still young. I was back at my parent's house. I stood in the doorway of my bedroom which looked the same as it did when I was kicked out. I know kicked out sounds harsh, but well…it was hard the way it took place. Mom said she never came in to change it around. At first, it was because of her disappointment in me for being gay, and then later it was because she missed me something terribly and did not want to disturb any memory she had of me to hold on to. For the longest, I could not understand how she could allow so many years to go by without trying to make up with me. My therapist helped me to understand that was not my work to do, but yet it was on her to understand that and deal with it.

I walked into the room which was warm and cozy. My favorite corner chair sat waiting to embrace me with its open arms. It was a mustard yellow, wide back chair with an ottoman. I remember I used to sit in that chair for many nights, thinking and pondering. I wondered where my life would go. I often thought about how it would be for me with my sexuality. Would I give in to it? Would it be something that I'd ever really get comfortable with? I was so confused and so scared of being found out. I went through great lengths to hide myself. I smiled as I reminisced over what used to be a very hurtful time of my life. I smiled because I had become a journalist and a storyteller - someone who shares truths. I became a truth-teller and it first had to start with me telling my own truth. I'm so glad I do what I do, even though I was not so happy with how I was doing it, I wouldn't trade telling the truth for the world.

It still felt a bit surreal to be back in this room. M childhood was a lonely one. Not lonely as in I didn't have anyone around, but lonely because of all the emotional things I was dealing with. If I think back on it long and hard enough, I can say that the way I was feeling with Tyler is how I felt as a kid. Being back at home would remind me of it sometimes, if I allowed it to. I shouldn't allow it to though. Perhaps it's all related, and this is why I was having such a hard time handling being alone in my adult life. I'm not that 10-year old kid anymore, the one that wet the bed up until he was 8 because he had anxiety problems. I'm no longer that kid that dreaded school because I got picked on a lot. Although I'm no longer that kid, my heart still longs for affirmation like I am that kid. When Tyler would not be around, it left me to feel like I was not secure.

I used to escape a lot when I was a kid. I would make up stories in my head and narrate my life all over again with my friends or the people in school that I had a thing for. They would be my good friends and we were in a singing group. All of the songs off the TLC, *Crazy, Sexy, Cool* album were ours. We'd perform those songs. That's how I escaped from the bullying. In my head, I'd tell these stories to myself to escape my reality. I taught myself not to feel what was going on around me. I taught myself a long time ago how to pretend like people weren't really treating me bad. That's probably why I hang on to Tyler even though having him does not serve me the way it used to. This is what quiet would do to me, the quiet of the house. As my parents lay sleeping, my thoughts forced me to reckon with my past that seemed to be manifesting into my current situation with Tyler.

I began to undress, and then I noticed a box on my dresser. It peaked my interest and I walked over. I opened it and saw a lot of letters. They were handwritten letters in what looked to be my mom's handwriting. I began to read them. I was immediately thrown into her thoughts from eight years ago.

My Son,

I miss you so much. I hope you are doing well with your studies. I still don't understand this gay thing. I know what my Bible tells me about it, but I also know what my heart tells me about you. I love you. I never wanted to be separated from you like I am now. I wish you would talk to us...

I stopped reading and put the letter back. I shouldn't be reading her private thoughts, even though it seemed like something she should have been saying to me directly back then. I think it would have helped a lot. I took a deep sigh and began to unpack my bag. Despite the up and down of my feelings lately, I was a bit excited about working on a new documentary. I couldn't wait to sit down in my chair and spend time with my thoughts. It sat waiting for us to reunite like old times with me wondering off into the Valhalla of my thoughts, pondering and thinking.

After I showered and got into my comfortable lounging clothes, I went downstairs to grab a snack. I knew I'd be up a while doing my preliminary brainstorming for my documentary. The house was dim and quiet. Mom and dad had already retired to their room. I walked toward the kitchen but the creaking of the hardwood floors would not allow me to be too incognito. For every creak and croak, I'd pause like a cat burglar trying not to get caught. In the kitchen, I shuffled around the pantry looking for something to indulge myself with. Then I looked over to the counter and found a stash of Oreos, which were always a favorite of mine. My mom also liked them with rocky road ice cream. Oreos and milk sounded good, but all they had was whole milk. I'd rather drink motor oil. I should've let them know to keep almond milk here for me. I snatched the Oreos and went back upstairs. At last, my chair and I would have a long night of getting reacquainted.

I sat in silence. I think I was trying to start with a title for the documentary, but that wasn't coming so well. I felt like a block was setting in. Thoughts of Tyler were in the back of my mind as well. It was moments like those where I missed what we had a few years ago. How did we manage to lose so much of our connectivity along the way? Had life began to be that busy? My thoughts were interrupted. I looked down to my phone which was vibrating. It was Tyler. I knew how to speak him up sometimes. I wish I had that power all the time. I picked it up to answer.

"Hey baby, what you up to?"

"Nothing, just sitting here in my room. How's L.A.?" I

asked.

"It's okay. I'm ready to get back to Atlanta. How are the parents?"

"They are doing okay," I said. "I miss you." I sincerely did.

"Good for them. I miss you too, love. I can't wait to see you."

"I can't wait to see you too," I said.

"Well, what are you up to?" He asked.

"So…listen, I have an idea and I want your opinion on it."

"Okay, I'm listening," he said.

By now, I had turned to the side in the chair with my feet propped up against the wall and my head rested on the arm of the chair. I used to do my best thinking this way.

"I'm going to do a documentary."

"Really? That's great! What do you plan to do it on?"

"I'm thinking about doing it on HIV/AIDs in the gay community, especially among black gay men. My problem with this is I know there are a gazillion documentaries about HIV/AIDS. I don't know how to make this one be different. What are your ideas?"

"I think that's a great topic. I wouldn't be too concerned with the idea that there are a lot of documentaries on this subject out already. The problem is still a huge one. Oh I know, tell it like a story. Here is what I think. I think the audience should be the gay community itself. Think about it. How many guys do we know that are really in the dark about this disease? They feel they are invincible it seems. Not only that, you should also paint the picture that those living with HIV can have a productive life. Tthey can be wonderful partners to have and they too can live on and get married and have wonderful careers as well. That should be your angle on this," he said.

"Wow, babe. This is why I love you. That makes so much sense. Damn, it seems like coming up with that shit was effortless for you. I still have so much to glean from you," I said with excitement. I had sat up on the edge of the chair by this time, leaning my pad on the bed, taking down the notes.

"Thank you, love. You are just as capable. You just have to believe in yourself more," Tyler said.

"I know, I know," I said. "I've just been in a stump lately is all, but I think this documentary is going to liven me back up. You know, make me feel like I'm doing something worthwhile with my life. The field reporting on dumb stuff is aggravating to my soul."

"You do honest work," Tyler said. "Don't downplay it. The most important thing about journalism, no matter how you are doing it, is to deliver the truth to the people. You play an important role in our community. Many people turn on the news to know what's going on in their area. You help give them that. Don't downplay it as something that is not building you up. Believe it or not, it is building you up. You'll see. I used to feel the same way you do when I was writing political internet articles for CNN, but I realize now that was the bridge I needed to take me to the position I wanted more, which is what I am doing now. Yeah, it keeps me away from home a lot, but I'm doing what I love," he said.

"Sometimes I feel like you love it more than you love me," I said. I didn't plan to say it, it just came up.

"What do you mean, Brandon?" He asked. I got up out of the chair with some anxiety because I did not know how this conversation was going to go.

"I miss you is what I mean. They have you away from home

a lot. I'm having a hard time adjusting to it. I need you home more. My parents told me that I need to focus on me a little more and I won't feel that way, but I don't know."

"I understand how you feel. I promise I am going to make it up to you when I can. I think your parents may be on to something too. Maybe this documentary will help you remove some of your focus on the loneliness," Tyler responded.

I was hoping he was going to say something a little more consoling. I guess I have to get what I can get.

"I hear you guys. When do you expect to be home?" I asked.

"I'm flying back in on Monday."

"Okay well I won't hold you, and I want to get back to my brainstorming. I really do miss you and I love you," I said. I didn't want to let him go but I wasn't in the mood to talk further.

Four

Chapter 4

I only stayed in Mobile for the weekend since I had to get back to work on Monday. My flight was landing and I had just finished watching *Love, Simon*. It's such a great movie about coming out. I was missing Tyler. While I sat in the back of my Uber ride back home, I flipped through my wallet and saw Orlando's card. "I meant to text him," I thought to myself. No better time than now.

Hi, I sent. Was he going to reply right away? I wondered if he was still doing his practice or had the Rainbow House expanded so much where he had to focus on it full-time. The Rainbow House was his charity when we first meet. I don't see how he was doing both a practice and the charity at the same time anyway. It just seemed odd to me. Why was I texting him anyway? My heart began to race and my eyes lit up. He had replied right away. I had become excited.

Orlando replied back with *Hey! I was wondering if I'd hear from you.* By this time, I had made it home. I fell back onto the sofa to engage with Orlando.

I've had a busy week and weekend. I'm just now getting to you. I had actually forgot, sorry," I replied. I tried to sound disengaged, but actually, a part of me was elated to talk to him. I looked across the room at a photo of me and Tyler. The picture seemed to stare back at me in the dimly lit apartment. There seemed to be a look of disapproval there. I stared back, and then I got up and walked into the bedroom to lay stomach first on the bed.

What are you up to on this fine Sunday? He texted.

I'm just lounging around. Just got off a flight not too long ago from visiting my parents.

Oh wow, that's good to hear. I take it that things are going well with you guys?

Yep, they are. We have a lot to catch up on."

You are most definitely right about that. How about we have some dinner, tonight?

I froze for a second. I pondered if I should I go? If I did, do I tell Tyler about it? Tyler would not have wanted me to go, but I wanted to go. I got up from the bed and paced back and forth in front of the foot board. I felt the anxiety boiling up against my rib cage from the bottom of my intestines it seemed. I had never entertained another guy before while being with Tyler. I knew that this open door would lead me down a path of no return. One part of me felt scared, but the other part of me wanted to see it out and find out if I could feel what I had been missing from Tyler all this time.

Soon enough, my pacing stopped and sat my phone down on the dresser with the chat thread lit up on the device as if it was patiently waiting for me to say, "Yes, I'll meet up with you." I walked away into the kitchen and stared into the fridge. Nothingness stared back at me, and that became a stark reminder that I was feeling like lonely person in that moment; nothingness from my partner and nothingness in my bed. I never understood why men cheat but in that moment, I fully understood why I wanted to. I closed the fridge as I began to reason with myself silently. My fridge was empty. I was going to go out to get food anyway. There's no harm in getting it with an old friend. "Yeah a friend who had you butt naked on his chaise lounge 5 years ago," said my conscious. By this time, ten minutes had passed and I had not responded back to Orlando yet. I went to grab my phone and made my choice. Cheating is a choice.

I'm free. Let's grab a bite. Are you still living in Buckhead?
"I am, same spot.
Okay, I live in Midtown.
OK. Let's hit up The Capital Grille.
I'd like that. I'm leaving now.
Bet, see you soon.

I wasn't actually leaving then. I had to freshen up, so I ran to the bathroom and quickly showered and put on my best scents. I felt like I wanted to be seductive that night.

I requested an Uber in case I decided to have a couple of glasses of wine. I was big on using Uber. My weekends were filled with Uber rides. I did enough driving during the week for work. I had arrived to the restaurant. Orlando had already reserved a table for us. I walked in and there he was sitting in the lobby area waiting. He had on a cream sweater with his hair curly. I smiled at him in adoration. He stood up when he saw me and greeted me.

"Hey you, I'm glad you could make it," he said. He gave me a hug. I got a whiff of his scent. He smelled like Paris in winter.

"I was surprised to see you the other day. I love this look on you!" I said with enthusiasm.

"I can say the same about you with your thick self. I see you've been hitting the gym," he said again, like he had already said at Chick-fil-A.

"Yeah, I try to stay fit since I'm on TV a lot. I can't be in these streets looking like shit dude."

"You'll never look like shit. So you're on TV a lot?" he asked.

"Yeah, I work for WSBtv. I do field reporting. You must not watch the news?" I asked as the hostess lead us to our table. We walked and chatted on our way there.

"Nah, I can't say that I do, not the local news. I catch CNN a lot though, but never local news," he said.

"Yeah, I've been trying to tell my producers that it's time to find ways to get to our audiences because people just don't watch the news like they used to," I said. Orlando gave me a look of confusion.

"So wait, weren't you the one saying that you didn't want to work for a station?" He asked.

"Yeah that was me, but life happens. I didn't really get to go out and do the things I wanted to do."

"But Tyler did, huh?" he asked.

"Yeah, he's at CNN? He doesn't get much TV time because he's out in the field. You may catch him here and there. He's a field reporter too, but he follows national politics. I think he's gunning for White House Correspondent if he can get it. He'd be a nice follow up to Abby Phillips. He'd probably have to start as a reporter first. I'm sure that White House correspondent spot is highly coveted," I said.

"Oh yeah, Abby Phillips is good. I love her presentation.

But, no, I haven't seen him on any reporting yet. I'm usually watching it during the weekdays during the day hours. If he did get that, it would be a really great opportunity. He'd have to move to D.C. though. You guys still together?" He asked. He looked at me with a look of hope in his eyes as if he was waiting to hear me say no.

"Yes we are together," I said as I looked into the menu.

"You know it took me a while to get past how you guys did me. I was really feeling you, like really, really feeling you, man. But like I told you when we all first met that I knew Tyler was the one for you. I was able to make peace with that because he really is the one for you," he said.

"Well, I'm glad to hear that from you. I'm sorry for what happened. You were just so smooth sir, who could resist all of that charm?" I laughed. "But, I should have been upfront with you. It's just things happened so damn fast. I couldn't keep up. It was so uncanny on how right you were about Tyler. As soon as he came out to his parents, we were ready to tie the knot it seems."

"That's because you two were already in a relationship with each other. His coming out just allowed you guys to finally be honest with each other. I told you when you two came over that night that it was so obvious that you two were more than friends, even if you two didn't realize it yet or not. I think it's a beautiful story, really, I do. I'm happy for you. That means you and he have been together a hell of a long time, right?"

"5 years dating, but almost 10 years total if you count the four years we played roommate in college. But longevity only means that things change though," I said. I looked back down into my menu and acted like what I just said wasn't going to reel in a ton of inquiries.

"Wait, what's up? Are you not happy?" He asked. Orlando looked like he was really interested in knowing if I was happy or not. I got the impression it was because he felt some sympathy for me. He's a therapist so that could be the truth or it really could all just be bullshit. He leaned in forward waiting on my reply.

"I am. I just don't think he is being so honest with me right now. I mean…I love Tyler…but he is never here. He is always on the road, and then my career is going nowhere really fast and that bums me out. I feel empty sometimes."

"Wow Brandon, I am sorry to hear that. It sounds to me like this is taking a toll on you. You deserve to be happy," he said.

"I mean, I think I am happy—no, I am content, but I could be happier I suppose. Tyler is a gem. I think we are just having the typical relationship pains since we've been together for so long," I said. Orlando listened intently. His eyes seemed to be fixated on my lips as I talked. I could not tell if he was fantasizing about kissing them or if he was doing this therapist thing again.

"I believe that you have control of your outcomes. If you feel that you are not happy, then you and Tyler should talk about that, or you should do something to make yourself feel fulfilled," He said.

"Well, what do you recommend I do?"

"Some people bury themselves in their work, but really you should talk to Tyler if you are having discontentment issues with the relationship. And if you don't want to do that then, there are other ways to manage your frustrations," he said.

I think I knew what he meant by that and I wasn't going to have him confirm it. If he was suggesting I go seek attention elsewhere, I didn't want to entertain that, especially with the idea coming from him of all people.

"I haven't really thought that far out yet. I just want to make it through the week. I do have some plans in the back of my mind though. I just need to put them on paper and make something pop. I want to do another documentary," I said.

"Oh okay, that's a start. What about?"

"About the AIDS epidemic among black gay men. You know black gay men have a 50% chance of contracting HIV. I would love to explore the psychology behind that and get a dialogue going about it."

"Well one thing I know is that you know how to get a dialogue going. I mean that last one you did was pretty good, and not because I was in it," he grinned.

"You are so full of yourself," I smiled. He smiled back and rubbed his chin with his hand.

"Then why are you here?" He asked.

"I wanted to see you," I said while I looked into his eyes.

"Aww, so I should feel special, huh?" He chimed back with that intense stare of his. When he speaks, sometimes it feels like the world around us stops, and it's just he and I, existing in some sort of paradigm.

"Not at all," I said.

"Why you playing hard to get? You were always so damn coy," he giggled.

"I thought that's what you liked about me back then, the chase," I said.

"I do like a chase. I like things that are a challenge to get," he said.

"Well, you shouldn't treat men like a game of conquest. That is so typical for someone like you."

"What do you mean someone like me?" He asked.

"I mean, you're handsome, you are successful and you have nice things. You can pretty much woo any guy you wish to woo. You are a type. Your type likes to play the field."

"Chile boo! Says the guy who has never dated, and the one relationship you have has been lasting for almost ten years if you count the 4 years you acted like you wasn't in love with the boy. What could you possibly know about how a player behaves?" Orlando retorted.

"I don't have to have experience to recognize game." I said.

"Is it because game recognizes game?" He asked.

"What?" I laughed. "No, what are you insinuating, sir?"

"I'm just saying. You might be quite the player yourself, but you've been tied down all of your life and you just don't know that you are capable of being one," he said.

"Chile, here you go," I replied.

"What you mean here I go? And where is the damn waiter?" He snapped. He looked around trying to spot someone. He was right though. We had been sitting here a minute longer than we should and still haven't even placed a drink order. I think I had read the menu front and back five times trying to avoid looking into Orlando's eyes a lot.

"Yeah we have been sitting here a minute," I said as I looked around too. "But as I was saying, I'm talking about you and your psychobabble. There you go trying to analyze me and shit," I said.

"My psychobabble pays the mortgages," he said.

"Mortgages? You have multiple houses now, and are you still doing therapy sessions?"

"I still have the condo, but I'll be closing next week on a house in Sandy Springs. I'm doing my practice full-time now."

"Really, so what happened to the Rainbow House?" I asked.

"It was never my plan to run it for a long time. I got it off the ground and once it became really successful, I hired a full-time manager, someone that could take the vision and make it grow. Now I'm the chairman of the board. My parents are still on the board as well. That frees up my time to be able to do what I love to do which is helping others and doing ministry," he said.

"Wait, what? You started a church, like a whole church?"

"No, not a church. I do a lot of work with HIV/AIDs in Atlanta, and actually, I'm glad you mentioned doing a documentary on it. I may be able to add some value to that. I also have a program that branched out of the Rainbow Homeless House. It's sort of ministry. It's Christian-based. I use Christian theology coupled with my therapy techniques to help those dealing with HIV, homelessness, and some other issues," he said.

"Oh wow, that's great. Awesome, actually. I just thought you were done with Christian ministry," I said.

"I never said that, I believe it was you that said that *you* were tired of it. I said that the way church is done needs to change. What better way to change it than to get in the trenches and make the changes happen. So, that's what I did. I offer ministry to gay people who still want a relationship with Jesus," he said.

"That's amazing. Good for you. How is it doing?" I asked

"It's going great so far. I see about 20 - 30 people a month. We are small, but growing. It's 2 years old. You should come check us out soon," he said.

"Okay cool. I will do that." The table got quiet. I pretended to look into my menu but I could feel Orlando's stare burning a hole into my forehead. I briefly peeked over the rim of the menu and there it was. That goddamned smile. I just smiled back and went back to my menu. I can't get caught up with this boy, not right now, not ever. His phone begin to buzz. Thank God for the interruption! I looked up at this point and I could see him still smiling as he reached over at his phone.

"I need to take this. I'll be right back," he said. He got up from the table to walk away.

"While you're up, grab a waiter or something, please," I said.

Orlando got up from the table. That should give me some time to fix my drooling. I was thinking about Tyler. I wondered what he is doing. Was he thinking about me? I didn't know. I wanted to know, but with him, so many things you just didn't know. I swear it seemed like the DL mentality never left that boy. He could be so guarded. I would have to pry simple things from him, and I was really starting to hate it. His parents still trip about the whole gay thing. I met them one time. They were not all too friendly. I told Tyler I never wanted to go through that again so quite naturally, to make me comfortable, we just never went see his family together. I met his sister though. She's cool. She was trying to move to Atlanta. She was always commenting on my pictures on Facebook. I loved that we had her support.

"I'm back. I'm so sorry. I had to take that call. Chrissy had a little issue with the house in Marietta today."

"Who's Chrissy?" I asked.

"She's the house manager for the Marietta location. The organization has four houses now. Oh and they are sending the manager over to our table."

"Wow! That's fucking awesome dude, but why is she calling you and not the CEO?" I asked

"My CEO is out on vacation so any issues are routing to me for the time being," he said.

"Oh okay. I was just wondering because I know it's been a minute since I took Non-profit Management. I'm pretty sure I remember the chair of the board not running the operations."

"You're such a geek. Who randomly points that out?" Orlando laughed.

"I'm just saying. I do have my MBA you know."

"Oh really, good for you! I knew you were made of some quality stock. Where from?"

"I got it from UGA," I said.

"Oh okay, smart ass," Orlando said.

"Says the guy running a practice, a church, and a non-profit organization." I chimed back.

"I'm not running the Rainbow House remember and I don't have a church," he said.

"I'm sorry to interrupt you two fellas. I'm Justin, I'm a manager here. I'm so sorry no one has come to serve you. I will be taking your order tonight and taking care of your bill. Again I am so sorry. What can I grab you to drink?" Justin asked.

I placed my order for a moscato and Orlando ordered a Bourbon Old Fashioned. The manager walked away with our drink orders and Orlando and I picked up on our conversation.

"I don't know why I got the MBA though. I haven't done anything worthwhile with it and here I am, making shit money with mountains of student loan debt," I said.

"Okay Brandon. Let me stop you right there because I'm hearing a lot of regrets coming from you. How's your appetite?" He asked.

"What?" I laughed. "Why you asking me that?" I asked.

"Just flow with me," he said.

"I mean…It's okay. I usually can eat when I'm hungry."

"Well, how often do you feel down and hopeless?"

"Hmm, it depends on what I'm doing. Usually three times a week at minimal. My weekends are a little better, unless Tyler is not home and I'm bored out of my mind."

"And when you are feeling down, do you cry or anything?" He asked.

"I don't cry, man. Why are you asking me all of this?" I asked.

"Hold on, bear with me. I know you talk about how you don't like your job right now, but what about other activities that you love to do. Have you discovered that you don't like to do them or does it feels hard to get motivated?"

"A little, sometimes. Not all the time. Like sometimes I can be all geared up to do something and then all of sudden, my mood changes up and I just don't feel up to it. Then when I get to that place, it feels so hard to get out of it. You think I'm depressed, don't you?" I asked.

"I won't diagnose you as that because this is not a therapy session, and typically a diagnosis can't be determined based on that type of direct questioning, but I will say that I think you are much so at risk of it and you should probably see a therapist about it. Are you still in contact with your therapist?" He asked.

"No I'm not. That was up in Maryland. Once my parents and I reconciled, I kinda stopped needing to see her. I stopped a lot of things including church. Anything that was helping me get to my center is gone," I said.

"You never stop needing to see a therapist. Even when

things are good, sometimes it is still good to have someone to talk to about things you know?" he said. "I mean, even I have a therapist," he said.

"Yeah, I know," I said.

"Well, can you be my therapist?" I asked.

"It's against my policies. I can't be your therapist because we have history, but I can recommend you to one that is phenomenal. You may have heard of her. She's on TV a lot and does radio. Her office is around here, down by Phipps. Her name is Spirit. Ever heard of her?" I asked.

"Yeah, I have. I didn't know she see's regular folk like me." I said.

"She does. Just because she is on TV doesn't mean she still isn't true to her calling. If you can get lucky and get on her case load, I think it would benefit you to set up an appointment with her so you can start figuring some things out with yourself and where you are now. I mean, a lot of time has passed for you and life happens every day, nonstop. A lot can happen in five years buddy. And then you aren't doing church or anything to keep yourself spiritually centered. Yeah you better do something about that," he said.

"I know. You are right. I will check her out," I said.

"Good for you," he replied.

Then there was that awkward silence again as he smiled at me. Orlando and I talked at the restaurant for a good little while. The manager had taken good care of us and our food was delicious. Chatting with Orlando was just what I needed. I had forgotten how easy he was to talk to and how well we communicated with each other. It reminded me of Tyler and me. Tyler and I could talk about everything under the sun. I miss him.

"Well sir it looks like they are cleaning up and we are the last ones here. I guess we should get up and get going," Orlando said.

"Yeah, you are right. I have to get up for work in the morning. I really don't want to go," I said.

"It's going to get better. Listen, I'd love to have you come to our next ministry session on Tuesday. You would love everyone. There are some really great people there," he said.

"That sounds good. Tyler will be flying back in on Monday, but I will let you know, okay?" I said.

"Bet," he said and rose from the table. I followed behind him and we exited together like the couple we never were.

Orlando and I stood outside and talked for about another hour. It's just like old times it seems. It's like he really gets me.

"So...any love interests in your life right now?" I asked.

"I have a couple of contenders. Nothing that's serious though. I have a guy that I'm into, but he's not from around here. He's cool people."

"Wait didn't you say you couldn't trust a guy if he didn't live in the city?" I asked. "Something about Beyoncé and baseball bats, remember that?" I laughed.

"Well after a while, you really get to see how shitty the pickings are around here and you end up just taking your chances with something long distanced, but it's been cool. Actually, the distance gives me the space I like, so it works. I like my space. I don't see how you sit here and complain about Tyler being gone so much. I'd love that. His absence would make me miss him, but at the same time it would allow me not to feel crowded. I think that would keep the relationship fresh," he said.

"But you do know that's not at all how a relationship will go. I mean...at least not in the long term," I said.

"I know and I'm working on that need to be alone thing I have going on, but in the meantime, it works for me. I don't need a man all up under me all the time. Why you asking me about my love life? It should have been you. It could have been you, hell it was you," he said.

"You know Tyler was in the picture."

"Ahem, was?"

"You know what I meant."

Yeah, and I know what you said too."

"Anyway," I said as I brushed up against him with a lean of my shoulder.

"I thought you had to get up early," he said.

"I do," I said and I looked away in the direction of my Uber ride who was in route.

"You know I could have simply driven you home, right? You don't want to leave, do you?" He asked.

"What makes you think that?" I asked.

"Cause you are still here."

"I don't have my car here, but you...I mean...you are still here and you have a whole Benz sitting right there," I said.

"You're right, I know why I am here still. The Uber excuse is cute, but you know the truth." He brushed his arm back against my arm. I could smell the fragrance of his cologne. I felt my dick start to rise. "Uber hurry the hell up!" I thought.

"The way I see it, your man is somewhere else right now. He should be here or else someone might slide in on his most prized possession," he said.

"You're right, he's somewhere right now, and you are a mess!" I said with a laugh. That's the charm that Orlando would lay on so effortlessly.

"I noticed he hasn't called you at all tonight. What's up with that?" He asked.

"I don't know. He'll text or something, I'm sure."

"Sounds suspect to me," he said.

"I can't do you right now Orlando," I said.

"What?" he asked with a look of fake surprise on his face. He was still brushing his arm against mine. The touch of his skin felt so good.

"I don't want to hear your theories about Tyler," I said.

"Well, I was right the first time," he said.

"Well you are wrong this time," I chimed back. *Where in the fuck is this Uber!*, I thought to myself. I took out my phone to check its status. The driver was 2 minutes out.

"Wait, I haven't even said anyth—"

"But you were thinking it and insinuating it. I know what you are thinking. You're thinking that Tyler is cheating on me." I said.

"I didn't say a thing. That boy loves you," he said.

"Yeah then why don't he act like it?" I asked. It seemed like my question was not only to Orlando but rhetorical to myself as I threw my head back and looked up at the stars. It was a clear night out.

"Are you really feeling that unloved?" He asked.

"I won't call it that. I just feel lonely," I said.

"I'm so sick of being lone-lay, every night while my man goes out with his hooomiiieeess. I just wanna know how it is to feel loved, to feel loovveeeee ohhh uuouhh!" Orlando sings into the night air interrupting the quiet all around us.

"So you gonna make fun of me?" I asked.

"Nah kid. I just thought about that song when you said that.

You just need some good loving. I mean, if he ain't around to give you what you need then go get it somewhere else," he said.

"What? No, I can't do that," I replied. My face turned up with shock and dismay.

"You can, you are just afraid to," Orlando said. He was looking away out into the skyline of Buckhead.

"Why would you suggest I cheat on Tyler? You are supposed to be a therapist," I asked him, trying to get him to turn my way. He turned to look at me with his shimmering eyes. My Uber was now a minute out.

"Yes, and as a therapist, I would tell my client that if they don't own up to their situations and accept some truths they are going to unwillingly "choose" to find someone else to fulfill their needs. Listen it's all textbook. Yes you can choose to cheat and you can choose not to cheat, but what you have to be more careful of are the little foxes. Cheating is a 12-step process in my playbook. The first time you felt alone and alienated was the first step being laid. That's all I am saying, and I am also telling you to stop sitting here feeling lonely because your man of 5 years is not giving you any attention. I know he works and shit, but maybe you two need to have a conversation about if this is working out or not. Listen, one thing I've learned is that loving someone is no good reason to stay in a bad situation, or in your case, an unhappy situation. It's just not worth it. I don't care how much you are in love. Love don't pay the bills and the absence of love doesn't give you what you need. Listen, can I be candid with you?" He asked.

"Yeah, sure?" I said. I looked at my Uber status on my phone. It was closing in, waiting at the red light.

"You are creating illusions for yourself. You want to desperately believe that what is sitting in front of your face as it concerns Tyler is not real. You are holding on to the old images of you and him backpacking through the south making that documentary. You have to see yourself for where you are now, and honestly, where you are now may not include Tyler like it once did. If you are not careful, those illusions are going to lead you right into someone else's bed. The heart wants what it wants, and so do the hormones. You can't defy nature with your illusions sir. So you say, 'oh I can't cheat, I'd never do that', well life has taught me that you don't know what you will do until you are put in the situation and sometimes the factors around you will make choosing and not choosing harder than you think," he closed.

I was silent. I had never thought about cheating on anyone before. It was just not something I felt capable of doing. Before I do that, I'd just tell Tyler that we are having problems and I need a break. Even still, I don't think I'd cheat during the break. I mean it was not like Tyler didn't pay me any attention when he was home. It's just that his time home was so scarce nowadays. I was so tired of not having anyone to go to movies with or to have dinners at home with. I just wanted some companionship or was I still building illusions again?

"So what are you thinking about?" Orlando asked.

"I'm thinking that I don't think I could cheat on Tyler, and definitely not do it on purpose either. It's not sex I want. It's the companionship I'm missing," I said.

"I hear you. Well listen, I'm here for you. I have advice for days, you know that," he said.

"Yeah I know. I better be getting on home now. My ride is pulling up. It's not a good luck for two black men to be loitering around in a parking deck in Buckhead," I said.

"Yeah, you are right. Well okay, give me a hug and I'll be on my merry little way," he said.

Orlando hugged me and it felt so good. I didn't really want to let go and it wasn't because it was him, but because it was a hug from someone. I just needed to be touched.

"I'll let you know about Tuesday," I said. I walked away as Orlando stood and watched. Tonight felt good in a weird way.

* * *

I woke up the next day with Orlando's last words on my mind. He seemed so sure that I was capable of cheating on Tyler. Was he right? He made some good theoretical points about what could lead a person to choose to cheat. It sounds like he was saying that the choices are made in small increments, and those increments start with little layers that are not cheating at all. It's like someone was trying to grab something off the top shelf. They would make all of these steps to get to that something like going to the garage, and going to the garage is not the same as getting something off the top shelf, grabbing the ladder out the garage isn't the same as grabbing something off the top shelf either. One could take that ladder and choose to use it to hang a picture.

This is how I process ideas that are foreign to me. I got out the bed to start my day by heading to the gym. I walked into the kitchen and made a smoothie and set it by the door so it'd be waiting for me when I walked out. My morning routine usually involved me going to the gym for some quick cardio. I'm not much of a weight lifter, but I'll do some small stuff from time to time. I don't like the muscle-bound look. I just like to be toned and lean and that works for me usually. The gym was on the 4th floor of our building. Once I got to the gym, I do my stretches and then get started on the treadmill. The treadmill is where I would do my thinking. That morning, I thought more on what Orlando and I concluded our night discussing.

I had to make what Orlando was saying make sense so I could see it the way he saw it. It did make sense, but what are my little foxes though? LIke getting something off the shelf, what steps have I put myself in to end up reaching for another man off a shelf? Could it be that every time I'm hurt by Tyler's lack of presence that it's the same as me going to the garage. What if I'm beyond that and now I'm in the closet with the ladder, climbing and climbing to that top shelf? Am I already at the top shelf about to grab what's there? Shit! Orlando's a good damn therapist. Wow what an analogy. After my workout, I showered at home and got dressed to start my day at work. The morning was beautiful. I had intended to go grab a breakfast sandwich, but I was running behind as usual. It's probably because of my racing thoughts. My thoughts were interrupted by a call.

Lamont, they guy who was in Tyler's and my first documentary called to let me know that a good friend of ours had died. It put a damper on my mood. I was leaving out of the parking garage when he gave me the news. Our friend who died had been dealing with cancer and he was positive. I think his HIV was managed though, but because he started treatment so late, he had some damage to his immune system. It just wasn't strong enough to ward off the cancer. It seemed like every year, I was attending a different funeral for someone in our community who had died from AIDS. HIV is HIV, and AIDS is AIDS. You can be HIV+ and be undetectable and everything, but if you get any other type of infection or issue, then more times than not, you are considered to have AIDS. They call these opportunistic infections. I still shudder at the thought of someone dying of AIDS. It's like, damn, no matter the medical advances that come, AIDS will still be the label for many who die with HIV. It's like there is no escape. What I do know is that the number one escape is to never get it in the first place.

I felt a jolt in my spirit and so I turned on my voice recorder and begin taking notes on the thoughts in my mind. They could be useful for my documentary. It was time for me to get that documentary going. I didn't know how I would pay for it, but what I did know is that I had to start it. It was necessary that I educate my community of gay men and women about the risks and dangers of HIV.

I recorded my thoughts as I filtered through the stop and go traffic of Peachtree road of Buckhead. Once I got to work, I put the recorder away. I parked and said a silent prayer to start my work day.

After stepped out the car, my phone began to ring. It was Tyler so I quickly answered.

"Hey my love. I wanted to catch you before you left out for work. How are you feeling?" He said.

"I'm good beloved. I'm just, you know, bummed out about Jonathan. I don't know if I can bury another person to AIDS, but I will be okay. Life goes on. I plan to go on in a different way, though."

"What do you mean?" Tyler asked.

"I can't shake this documentary I want to do, but I quickly realized that I don't have the money to fund it."

"Don't worry about that. I will help you. I was actually thinking about it and I looked up some grants that you can apply for."

"I don't know how to write a grant."

"You should," Tyler replied. "I mean, what did UGA teach you in that MBA program?"

"Well, it wasn't grant writing I can tell you that," I said.

"Well take a course on it. It can't be that hard. I'll help you out with it. I'll help you out with it all, okay?"

"Okay, thank you. I really appreciate your help."

"It's no biggie. I love you and that's what I am here for."

Sometimes, Tyler is the best boyfriend I could ever ask for and then other times he is not. I just don't get him. I can't put my finger on it but if I had to describe my experience with him over the past couple of years, I'd say it feels like dating a married man. Sometimes I get affection, and sometimes I don't get him because he makes himself so emotionally unavailable.

"What will you call it?" He asked.

"I haven't thought that far out yet. Maybe I can get your help with that part."

"Sure thing babe, you know I'm willing to help any way that I can."

"I know. I don't want to take away from your responsibilities with CNN. I won't be expecting your help on it, not the way we did *The Bow*," I said.

"Wow, look at you all grown up. I'm proud of you dear. This is definitely something that I think you should do. It will reignite you and perhaps pep you up some."

I sat on the edge of the bed wrapped in my towel. "Oh you have?" I asked. I wasn't expecting him to speak on that.

"Yes. I may not be home as much but I can always feel you, Brandon."

"Honestly Tyler, I didn't think you really cared. I mean, I don't expect you to be all up under me, but I miss you a lot. You're always gone. I know you have to work to help take care of us, but sometimes I'd rather we be back to when we were struggling. At least we were together a lot."

"Wow, I didn't know you were feeling like that honey. Why didn't you say anything?"

"I don't feel like I should have to say anything. Some things I feel like a person should just know if they are in a relationship. It's like we have become complacent with each other," I said.

"I'm sorry, Brandon. It is not my intention to make you feel neglected. The weather is all clear and we are expected to take off in a couple of hours. I think we should do something together when I get home. How does that sound?" He asked.

"I'd like that. What do you have in mind?" I asked.

"I don't know. I feel like we have eaten at all the restaurants in Atlanta. Don't worry about it. I will plan something for us to do. How does that sound?"

"That sounds good to me honey. What time will you be back in?" I asked

"I'll be catching a flight back around 9am west coast time. I should be landing there about 3 or 4ish," he said.

"Great! I can't wait to see you babe!" I said.

"I can't wait to see you too. Do know that I love you very much. I know that I am not around much, but I do really care that you are not feeling fulfilled," he said.

"Thank you dear. That's what I needed to hear from you. Thank you. I love you too. Ok, well I'll let you go because I know you have to get to the airport," I said.

"Yes I do. I'll let you know what we will do tonight. Just make sure your fine ass is right for your man," he said.

I felt something go all over me. I blushed and said, "Okay love!"

"I will text you when I am boarding the plane. Think of me."

"I will. Bye love," I said.

That man still makes my heart skip beats. No sooner after that, my phone chimed.

Good Morning, You, it read. It was Orlando. Why did I even open this door again? I waited before I replied. I wanted it to seem like I had gotten caught up in starting my day. I also didn't want to seem inviting, although I guess one could say that ship has already sailed. Have you ever had chemistry with someone that was so strong that you just couldn't deny that it was there? Yeah, that's where I am with Orlando. You would have to be around him yourself to see exactly what I am talking about. Whew, this boy is something else. And, it's like he knows it too. I can tell that he doesn't try to do this stuff on purpose. It's just genuinely how he is. I've never seen anyone so charming before. I mean, my Tyler is charming in his own little way, but Orlando had him beat. I must admit that. That's why I must be careful. I got settled in the little office that I share with a couple of other journalist. It was split out with cubicles that each had stacks of papers all over them. We always had mountains of work to do.

I replied back after three hours. By this time, I was out in the field working. Jamie and I managed to catch a break in between stories and that's when I sent my good morning back. Orlando was absolutely right, again. I am coy as fuck. I like this little cat and mouse game we play. I shouldn't be playing it anyway.

"So Jamie, I have decided to go ahead and do the documentary. What do you say about being my producer? I could really use your help."

"Wow that was quick. Just the other day we were talking about this. What made you change your mind?" He asked.

"Well, it wasn't a matter of me changing my mind, but more a matter of me making the decision to move forward. I have realized that I do have the power to change my outcomes and sitting around bitching about things won't do much to change my outcome. Also, I had a friend who died early this morning from AIDS-related cancer and after losing him, among so many others in the past, I decided it was time to get off my ass and do this. So do you want to be a part?" I asked.

"You know I am down for it. Have you discussed this with Janice yet? You know she is going to want to have some input on it," he said.

"I have not yet. I plan to meet with her on Thursday. I don't think she will have an issue, but I guess we will see. But at any rate, what should we do for lunch?" I asked.

"I kinda got a taste for some Mexican," he said.

"Okay, cool, Mexican it is. Have you ever been to Uncle Julio's?" I asked.

"Yeah, a couple of times. They are pretty good. We can go there."

The restaurant was a short ride from where we were currently covering a story. Once we arrived, we managed to find a parking spot. The lunch time parking for most restaurants in the city is usually scarce. Once inside of the restaurant, Jamie and I got a table out on the deck at Uncle Julio's. The weather was nice and the hum of Peachtree Street was as usual. Atlanta has really grown on me and I really like it. Even with all of the eye candy that is around, I have managed to not get into any trouble. I just hope that's the same for Tyler. I know he loves me and things but sometimes I can't help but wonder if he is truly faithful to me. I guess time will tell. I am not one of those who will snoop through phones.

"What's on your mind over there?" Jamie asked.

"Oh nothing. Just thoughts. You know how I am," I said.

"How are things on the home front; where is Tyler?" He asked.

"Tyler should be landing in a couple of hours," I said.

"Oh that's great. So you two will be M.I.A. for a while I bet."

"Why do you say that?" I laughed.

"I'm just saying, If I was days without my man, I know what we would be doing by the time he came back home. The phones would be on do not disturb."

"Jamie, you wouldn't know what to do with a man," I said.

"I resent that. You assume I'm straight?" He asked.

"Well I mean...I don't get that vibe from you but even if you were gay, what would you know to do with a man?" I laughed.

"I'll take that as a rhetorical question. But just so you know, I would know what to do with a man."

Jamie was a child compared to me. With me knocking on the door of 30, Jamie was 23 and very good at his work. He went to Georgia Tech.

"Brandon, can I ask you something?" Jamie asked.

"Always, what's up?"

"How did you know that you are gay? Like when did you know for sure?" He asked.

"Well, for me, I have always known that I was gay since I

was a small child. I just knew that something was different about me. I couldn't identify what it was, but I knew I was different. I had a hard time relating to other boys in the normal way. Like, I was not interested in sports. I was quiet and soft spoken. I was never an assertive person, not until I got older. I don't know, I guess I just always knew," I replied.

"So you did not go through a period of second guessing yourself on whether you was gay or not?" He asked.

"Do you mean if I have ever been attracted to girls and was maybe unsure if I was gay because of that?" I asked for clarity.

"Yes, exactly," he said.

"Umm, no. I've always known for sure that I liked boys. I had a girlfriend once though. I really did love her. It was grade school stuff though, but even with that, I can't remember being physically attracted to her. I think it was the friendship that I was fawning over and the fact that an actual girl had taken interest in me," I said.

"Wow, that's interesting. So you don't think that you're bisexual or have been at any other point in your life?" He asked.

"No, I can honestly say that I have never been in that type of limbo as it concerns men and women."

"Intriguing," he said.

I just looked at him with a blank stare. I wasn't quite understanding where this line of questioning was originating from. It seemed like Tyler was on the other side of the table from me.

"So...where did that come from?" I asked.

Jamie just looked at me and smiled. He's a rather nice looking guy.

"Oh nothing. As they say, if you want to understand

something that you know little about, then just ask," he said.

"I've never heard that but if you say it's a saying, then it's a saying," I said. I stopped my probe, but my mind was still wondering. Perhaps I was just obsessed with men who are down low. It could have been a subconscious thing because of my experience with Tyler.

"How do we get this documentary going? What is your plan for it? What about HIV are you attempting to investigate?" He asked, casually shifting the conversation.

"I have no idea honestly. I will have to take some time and organize my direction for it, but first, I will need to speak with Janice. Tyler did help me out a little with it last night. Once he is here, we will dive into it deeper," I said.

"You really think she is going to allow you to do it?" Jamie asked.

"I don't know. I guess we shall see," I replied.

"Okay, well, cool. Let me know how that goes when it happens," he said.

"I just don't know how I got so far behind. Tyler is out living it up, doing his passion. I was supposed to be there with him. I don't know how I ended up with a random ass 9-5," I said.

"Well, honestly, Brandon, I wouldn't consider it a random ass 9-5. I mean, you are still working in your chosen field. It's not exactly in the way you want it to be, but you are doing what you are called to do. Most people are in the same situation with their chosen field and what they actually start out doing. This is just a stepping stone, and who knows what it will lead to? Don't compare yourself to Tyler. Tyler has his own journey, just like you do. If it's meant that you two do that journey together then it'll happen. In the meantime, take this for what it is and make sure that you are building yourself in the process," Jamie said.

What Jamie just said was thought provoking. It almost made me wonder if somehow the universe was speaking to me in a deeper way to give me a deeper message about Tyler and me. Not only did I feel a way about not being on Tyler's level when it comes to my journalism, but I also had been feeling a way about the trajectory of our relationship. What I heard in what Jamie said that I should not focus so much on Tyler and me being together because it may not be meant for us to be. Or am I just reading too much into it?

"Thanks, Jamie. You just might be right. Oddly enough, Tyler said some of the same stuff to me last night." By this time we had finished our lunch. It was about time to head back to the office. No sooner than by the time we got back in the car, my phone starts buzzing. I looked over at Jamie with bewilderment. "It's Janice," I said.

"Janice? I wonder why would she be calling you," he said.

I put my finger to my lip as I answered the phone.

"Hi Janice," I said.

We chatted briefly. I ended the call with, "Sure thing, see you soon."

Jamie looked at me with inquiry.

"I have a meeting with Janice before we head out," I said to Jamie.

"Oh, really? What is it going to be about?" he asked.

"I'm not too sure, although, I think I have an idea," I said.

"Well, what do you think it is?" He asked.

"I have no clue. You know how I've been showing disinterest in the assignments they send me on, well I think she's going to ask me about that," I said.

"What makes you so sure," he asked.

Chapter 4

"I just know. I'll let you know how it goes. She wants to see me once I get back," I said. I started up the car and we headed back down Peachtree toward the station. My anxiety tried to flare up, but in my mind I just told myself to be cool. I really did not have anything to be concerned with. But just as Alec predicted she asked to see me and because he had already warned me of sorts, I have a little bit of an idea that she may want to discuss my career here. I think I'm just going to use this as an opportunity to share my desires with her and see where it goes. Janice is usually easy to talk to but she can be cutthroat so I'm really not too sure who I'm meeting with, the nice Janice or Janice the pit bull.

Five

Chapter 5

J amie and I arrived back to the building. After we got back into the studio and unloaded our footage, I prepared for my meeting with Janice. She was right down the hallway from our area.

"Okay, here goes nothing," I said to Jamie.

"I'll say a prayer," he said with a smile.

I approached her office with a slow knock on her door.

"It's open," she yelled.

I went in and she motioned me to have a seat.

"So, Brandon. I wanted to meet with you to talk about your work," she said.

She went straight to the point which was a bit concerning for me. No small talk, no good morning, no nothing.

"Okay, what about it?" I asked

"Here at WSB, we take pride in our teams and the content they deliver. Are you happy with your role here?"

Her questions caught me off guard. I was not expecting her to ask me that so bluntly. I hesitated a little and then answered, "Honestly, no, I'm not. I mean I know that this is a part of the career path, a boot camp of sorts, but I dunno. I'm not happy with the type of stories I am sent out to cover."

"Hmmm," she said and jotted down some notes. "Tell me more about that, the type of assignments. What type of assignments would you be interested in?"

"The assignments do not challenge my talents. Don't get me wrong, I love reporting news, but I also like discovering news...meaningful news. I just don't think reporting on local crime stories and other local things is up my alley. Honestly, I've become quite burned out with it. When I was wrapping up my undergrad program at HSU, I envisioned myself being a backpack journalist actually," I replied. She looked at me and leaned back in her chair with a rock. Her eyes were locked intently on me. She is one that looks you straight in the face during a conversation as if she is reading your soul. The chair popped forward as her stare broke and her eyes brightened a bit. Was it empathy I saw? I don't know. I just hope she wouldn't yell, "You're fired, get the fuck out!"

"Interesting. Listen, I totally understand your sentiments. My first job out of college was working for a small newspaper press in my hometown. I lived at home with my alcoholic father, and it just wasn't my ideal situation. But thanks to my mentor, who was the editor of the paper, saw potential in me. She helped me expand my talents and eventually, I would help her create and develop a magazine for the local area. She made me the editorial curator and it was the open door I needed to jump-start my career. That one little opportunity lead me to New York, working for The New York Times, helping them roll out their online presence, since this was around the time the internet was becoming hot and popping. Fast forward to today, and I'm here at WSBV being tasked with helping the station find new ways to draw in viewers. Here is where you come in. I know a little about your background. Actually, I'm lying…I know a lot about your background, and I know investigative journalism is your wheelhouse. So I've been thinking, our first job is to report the Atlanta news, and we will always do that in the traditional way, but I also want to add some more elements to how we do that."

"Okay, I'm listening. What ideas do you have?" I asked.

"Well, that's why I have you in here. I saw your work on *The Bow* documentary and some other items from your portfolio. I feel that you would be perfect to help lead this part of our crew. Here is the plan: We are going to begin doing an investigative session of our news program where we do some investigative journalism to bring stories to our viewers on things that affect our community here in Atlanta - like the recent fiasco with voting machines during the Governor's race. People want to know what really happened, they want to hear the story behind things that are taking place in our community," she said.

I begin to smile a little, although I wanted to be coy.

"This sounds exciting. Are you offering me a part in this?" I asked.

"Yes, I am offering you a promotion. How does Executive Investigative Director sound?" She asked with a grin. It was as if she knew she was turning my stove on.

"It sounds like music to my ears!" I replied excitedly. I was so excited I dropped my phone out of my hands which were sweaty due to nerves. I reached down to grab it in embarrassment. "I'm so sorry," I said.

"It's okay, Brandon. I figured it would make you excited. The other executives and I reviewed this proposal and we found you to be the perfect fit for this. You are raw talent sitting in our midst and I want to develop you. You will have a team of journalists who would assist you. Your role would be to come up with investigative stories for them to follow and do research on. I kinda want these to be produced in a 20/20 type of format. We are allotting you with a 30-minute time slot for these shows. Right now the show will air twice a week. We are expected to launch in three months, so this gives you time to interview and hire your team, begin selecting stories for them to investigate and start producing. Now you are given about 90% authority to run this area but you will have to pass all stories through me for approval. My best suggestion is for you to brainstorm a list of about 5 stories to get you started. You would be responsible for doing some light research, you or your team, and then sell the story to me for approval. Any questions?" She asked.

"I'm sure I have plenty, but I'm so shocked right now I can't think of any. Okay so you said I can pick my own team. Do they have to come from within or off the street?" I asked.

"They can be from within or off the street. You may post the positions and invite internal associates and use some of our recruiters to pull in outside candidates and begin building your team. I will assist you with that since it would be your first time doing that sort of thing," she said.

"Awesome, okay, I do have a question," I said.

"Sure, what's that?" she asked.

"It sounds like this role has some management duties as well? I don't have any supervisory experience," I asked.

"You have a MBA from UGA - that's enough for me and besides your concentration was project management, I am confident that you are prepared to run this team and the projects this team will produce, and I will mentor you along the way. So what do you say?" She asked as she stood up with her hand extended.

I stood up and reached out and shook it and said, "I most definitely am interested, but I feel I need to talk it over with my partner first. I just want his thoughts about it."

"You mean Tyler? Oh sure, take the time you need. I'll be here when you are ready. In the meantime, let me show you what we are offering as salary for this role," she said.

She slid a piece of paper over to me and I must say, it was a pretty substantial increase from what I was currently making. I was all smiles.

"Well this certainly should make this offer much easier to accept, as if it wasn't easy before," I said with a giggle.

"Thank you so much for this. This is exactly the open door I had been looking for. I won't let you down. I will have a decision to you first thing in the morning."

"Great, just stop by my office and we can pick up from there," she said.

I walked out of her office and just fell to my knees with thanksgiving in my heart. I could not wait to tell Tyler. "Thank you, Jesus!" I shouted and I didn't care who heard.

* * *

I texted Tyler right away.

Baby, have you landed yet? Call me once you are able.

I assumed maybe he was still in route. I didn't know his flight number to track if he had landed yet or not.

I went back into my office area and met a patient Jamie waiting for me to return.

"So, spill the beans. What did Janice want with you?" Jamie asked.

"Oh nothing, just a little talk about my job here and…a big fat ass promotion!"

"Shut up! For real? Wow, so tell me about it."

"Well, I have not officially accepted the offer yet, but I am very sure I will. Man, Jamie, it's like she's been reading my thoughts and listening in on my conversations. She begin asking me about how I felt about my work duties. I just told her the truth. Well it's said the truth will set you free, and free indeed is what it did. She begin to talk about a new thing she wants to do here and she wants me to head it up. She offered me a position of Executive Investigative Producer. I'll get to do some investigative journalism!" I said excitedly.

"Wow that's great. Shockingly great. I'm happy for you."

"Yes, a shock it was, and thank you so much."

"Aww man, so we won't be working together anymore?" Jamie asked. He looked genuinely sad. It kinda threw me a little.

"Oh wow, I didn't even think about that. Don't worry about it. I think we can still ensure we work together some, but in the meantime, we have work to get to today so let's hop on it."

I'm still trying to figure Jamie out. A part of me feels like he is suspect. My gaydar is usually not off. Sometimes I think to just flat out ask him, but he's a coworker and that would be sexual harassment. I'll try to get it out of him another way.

Jamie and I were headed to an apartment complex to report

on a water main break that hadn't been fixed in two days and the residents had been without water. We were supposed to be done today, but another crew was caught up in traffic and we were nearby. The station always wants to be the first on scene.

"Have you told Tyler about your good news yet?" Jamie asked.

"I haven't spoken to Tyler yet, but I did call him. He hasn't called back. I think he is still in the air."

"Oh he didn't arrive yesterday as scheduled?"

"No, he didn't He says there was some weather that caused his flight to be cancelled, or something like that."

"You must really trust him. I think I'd be questioning all of these mishaps that seem to happen with him."

"Is that right?"

"Yes, it just seems odd. Don't you think its odd?"

Here was my opportunity to see if I could get inside of his head. I find it strange a straight man would consider the behavior of another man odd.

"I don't give it much thought. The way I see it, what's done in the dark will make its way to the light."

"Sometimes," he replied.

"What you mean by that?"

"I'm saying, sometimes people get away with their shit. Some secrets are well hidden. Trust me, I know."

"Do you? Expound." I said.

"Let's just say, I've helped some people cheat before and the mate still doesn't know a thing."

"Helped as in you were the one they were doing the dirty work with?"

"Yes."

"Okay, so… you think Tyler is out cheating on me?"

"It doesn't matter what I think. He's who you want. If he is or isn't, you're still with him, right?"

"So you're saying I shouldn't be with him?"

"No, I'm saying if you feel he is cheating, just ask him."

"I can't do that. I don't have any real reason to ask him something like that." I said.

"Seems to me if you are having doubts, then that's reason enough. What if he is cheating? What if he tells you, yes he is, are you prepared to handle that?"

"I think so."

"Hmm." Jamie said nothing further nor did he look my way.

"Wait, what was all that about?" I asked.

"Nothing, I personally don't think you would be ready to handle that. You don't seem like the type that would understand the dynamics of infidelity. I don't even believe you yourself would be capable of cheating."

"Don't be so sure about that," I said. I looked at him. My eyes were still talking although the words of my mouth had stopped.

Jamie looked at me with his mouth open wide. He is one cute red-headed white boy.

"You are fucking lying! That's hard to believe, especially as much as you go on about Tyler. When did this happen?"

"I don't know what you're referring to."

"You know what I'm referring to, sir. Tell me about it."

"I'm astounded how you want to hear about my gay escapades. Is there something you want to share?"

"Maybe, but umm, you first. I asked for your dirt first."

"Can't believe I'm about to tell you this." I said. Actually, I could believe it. That's how I was going to get that little ginger stud muffin to tell me his tea.

"So, last night, I had dinner with an old friend. One thing lead to another and we ended up having sex. I got up today. I didn't feel much guilt about it. He's an old flame, so maybe a part of me always wanted it to happen. I also am just so sick and tired of Tyler not being here for and with me. I know that doesn't justify it, but oh well. What's done is done."

"Damn, just last night. So this just happened, you still probably smell like him!" Jamie said as he grabbed my arm and leaned in for a sniff.

"Chile hush. He smells like a god on Christmas morning. You'd know if you still smelled him."

"Maybe, I mean you smell good most of the times anyway so I wouldn't really notice," he said.

"Hmmm. Well now you know, I'm not perfect and yes I understand infidelity more than you think. But that doesn't mean that I will automatically just know if Tyler is cheating just because I have."

"I guess you are right. So, is this going to be the last time you do it?"

"Well, I definitely don't plan to make a habit of it. The guy I did it with, he's so something…charming, debonair, cultured. He is everything. If he texted me now and wanted to hook up, I'd probably have to fight to say no."

"Wow, so he was that good huh?"

"No, it's not that. I mean, shit yeah, he's good plus some, but no. I would rather say that we are good together and that's what makes things tough. We actually have history."

"So he's an ex?" Jamie asked.

"No, not really. Okay, so when Tyler and I first came down here to shoot *The Bow* after the Storm a few years ago, we met this guy. He and I hit it off. Tyler was DL. At that time, I didn't even know for sure he was gay. I mean, I suspected it, but I wasn't sure about it. Well me and this guy started dating a little, but it was short lived because by the time we had finished shooting the documentary, Tyler had come out to me and confessed his love for me. I chose Tyler and broke it off with the guy. I ran into him last week at Chick-fil-A."

"Chick-fil-A? You eat there?" Jamie asked.

"Yes, what's wrong with that?"

"They hate gays, Brandon."

"Their politics have nothing to do with me directly. I'm sure the rich people that own this station support conservative interests as well. I'm not going to quit my job because of the notion."

"I suppose," Jamie answered. "Back to you though. So Tyler was DL? Was he straight before?"

"No, not really. He was just really hiding his sexuality. He struggled with that a lot. Honestly, I think he still does," I said.

"Well do you ever ask him about it?" Jamie asked.

"No, I don't. When he's with me I don't get the vibe that he is still struggling."

"But he's hardly with you though."

"That's true. I mean it's not like he's been AWOL the whole five years that we have been together," I said.

"Do you think that you are a good read of people?"

"I think so, sometimes. What makes you ask?"

"Just pondering. Can I may speak freely?" he asked.

"Sure, that's why I asked what made you ask."

"First, this mystery guy seems like trouble. Do you really want to throw your relationship away on that? Is he that good in bed? Is it worth it? Honestly, you should consider if he is just trying to get back at you for breaking up with him. You know, some people don't like to see others happy. I don't get a good feeling about him," Jamie said.

"You haven't even met him before," I said.

"I don't have to. I just know what I sense. Second, what if Tyler is still struggling with his sexuality? Are you sure he's not in that space still? Yeah, sure, he's okay with you, but what about the totality of it?"

"I don't give it much thought," I said.

"Yeah cause you're always in your own head about the relationship. Have you ever considered that perhaps he is distant for reasons that may not have anything to do with you in the way you think it does? He could be dealing with something."

"Nah, I think that's a bit of a reach. I would know if my baby was depressed or dealing with something."

"Would you?" he asked. Jamie was starting to get on my nerves a little bit and I know why. He was forcing me to think beyond the surface or perhaps my own selfishness about the people in my life.

"You sure are going in hard with your questions here sir," I said

"We work in the world of journalism. We get to the truth. If I can tell you a hard truth about you I will."

"You can, go for it."

"Brandon, you're self-absorbed. I'm not calling you selfish, but you tend to get stuck in your own head about things and you fail to see what's right in front of you sometimes. You're criticizing Tyler for being detached, but you're just as detached as he is. I think you pay attention to what you want to pay attention to and when you do realize things, you don't speak on them because you make things about you when you think about them. Sometimes, confronting an issue head on will work out good for you."

What the fuck? I thought to myself. He is clocking me like a state patrolman.

"Well you sure are introspective today. So let's say you are right, How—

"Oh I am," Jamie interrupted.

"Ugh, anyway, let's say that you are right. How about this for straightforward confrontations on what I pay attention to: I get a feeling that you may be interested in men yourself."

He sat quietly for a few seconds and then he broke the silence.

"Your vibe is correct. Why didn't you ask me sooner?" he asked.

"I don't make it a habit of assuming people are gay or straight. Nowadays you can't really tell and especially with you white boys, it's not easy to clock you guys."

"I have been gay since I could walk and what does me being white have to do with anything?"

"Here's the deal, Jamie. White guys, well white families in general are usually more open emotionally. White mean are typically not taught to have to prove their masculinity. They are allowed to be sensitive in a way that black men aren't. Black men have to spend most of their lives proving their masculinity. A lot of that comes from the effects of slavery. So essentially, black men are not taught to embrace their emotions. We are taught those types of things make us soft and gay. But because white men in general are just more aware of themselves and how they fit into society, they tend to be more sensitive and emotional. in other words, you don't see hyper-masculinity among some cultures like you do with the black culture. So for that reason, it's not always that easy to tell if a white man is gay based on some of the same factors that I am able to tell that a black man is gay. Does that make sense?"

"It makes perfect sense and so eloquently explained."

"So why didn't you feel you could share with me that you are gay?"

"The same reason you don't share it with people. It's just not something you walk up to people and share. Don't allow the fact that I'm white to cause you to believe that our struggles in the LGBT community are different. It's not that much different. We get ostracized by our families just as much. We are shamed just as much and face suicidal rates just the same."

"I will be the first to admit that I need to work on not thinking that black gays have it the worst compared to other races, but...but Jamie, it is different for black gay men. Imagine all that you and your counterparts face as white gay men and then add to it discrimination and prejudices because you are black and then...on top of that, add the hate that your own race of people project on you for being gay. Many in my race consider me to be dirty and a part of some agenda to keep the black race down, as if my being gay somehow equates to Jim Crow or something. I'm just saying, I think it's bliss for the white gay man in America"

"I get that, Brandon. And I don't aim to discount your experience as a black man who happens to be gay, or a gay man who happens to be black or just simply, a black gay man, however people choose to see it. I think for me, I'm just a little lethargic of dealing with the notion that my whiteness somehow diminishes the experiences I've had as a gay man, just because I am white. Now yes, in general, the white race is privileged beyond measure and I would be amiss if I did not acknowledge that, but not all of us whites have gotten the better advantage of that privilege. Just like you get offended by racist comments from white, I get just as offended when nonwhites assume that I benefit from white privilege. Not all white people are experiencing that bliss you're talking about—at least not the way you are blanketing it. I do have privilege, but not when it comes to how I've been treated for being gay in my own family."

"You're right, Jamie. I'm sorry. I apologize for diminishing your experiences because you are white. It's reverse racism and it's not right of me to do that and I am ashamed to have done so. I don't want you feeling that I look at you and feel you have some type of privilege that separates you from understanding me or my experiences. I think we can work to ensure that we learn from each other more. Don't be mad at me. Give me a hug," I closed with a smile. I could tell that he was genuinely upset.

He leaned in and hugged me and then looked out the window. Maybe he was still mad. I continued to drive to our story. We had arrived. I parked and we just kinda sat there in silence. Then I felt him grab my hand.

"I accept your apology. I want you to know that I've really enjoyed being around you all this time. Although I wasn't sharing with you things about me, being able to see you live your life open and confidently has been a great help to me. I'm actually happy that I can show you more of me and hopefully that means we can grow closer as friends, and the racial disconnections will go away."

I was kinda shaken by what he said coupled with the soft

warm touch of his hand. I felt myself being aroused. This is definitely something I will have to get used to with him. He is so open and sensitive, and I'll have to learn not to interpret it as him coming on to me.

"Thank you, Jamie. I'm looking forward to that," I said with a smile. I could see him blush a little. "Now let's go get this story done," I said.

Six

Chapter 6

I had just found out Tyler won't be making it in today. His flight was delayed due to some storms. *I guess I'll be landing sometime early in the morning. I'm sorry love. I know you were looking forward to our time together this evening. Keep the sheets warm for me. I love you.* Tyler texted.

I guess he couldn't help the weather, but man I was getting sick of these types of texts. I was also a bit annoyed that he didn't call like I requested. It had been a long day and I was tired. I decided that I'd go make some time for myself at the spa. I just needed to relax. I have so much on my mind that I am dealing with. I had gone down to the gym in our building to do some working out. Aftwards, I sat in the sauna. As I sat in the sauna, my phone began to buzz. It was Alec.

"Hey friend, what's up?"

"You were on my mind. How is it going?" Alec responded.

"It's going. I'm trying to keep my thoughts positive, but you know, things are getting a little tough for me. I…I don't know. Guess who is still not home yet."

"You mean to tell me that Tyler still got his ass in L.A.? Brandon, what's really going on with y'all?"

"He was supposed to come home today, but the weather caused his flight to be cancelled. I guess he will be here sometime tomorrow. This shit is getting crazy. I'm feeling lonely and down."

"Well honey, don't let it get you down. Such is life. Listen, you want me to come up there to visit you? I mean, I owe Londell a visit anyway."

"Who is Londell?" I asked.

"Londell, honey! You know…oh I guess I didn't tell you his name. That's my boo thang I was telling you about. I plan to come up to see him in a couple of months. I'd love to have you guys meet. I think you will like him."

"Oh okay, well cool…sure…I look forward to that."

"Well damn honey, if I had to go by your tone, I wouldn't think you were happy about it."

"Don't mind me. I'll be alright. I just got to get my shit together."

"You need to go talk to someone. A therapist, life coach or something honey."

"I will. I got a referral to someone the other day actually. I'm going to call her and set up an appointment."

"Good for you. I just hate seeing you in this type of aura. It's not cute chile, but you know I am always here for you, and I love you. Well, look, I got to get back out here to work. I swear these people act like they can't do what they supposed to do without someone watching over them every second. UGH! I need another job."

"Thank you, Alec. I love you too."

"Okay love, gotta go, Bye."

Talking to Alec made me feel somewhat better. I got up from the sauna and showered and headed for home. I texted Orlando to see if he was free. I figured I may as well have dinner and not have it alone.

Grand Lux? 7:00p? I walked away from the phone as if my fingers had not just actively plotted dinner with my ex.

A little while had passed, and he finally responded. I thought I would have to go somewhere alone.

Hey! Sure! I'd love too. I'll meet you there. Phipps location?

Yes...that's the only one I know of." After sending that response, I sat on the edge of the bed and stared at the wall which stared back at me, faceless. I was faceless too. I needed attention and at that moment, I didn't care who it came from.

* * *

I drove this time. I went to secure a table. The wait times are usually bananas but it was early in the week and it wasn't as busy although there was still a small 20-minute wait. I put in a reservation for a table and sat down. Soon enough the essence of beauty which is Orlando McIntyre came walking through the door. "Why is this man so fine to me?" I said to myself.

"There he is!" he said as he walked over and gave me a hug, smelling like Armani Code. He was dressed to a T. He had on these light blue, stone washed, slightly tattered jeans, a canary yellow shirt, with a white knitted sweater of some sort. The sweater was very different. It draped down to his mid thigh. It was a becoming look on him.

"Wow you look great," I said out loud, which I didn't intend to. He just laughed and smiled.

"Thank you, I try. You look good too, as usual," He said as he sat down next to me. "Can I admit something?"

"Umm, sure," I said, not knowing what he was about to say.

"I was so surprised to see your invitation, and for it to come across so definitively. I was happy to see it, but surprised."

"Why is that?"

"Well, I remember you said that Tyler would be back tonight. I honestly didn't think I'd hear from you much this week because of that."

"Spoken like a player," I said.

"No," he said with a laugh. "You have to understand that I just have a mindfulness to the psychology of people. I figured you'd be spending and devoting your attention and time to him. So why should or would I interfere with that?"

"What if I wanted you to interfere?"

"What does that mean?" He asked.

"Nothing, don't worry about it," I said with a grin. I pretended to look off into the restaurant to people-watch. The hostess stood looking intently into her computer screen. Waiters rushed to and fro from the kitchen, to the bar, and then to the floor. It was a typical night.

"You are so hard to figure out," he said, interrupting my people watching.

"I know, that's the point," I said. My phone vibrated and I looked down thinking perhaps Tyler was messaging me, but it was the automatic messages for our table. It was ready. "We should get moving to the hostess' desk."

I got the hostess attention and I could feel Orlando standing behind me very close as if he would wrap his arms around me in any second. He didn't though. Our waiter came to escort us to our table.

We took our seat and there we were.

"So, how was your day today?" He asked.

"It was okay. I did a story on a robbery at a Walgreens in Cobb County."

"Interesting…What happened?"

"The store was robbed," I replied with a look of confusion.

"You and your smart-ass mouth."

"What?"

"Nothing sir."

"Okay, the guy robbed the store, he ran away on foot. The police are still out looking for him. I'm sorry for the sarcasm."

"No need to apologize. I recognize it's your boredom with your work that fuels it. I didn't take offense, but what I would suggest is that you be mindful of how you speak about your job or anything that relates to it. You don't even realize how the way you feel about it comes across. Energy, energy, energy. Always be mindful of your energy."

"Why are you always so damn preachy?"

"It's just my nature. I'm a caregiver. You know my work and my background."

"I guess."

"Well listen, I'll be attending an AIDS Coalition event next month. I have a plus-one ticket. I'd like for you to come. I think it will give you some opportunity for your documentary."

I just sort of looked at him in that moment. I wasn't expecting the invitation, but moreover, it represented how much he pays attention to me. He always did seem to do that so well. Tyler used to do that. I felt a bit of warmth inside when he said that. Wow, to think of me in that way and my interests. I hadn't even mentioned to him that I had officially planned to start the documentary process.

"Thank you so much for inviting me. Let me see what my schedule will look like and I'll let you know."

"Check your schedule or check Tyler's schedule?"

"My schedule, why would I need to check Tyler's schedule?"

"Let me ask you something, Brandon. Does he know you are here with me tonight? Did you tell him about the other night? What are you doing here with me? What do you want from me, Brandon?"

"No," I said as I looked away. I was not expecting this line of questioning, but if I can recall correctly, Orlando has never been one to beat around the bush on anything.

"Why doesn't he know?"

"Why does it matter, Orlando?" I asked.

"It matters plenty. You know how we vibe with each other. This is a situation waiting to happen and you know it. You are here for a reason."

"I was with you the other night because we ran into each other and you asked me out to dinner and-"

"And you could have said no. Don't make this about me and not about how you feel."

"Oh so you think I feel something?" I rolled my eyes at his assumption.

He chuckled and said, "I don't know, that's what I want to know. Why are you here?"

"Tonight, I am here because Tyler is not," I replied. I looked into my menu. It was starting to feel tense for me.

"So you are here to make yourself feel better and you are using me to do it?"

"No, it's not like that."

"Then what is it like? Hey, look at me. Seriously, what is it like?" He asked.

"I don't know, stop badgering me." I said in a frantic.

"You see, Brandon. You have a lot of internal work to do. I am an indulgence for you right now. You have been dealing with depression, you're lonely and you are frustrated with your job. An affair is a convenient escape for you. I can't be that escape."

"I'm not asking you to be my escape."

"Then why are you here?"

Orlando was really making me think. I knew that I couldn't tell him that I was here because I just wanted to have him make me feel good about myself, if not just for a moment.

"Umm…I'm here…because…I miss feeling what I feel when I'm around you. Tyler used to make me feel that— the excitement, the jitters, all of it. I really have been missing that. I feel like I'm in love with a ghost. Having you show back up in my life, I dunno…it's like now I feel like life doesn't have to be so bland and empty feeling for me."

"I get that, but why do you think you should or could take this type of gamble by being here with me, knowing that we have history. You know what our chemistry is like."

"You know, your ass is asking a lot of questions about me and my motives. What about your motives. Why are you here? What do you want from me? Don't make it seem like I have you here all on my own agenda," I said.

"I'm here because you know like I've always made it known to you that I consider you to be a special person. Even though you fucked me over, I still never really got over you like that. I always marked you as, "the one that got away."

"So why sit here and make it seem like its all me then?"

"I wasn't, I was just seeing where your awareness is. Some people cheat on purpose and some slip up and do it."

"So you think I'm cheating?"

"If Tyler doesn't know you are here and you don't plan to tell him you've been out with me twice, then yes, it's cheating on some level or another. Now whether you are doing it on purpose or not, I don't know. That's why I asked you the questions I did." He sat back in his seat and motioned for the waiter.

"Well, what do you want it to be? Do you want me to be here on purpose or do you want me to be here in a subconscious sort of was?"

"There is no right way to answer that, because it indicates in either way that I want you to cheat on Tyler with me," he said.

"But I still want you to answer though," I replied.

"Well, okay…I want you to be here on purpose. I have so many different reasons why I say that."

"Okay, so tell me wh—"

"Have you fellas had time to look over the drink menu?" The waiter asked.

"I'll take a glass of the Kim Crawford Sauvignon Blanc," Orlando replied then he motioned the waiter to my direction for my drink order.

"I'll take a smart margarita please, on the rocks with salt, thanks," I said.

"I'll get those orders in for you. Are you two ready to order?"

"Give us a few more minutes—oh but can you bring some Thai Shrimp Spring Rolls?"

"Yessir, I'll get that right out, and for you sir, any starters?"

"I'm sure my guest doesn't mind if I nibble on his," I said with a sly smile.

"Okie dokie," the waiter laugh as if he caught the innuendo.

"So like I was saying, tell me why you say you have many reasons to want me to be here on purpose?" I asked.

"Well, for one, I don't want someone using me to make themselves feel good and then I get hurt. Two, honestly, I don't give a fuck about Tyler, I don't care about his feelings, but I feel like if you are here on purpose, then you know full well what you are getting into and you've already considered Tyler's feelings and have taken responsibility for them for yourself," he said.

"Wow, okay," I said with a look of bewilderment. I need my drink now. I was utterly shocked. I guess Orlando really is a player. That should have been my queue to get my ass up from the table and walk away, but I was already caught up in the devils web and I couldn't feel the urge to get up and walk out of there right then and there.

"What? Are you shocked? You are not a little boy anymore, Brandon. You are almost 30 now, right? This is Atlanta, it's how it is. Listen, don't play this game if you aren't ready. That's all I'm going to say," Orlando said. He leaned his back flat against his chair again. I notice he does that a lot. It seems like a power position he likes.

"How did we get to talking about playing a game?" I asked.

"Because, look Brandon, I am a grown ass man. I am an executive and a community leader. I have friends in high places and friends in common places. I know power and power knows me. Hell, I AM power."

"What does that have to do with anything, Orlando?"

"What it means is you are dealing with someone who is

among the elite, this type of thing goes down with our type all the time. So for us, we get straight to the point. I'm not interested in coy games with you or anybody. I know you have a man, but I also know you have seen me twice in two nights. There is no sense in beating around the bush. I know what this is and you know what this is, although you aren't ready to admit you know what it is. I'm just trying to move the process right along to where we want it to go."

"This is a lot, Orlando," I said.

"It's not. You are making it that way. You are trying to maintain your innocence but honestly, that went out the window yesterday," he leaned in towards me with his arms and elbows on the table and whispered, "There is no more morality for you to cling on to."

"So I should just start seeing you on the side like a side piece?" I asked.

"No, I'm nobody's side anything."

"It doesn't have to be riddled with labels and whatnot. I mean, just like we have seen each other last night and tonight, if we happen to fuck tomorrow night and the night after that, it is what it is," he said.

"I'm exhausted with this," I replied

"That's cause you are resisting. Stop resisting. You know you want this. I can give you everything you have been missing out on. On top of that, you get to keep your man. I'll just be a convenient buffer for you when he's not around. I mean, damn, how many more 'I'm late baby' texts can you tolerate? Or how many more times will you go to bed with a hard on because your man is never home. This doesn't have to be complicated," he said. Orlando was closing in on his deal like a car salesman trying to convince a man's wife why she should be okay with him shelling out their kid's college tuition on a Corvette.

"But it is complicated, Orlando," I said.

"It's not and to show you it's not, let me prove it to you."

He leaned over the table, nearly knocking over the candle centerpiece, and pulled me into a sultry, wet kiss.

"See how easy that was, and there is more where that comes from," he said with a sly smile.

I instantly became aroused. I couldn't resist, and I kissed him back. I didn't know if that meant I had finally given in, but that kiss was everything and my inhibitions were gone. I had fallen into his spell and the rest would change my world forever.

* * *

Dinner was over and Orlando and I walked out of the restaurant together. He was a lot tipsy after finishing what started out as one glass to a whole bottle of wine by himself.

"I hope you didn't drive, sir," I said.

"No, I Ubered. I knew I would have a good bit of drink tonight."

"Well I drove, I can take you home since your condo is nearby," I offered.

"That sounds like a plan," he said.

We walked to my car that was parked nearby.

"Nice ride. You are definitely a BMW type of guy. It fits you."

"Thanks, it's been good to me. I was afraid of getting a BMW because of the horror stories I've heard, but I've managed to do well with it." I continued the small talk, trying not to think of how this night could possibly end with an inebriated Orlando who was ready to get into my pants. "So you still an Audi man?" I asked.

"And you know it. But I actually scored a good deal on a new S Class," he said.

"Oh you fancy I see," I said. We were traveling to his condo which was nearby.

"Are you going to come up to the condo?" He asked.

"Do you want me to?" I asked.

"Duh, that's why I asked," he said.

"Yes, I'll come up for a second."

"Okay, won't be a second, but sure."

"What?"

"Oh nothing. You can park in the parking garage. So, umm, yeah pull up over here and I'll tell the guard so he don't boot your shit," he said.

I was a little nervous because I knew what type of trouble he and I would end up getting into because we really shouldn't be alone like that. Orlando was right at the restaurant. I needed to be honest with myself. I wanted to do this and I may as well be present in the doing. Tyler has been dropping the ball with me and, ugh, I just want to feel loved.

We went through the whole parking process and got out. We arrived at his floor. He looked like he was super exhausted. Once inside his condo, everything seemed to stand still as I remembered back on the last time I was there on his sofa with him all over me. It was something about that memory that just did it for me and all of the little decency I had for my relationship dissipated. Orlando had gone to his bedroom. I'm assumed it was to change or something. I was feeling edgy so I went to find him.

He was standing by his bed with his shirt off and taking off his watch facing the window. Being on the 29th floor meant no drapes and a wonderful view of the Buckhead skyline. I walked in and stood behind him with my breath on his neck. He just stood still and relaxed his head back on the left of my shoulder. I begin to massage his waist with my hands while sniffing in the Armani Code cologne. I was rock solid at this point and my protrusion impressed against his back. His hair was soft against my shoulder. Orlando is slightly shorter than me, but my nose was right against his ear. I kissed him softly on his exposed neck while pulling him in tighter against my chest. He seemed to melt a little, like he was releasing all control of his body and giving it over to me. He turned around and kissed me and an explosion seemed to happen because we got lost in a rage of passion as my shirt became a weapon across the room. I pushed him back onto the bed. By this time, his pants were off and his red boxer briefs hugged his muscular thighs and protruding penis. The Last time he took control, this time, I took control. As I hovered over him, the warmth of his breath on my chest made me forget for just a moment about any inhibitions that I had about this whole episode. All of the hidden thoughts I had in my mind about him before had manifested into this moment. If I were not troubled by them then, why be troubled now? The action was already taking place in my heart whenever I fawned over his beauty.

By now, he was completely nude as he stood up on his knees straddled over my waist as I was now laid back on the plush gray duvet that had seemed to explode with color all of a suddenly. As he scooted forward, his dick bounced on my nose and slid into my mouth. I grabbed his thin waist as he tightened his balance with his athletic thighs. After sucking him into fits of moans and shrieks, I stood up with him straddled around my waist and walked over from the bed to the chaise in his room. I gently laid him back on the chaise, the same way he laid me back on it several years ago. He spread his legs open as to invite me into the Taj Mahal. I could smell the sweet smell of his cologne radiating from his body even more now.

"What you waiting on papi?" His penis was throbbing and he was wet. I knew he was primed. One moan after another marked the various ways I molded myself with his body. We performed like pancakes on a skillet: brown on one side, ivory on the other, now flip. He felt like a glove that was a perfect fit. It was 11:15pm. Orlando was out like a light. I sat looking up at the ceiling with him asleep on my chest. What had I just done and why could I not feel any regret about it? The only thing I did feel regret about was not using a condom. We got so caught up and one thing quickly moved to another and then there I was, releasing into him as he screamed in a fit of passion, scratching at my chest, me pulling at his hair.

He eventually woke up and said that I should not stay the night.

"I know you are new to this type of thing, but you never stay the night. You stay the night with people you are building a relationship with. We are not doing that, right? You still want your man and if you still want him, then you better go home and sleep in your own bed."

It was so uncanny how he is able to separate himself from this experience as if it was "just sex". I shouldn't care. If what we were doing was going to be what it was going to be, I had to develop some thick skin and make sure I didn't fall in love.

"Okay," I said.

I got up and I looked for my underwear. They were behind the nightstand. Not sure how that happened. I got dressed and he put on a robe. I looked at him and he looked at me with a smile. Then he walked over to me and kissed me softly.

"This was nice. It's not just sex for me, because it's you. I don't want us to complicate things either. I know Tyler means the world to you so, I don't want to break that up, but this is what we've done and may do again and again and again, it's fun. It's to help you manage the loneliness and for me to get some good sex out of it," he laughed. "I'm just joking about that," he said.

"It's cool. I can handle this. I'm not as weak as you think."

As I drove home, I thought very little about Tyler, but thought a great deal about my night with Orlando. It was the sex that I kept replaying in my mind. It felt so good. I couldn't' shake the thought of it. I was already thinking of the next time it would happen.

Seven

Chapter 7

‿୧ଵଵ୨‿

My workday was wrapped up and I was sitting in a bit of traffic on Peachtree Road. It's been a week since I've seen Tyler and when he is here, we hardly spend any time together. I figured tonight would be a good night to have a nice dinner with him and I'd use that as a moment to share my good news with him as well. I'm not much of a cook, but I'm going to try and put something together.

"Hey love, I got your message. We just landed. What's up?"

"Hey babe, it's good to hear you. I just wanted to see when you would be home but looks like you were probably in the air when I called. I hope you didn't make any plans for this evening. I want us to have a nice dinner together. I'm going to cook us up a meal tonight," I said.

"You, cook? So you're mad at me?" Tyler asked with a chuckle.

"Don't be slick. My cooking is not that bad. As a matter of fact, I'm going to surprise you good tonight. It'll be the best food you've ever eaten. You just wait and see."

"Okay, dear. We shall see what this will be. I guess I should be there in a couple of hours. I have to stop by CNN after I leave here," he said.

"Damn, don't they know you have a whole life outside of them?" I said quite snappily, before I knew it.

"Yes they do. I just got to get my itinerary for the next month."

"Well, hopefully they don't have you traveling all around the world. I miss you."

"I know, love. I miss you too. We will discuss it more when I get home. Hopefully the schedule will have me be a lot closer in the coming weeks," he replied.

"Okay, dear, well hurry on home. I love you."

"I love you, too."

A smile whisked across my face at the thought of Tyler coming home and spending some quality time with me. I was happy that I'd get to spend a lovely evening with Tyler. I was so giddy that I scurried out of the apartment in a hast and forget my wallet. I had gotten down to my car in the parking deck before I realized it, and then had to go back up to the apartment. The day felt nice. For just a moment, I felt a little hope and not the usual despair. As I was headed to Sprouts to do grocery shopping, my night with Orlando came into my view like a haunting flashback. I still hadn't felt guilty for what I'd done. I had told myself that it was a one-time thing. Just a hit and run, and if Tyler ever found out, I could chalk it up to sexual urges and his absence. That's what I told myself, even though deep down, I knew all of it was lies. I didn't want to be thinking about this like that so I blasted the radio with a little Rihanna. Once I got to Sprouts, my brain froze. I could not think of anything to prepare. Soon as I walked through the automatic doors and looked at all the aisles and produce presenting themselves, I panicked.

"Tyler is right. I can't cook worth a shit. I had no business talking about making a romantic dinner," I said out loud.

Maybe some seafood will do the trick. I walked over and saw some lobster tails chilling in the cooler. It immediately took me back to that date night I had with Orlando when he prepared them for me several years ago. It was so nice and so good. If only I had those type of skills. My phone rang and as I spoke of the devil, it was him calling. I picked up.

"Hello…"

"Hey sir, hmmm you sound good the day after," he said. His voice was chilly and it sounded like it vibrated every time he used it.

"Chile," I replied.

"What are you up to? Do you want to have dinner again tonight?" He asked forwardly. Everything with him is forward.

"I'm sorry, I can't. Tyler is here and on his way home from the airport. I'm supposed to be preparing dinner for us tonight, which I have no idea what to make. I'm not good at this," I said.

"Awe, well that's…um…cute I guess. How about I give you some ideas. What does he like?" He asked.

"He's not a cultured kind of guy. Well, he may be now that he travels so much. I dunno. I do know he likes Cajun foods."

"Okay, well that's good enough. Nothing wrong with a little Creole. Perhaps then you should do a New Orleans style dish.

I'm thinking a Blackened Snapper with Crawfish Étouffée," he said.

"Oh my. That sounds so good, and that just rolled off your tongue like you make it all the time."

"Well I have made it a couple of times. It's one of my favorite New Orleans style dishes, and it's quite easy to make."

"Thank you so much. You are a life saver," I said.

"So basically your side piece just helped you decide what to cook for your man."

"Don't make it sound so bad."

"I'm just saying. You know you tend to pretend like shit isn't happening. That old church mentality is still with you."

"Can you not psychoanalyze me right now, please? Besides, don't you need to be preparing for your ministry tomorrow tonight?"

"Don't be worrying about me and what I have going on. My plans for tomorrow night's gathering are already prepared. It's just a shame my bed is not going to be popping like it was last night again tonight. Boy you fucked the shit out of me. I was pleasantly surprised. I didn't know you had it in ya," he laughed.

"I mean…what can I say?"

"Say when is the next time I can get some more."

"I don't know, Orlando. Tyler is in town. It will have to wait." I was supposed to say never again.

"Really? Does it? Atlanta is a big city sir. My S Class has a huge backseat too. You ever had sex on Mercedes leather? I'm closing on my house next week. I'm thinking you and I break it in with a little romping in the foyea."

"Foyea? Why can't your bougie ass just say foyer like the rest of us?"

"You wasn't complaining about my bougie ass last night when it was riding your dick."

"Oh my god, you're so vulgar," I said.

"And you like it."

"You're right," I said with a laugh, then I pulled my phone away to look at my screen. Another call. "Anyway, I have a call coming through. It's Tyler's sister. I wonder what she wants. Let me take this," I said.

"Alright sexy. Don't you wear Tyler out too bad tonight. I need you to save some of that energy for me," he said.

"You are too much, bye sir." I answered the line with his sister on it. She and I were tight, somewhat. I continued to do my shopping as I said hello.

"Hey Love! I hope I didn't catch you at a bad time." She is always so bubbly.

"No you didn't. Headed home to make dinner for Tyler and myself. What's up?"

"I was just wondering how Tyler was doing. I reached out to him a couple of times about coming down to visit and well… I haven't heard back. Is everything okay?" she asked.

"I'm shocked to hear this…well…not really I guess. Tyler has been acting a little distant lately. You know he's not one to share his feelings."

"You're right about that. I was just concerned. Did you know he talked to mama last week. It didn't go well." She said.

"Awee, no, I didn't know that. What happened?" I asked.

"You know they were going in on him about the gay stuff. I just hate it for him. I tried to reach out to him. You know, he and I used to be so cool. It's like the last few years, he's such a different guy. Why do you think that is?" She asked.

"I have always known that Tyler still struggled with accepting his sexuality and the way it severed his relationship with your parents. He doesn't talk about it much, and I know it's something he doesn't really like to talk about, but I feel he needs to talk about it. What I do know is unresolved issues like that show up as symptoms of depression later and…well… no one wants to deal with depression," I said.

"My dad deals with it. He's bipolar. It nearly destroyed our family. I can believe that Tyler could probably be dealing with some aspect of it. Maybe that explains his ambition," she said.

"You think ambition is a sign of bipolarism?" I asked.

"No, not at all. I'm just saying the high ups and then downs, and besides, I know mental illness can be hereditary. My grandmother was bipolar, now my dad. I dunno…I think Tyler may be predisposed to it," she said.

"I don't want to think of Tyler being bipolar. I hope he is just simply having a hard time dealing with the situation with your parents. I mean…I don't know much about it though, but it seems extreme. He doesn't exhibit those types of signs. I think it's just a phase or rough patch, you know, having to manage the rejection of your folks," I said. I honestly did not want to think that he could possibly be manic depressive. I hadn't seen him be up and down in that way, but then again, his ass is never here. I didn't think he was bipolar, but I'm also not a therapist either.

"Yeah, I can get that. I just wanted to know why he hasn't responded to me. I wanted him to receive me when I visit. I'm thinking about going to Georgia State to advance my nursing career. I want to be a Nurse Practitioner," she said.

My face shined. "Oh that's great! Good for you. I tell you what, I'll mention it to him over dinner tonight. You know he is a sucker for education. Once he hears that, he'll be excited to call you back," I said.

"He better! You tell him if he don't, I'm going to tell mama on him."

I chuckled. "I sure will. I can't wait to have you visit! He should be home shortly and he and I will talk. Thank you for calling," I said.

* * *

I got home and showered and got cleaned up before I started dinner. I must say it came out quite well. Orlando must've rubbed off on me through the sex. Hmm. Tyler was still out. His couple of hours had turned into four. That was probably why I was sleeping with Orlando. By this time, I had already had two glasses of Zinfandel. I went over to the study and begin to look over some plans that I had jotted down about my upcoming role. I had so many ideas that I wanted to pursue. I also wanted to do a special on the HIV epidemic, but I didn't want it to be cliche'. I know that one out of two black gay men are at risk for HIV, but I don't want to feed the narrative that exists that HIV is a gay disease, because it is not. Perhaps I could have approached an angle that would spread awareness of the disease and educates people. It was now 9:00pm.

Sir, where are you? I texted to Tyler with a disappointed emoji.

I'm on the way, I got tied up at the office. **smiley face**

I sent back the rolling eyes emoji.

Boy he can sure fuck up a good evening. I sighed. I

texted Orlando. I just wanted to not feel disappointed and he normally makes me feel really good.

I'm sure you are looking good and sexy right now. I typed

Then there appeared the bubble with the three dots. I guess he was available. I was happy to see that though.

You missing me already, daddy? he responded.

A little bit.

What's going on? I thought you and that man of yours was having a romantic dinner?

Yeah, about that…

Okay, yeah, so…

His ass is not even here yet. I cooked about 2 hours ago. I've been sitting here waiting ever since. I don't know what has gotten into him, but I'm about sick of this shit for real.

Babe, you will have to lay down the law with him. I mean, fucking me isn't going to tell him how you feel. You need to open up your mouth and talk.

At least fucking you makes me feel something good.

Is that right?

Yes, you felt like velvet. I've been thinking about it so much.

Aww. So when is that man going to be gone again. I can't wait to spend some more time with you.

I don't know. He is supposed to get his new itinerary today, he claims that's what he went to CNN for.

I hope they send his ass to Alaska. Then I'll have you to myself.

I just want things to be right with him and me.

That ship has sailed honey. The way you fucked me last night shows it. As a matter of fact, you made good love to me last night. I call it fucking to keep the boundaries, but I must say, it was a really good feeling to finally have you. I never really got over you, Brandon. And being with you, smelling you, all of it just brought back a flood of memories.

Orlando you can't be saying stuff to me like this. You know I'm in a vulnerable space.

I know, but it's the truth. Okay, I'm sorry. I get that you and your boyfriend have some issues to work through. I can respect that. I just wanted you to know that I've been thinking about you all day, the way you felt all over me last night. How you caressed my hair and sucked softly on my neck. You got my mind tripping.

So I was that good, huh?

Boy you were fucking amazing.

I heard the door lock shifting.

He's here. I'll chat back with you in a few.

Okay love. I'll be thinking of you.

I thought if I should delete the thread, but I didn't have time to do so. Tyler was making his way in. I can't believe I'm having to delete texts now.

* * *

There he was, backing into the apartment with his luggage. He looked tired.

"Oh, hey babe. Listen, I'm so sorry. I got to the office and I got tied up. Wow, it smells good in here."

"Yeah, I made us some dinner. It probably needs warming up now." I tried not to sound dry, but actually act as if I was enthused to see him. I really was happy to see him. I have missed him, and despite my situation with Orlando, I still love Tyler. I consider Orlando to be loose ends that I never tied up. Right now, I'm just kind of playing with the strings until I'm ready to tie them up.

"Baby, I'm really sorry for being so late. How can I make it up to you?"

"Don't worry, I'm just glad that you are here," I said.

"Have you eaten yet?" He asked.

"No, I have not eaten yet. I wanted to wait for you. Let me go warm up the food and we can eat. How about you go freshen up. I'm sure you need to unwind a bit after all the traveling and things," I said.

I walked towards the kitchen, leaving him with an unsuspecting look on his face.

"Okay, that's actually perfect. I'll go shower."

I went into the kitchen. "Let me try and get myself together. He's been on the road for a week and I know he is going to want some ass," I said under my breath.

I heard a phone buzzing. I thought it was mine but it turned out to be Tyler's. I went over to silence it but I couldn't help but notice the name, Alan Winters. Three messages back to back. I'm not usually one to get suspicious or jealous, but I'd been in such a raw space lately, my mind was everywhere. I felt threatened by this name, Alan or perhaps it's just me and my guilt because of what I had been doing. If Tyler was cheating on me, at that point, I believed I deserved it. I just walked away. I needed to clear my thoughts. Then, I heard buzzing again, but this time, it was my phone. This time it was my "Alan", as in Orlando, but he was calling me instead of texting. I peeked around the corner into the bedroom to see if Tyler was still drowning out the noise with the shower running. I tipped towards the balcony and softly answered. I heard Orlando's voice come across.

"Hey, is it safe to talk."

"Yeah, he's showering, I got a few seconds."

"Okay, so, how's it going and how are you feeling?" He

asked.

"I'm feeling a little uneasy. Honestly Orlando, my feelings are all over the place. I'm thinking about you and then names popping up on his phone and it has me paranoid as shit. I shouldn't be in this head space at all."

"I understand how you feel. I wish I could console you right now," Orlando said.

That was that sweet, charming side of Orlando that had me hooked from the very beginning. He was so supportive and so present, and even though he was way more successful than Tyler, he never seemed to let his work take priority over me. It's like he valued having a man. What was I doing? Was I really comparing him to Tyler as if I wanted to find out if the grass was greener on the other side?

"I wish you could too," I replied. I felt my heart get warm a little. I was letting my guard down with him and that was no good.

"You are going to get me in trouble," I replied.

"You are already in trouble, Brandon."

I rolled my eyes and shooed him off the line. I couldn't get caught by Tyler. I returned into the apartment. The shower was still going so Tyler was not out yet. I begin to plate our food and prepared to set up the dinner table. It was 9:45pm. A picture came through on my phone. It was a beautiful picture of Orlando, oh my god, in nothing but a towel. The caption read, "Next time, I'm taking the lead xoxo." I felt my dick get hard. I don't know why he was doing this to me.

* * *

Buzzz, Buzz, Buzz...Buzz, Buzz, buzz. Tyler's phone again.

This time it was a call. I walked over to silence it, but it was a Facetime call. Alan again. Who is this Alan person? I silenced the call, but then immediately picked up my phone. I need to find out who Alan Winters is, or at least see what he looks like. I went to Facebook and searched. Two names popped up, one was mutual friends with Tyler. This must be him, I thought to myself. He was attractive, very attractive. Looks like he worked at CNN. "Yep, this is definitely him, and he is definitely gay, I said out loud. The picture was of a white guy with dark brunette hair. He looked like he could have been German to me. Tyler is so Afro-centric, I would have never pegged him to be an interracial dater. My mind is crazy, I've already put Tyler in a relationship with someone else.

Tyler walked in and I quickly put my phone away.

"Hmmm, this looks good, honey," Tyler said. He came over to my side and kissed me. Then he walked over to his phone which had been screaming for his attention for the last 20 minutes. I watched him from behind. I just wanted to see his facial expressions. He opened his phone and looked like he was reading some text message. Did this boy just smile? My eyes stretched at the sight. He smiled like he was in love. I felt my heart drop into my lap. I can't believe what I'm going through. How will I get through this dinner with thoughts of him cheating on me with what looks like a buff Instagram Model and thoughts of my passionate night with Orlando which is far from over. I need a drink. I poured myself another glass of wine from the bottle I had earlier, which was just about empty.

He sat down and we said grace. Things started a bit quiet at first. Then I broke the silence.

"Well, babe, I got some really good news today at work."

"Is that right, what is it?" he replied.

"You know I've been burned out with the work I've been doing. So today, Janice called me into her office and she offered me a new role. You are now looking at their newest Executive Producer of the Investigative Team. I will run their investigative journalism department. I finally will get to do some investigative journalism and not chase after robbers and the latest apartment building they've shot up."

"Awesome! I'm really glad to hear this. You deserve it. So when do you get started?"

"I have to pick out my team and pitch my first five topics. She didn't give me a start, but I think the shows will launch in a couple of months, but I'll be doing my first set of investigation soon," I replied.

"So what ideas do you have?"

"I'm still thinking on that. I want to do impacting stories. What do you suggest?" I asked.

"Let me think. Investigative stories can be tricky. You have to service the viewing audience so that means you will need to investigate things that actually matter to them. It'll have to be about things in the area. Perhaps looking into the election situation. Do some investigating on how the polls are managed. That'll be a good start. You could use this to test out your documentary idea on the HIV epidemic or actually anything regarding healthcare. That's always a hot topic. And, I'm sure things will pop up around the city that will spark some ideas." Tyler added.

"Yeah, I thought about the HIV thing. I figured it was cliche."

"But it's a cliche reality that needs to be talked about. It's a real epidemic you know."

"Yeah, I know. Well I do have to have five stories to lead

into the launch with so that can be one."

"Well, certainly let me know if I can help you in any way. I'm so proud of you, boo," he said.

"I will. So, did you get your itinerary? Why did they have you at the station so long after your flight. I thought you were just going to get your itinerary? Was there a problem? Were you able to get it?"

"Yeah, I did. It's umm…well…it's not a good one. They want me on a few campaign trails. I'm going to be in DC for the next three weeks or so. I'm sorry baby. I know you want me home more. The good news is that I don't have to leave for another week so I'll be right here, home with you."

I needed to use this moment to share how I feel, but I did not feel like having an argument, and besides, what would it change anyway. It's not like he can tell them no. I guess Orlando hit the nail again. It doesn't do any good if I'm not going to say anything. Wow, that thought seemed to echo in my head and the next thing I know I found myself saying more than I thought I'd say.

"Tyler, let me just be honest with you. I know I touched on this the other night, but I've been in a bad space. Some of it has to do with your absence, and some of it has to do with how burned out I had become with work. I…I don't know. I just know that I need you. I'm glad to hear you will be home all this week but that will not help me feel less abandoned after you leave. And not only that, like tonight, you were supposed to be here way before you got here. You know I'm not one to think you are doing anything wrong, but I mean…I'm only human as well."

"You thought I was out elsewhere, besides the CNN building?" Tyler asked.

"No, I did not think that. But that doesn't mean that I did not get upset sitting here waiting for you."

"So that's the elephant in the room, huh?"

"What do you mean?" I asked.

"I could tell something was off when I got home. Your energy is very different," he said.

"Well, yeah. I mean, you're never here. I've started to build up a wall, maybe a little resentment. I don't want to feel this way, Tyler."

"What do you want me to do? I can't quit my job and you know this is what I've dreamed of."

"There sure are a lot of "I" statements in that. Last I checked, this is a two-party event we have going on here. I get you have your career, but is it worth losing me over?" I asked. He sat up straight in chair. I don't think he ever considered that.

"Lose you? I didn't think it had become that serious. What's the talk about me losing you? No, nothing is worth me losing you. I also cannot lose myself especially if I haven't even fully found myself yet."

"I know and I want you to become everything you set out to become. I wouldn't want you to lose yourself, but I want you to make more time for me. Building your career does not mean you have to lose me in the process. I need you to make more effort. I know some of the time away you cannot control, but I believe there are things you can control, like tonight.

"You are starting to sound like a nag. I mean if the shoe was on the other foot, I would be understanding of your schedule."

"Well the shoe is not on the other foot and yes, you may be able to deal with being left alone because you like your alone time anyway, but me on the other hand, no! If I am in a relationship with someone, then I want to reap the benefits of that," I said.

"Well, Brandon, being in a relationship isn't about all of this lovey dovey shit you are always trying to get. You need to grow up, man. We are not 20 anymore. We are almost 30 years old, we both have careers and we have adult shit to do. Sometimes that means we can't act like Cliff and Clair Huxtable."

"I don't think getting a little time with you has to equate to all of that. I'm just asking for a little more of your attention, and I damn sure don't want to have to sit here and defend my feelings to you. Sure, you may not understand them, but at least don't sit here and make it seem like I'm being some type of crybaby bitch about it. You got me out here looking like a fool, Tyler. Everyone is questioning me about why you are away so much. Frankly, I'm running out of excuses. I'm tired of making those same excuses to myself. Like tonight, I'm sitting here wondering where you are and here I go always thinking to myself, 'Oh he must've got caught in traffic, or maybe he got held up at the airport.' I'm getting really tired of this, Tyler."

"Okay, okay...I hear you, and I'm sorry about tonight. It won't happen again, I promise."

"Don't make promises that you cannot keep," I said. I feel like Tyler and I have been having the same conversation over and over again and nothing changes. He will leave out of here in a week on his next assignment, and it'll feel like he does not exist all over again. He apologizes, we have sex and then it's back to the same shit. I'm tired. Sometimes I just wonder how much longer we will last. He got up from his seat and came over to wrap his arms around me.

"Look, baby, I'm sorry. I know I've been absent. I don't want you sitting around here like a Vietnam housewife and I'm away at war. I will try to be better. I've been under so much pressure lately. I haven't been feeling my best. I've been feeling down lately, and I don't know why."

"What do you mean you've been feeling down?" I asked.

"I don't know. It's just, I've been feeling down."

"What do you think brought that on? What have you been thinking about?"

"It comes and goes. It started the other day. I find myself not wanting to get out of bed in the morning."

"Do you think it's health-related or perhaps it's something you're not talking about."

"I think my health is good, and I'm not really sure about me not talking about something."

"Well, sometimes we can be triggered by something. Are you happy with work?"

"Yeah, I'm pretty content with work. Things could not be better in that regard."

"Is there anything else you may not be happy with?" I wondered if he was not happy in the relationship. I didn't want to say it, but I am very curious though.

"I can't think of anything. I know my problem is that I detach myself from my feelings. There could very well be something going on and I am just not allowing myself to open up about it," he said.

"I agree with that. You can be a mystery at times. Let's see… you're okay with work. So what about being away from home so much. Do you think that bothers you?"

"I've gotten used to that. Yeah, I miss having you around, but I don't think it's something causing me to feel down."

"Hmmm, OK then. Well, have you talked to your sister?" I already knew the answer to this question, but I just wanted to see what he would say.

"I haven't talked to her."

"Well I did. She called me today and asked about you. She said she had been trying to reach you. You ignoring her or something? What's going on?"

"No, I'm not ignoring her, at least not on purpose. I'm usually on set when she calls and I simply forget to call her back."

"Tyler, I really do think you bury yourself in your work on purpose. I'm not Dr. Phil, but I don't know, I feel like there is something really going on with you that you are not talking about," I said.

"If I am, I don't know what it is. And, I just like to stay busy. I don't think I bury myself in my work. Like I said already, I can't help my job."

"But you don't mind it either. It's a welcomed inconvenience for you as far as I believe."

"I don't think it's that big of a deal."

"It is and you should talk about it. You don't know what's hurting you until you get it out."

"Nothing is hurting me."

"Then why not call your sister back? Why avoid coming home to spend time with me? What are you hiding from or more rather, what are you hiding?" I asked.

"I feel like you are probing and it's getting on my nerves," he said.

"So I'm irritating you about what I'm asking? I think that's even further proof that something is going on with you and you know it. You need to find out what it is, not for me, but for yourself. If you're not going to talk about it to someone, then you need to write it out in a journal, write a book or something."

I sat and watched Tyler sit in silence after that. He looked at me but it was as if he was looking beyond me at something behind me.

"Well…?" I said

"I know. I just…" He started to cry. It completely caught me off guard. I immediately jumped out of my seat to console him. It broke my heart. It's something when you see the person you're so used to seeing be strong break away. I held him tight.

"It's okay, love. Let it out."

Eight

Chapter 8

⚜

My night with Tyler that evening was exhausting. Conversations with him are always very intense either in a good way or a bad way. That time it was different, but still exhausting. I remember when Tyler and I were on the road together doing our documentary. He was a mystery then just like he was last night. It seemed like the traumas he was dealing with never left. I learned something new that night. I learned that the coming out process can be a motherfucker. It is no easy feat. It's never a one-time event. It's series of months and years of slowly coming to terms with oneself. Some of us didn't become whole until well into our thirties. We had been coming out since we were teenagers. Over the years, I've helped many young gays come out. I've held their hands and cried with them. Some I've sat with them as they told their parents their truth. Someone like Tyler can come to a detrimental end with trying to reconcile their sexuality with their world. You see, Tyler's fundamental Christian family would have no parts with him because he was gay. I slowly began to understand what I was dealing with, why he was always away and why he was avoiding his sister. I believe Tyler hated himself. I believe he used ambition and his success as a way to camouflage all that he was facing. He was high-functioning in his depression.

Depression doesn't look the same on everyone. Depression isn't always shades drawn, hair undone and no baths for days. Sometimes it's the overachiever. Sometimes it's the person that has to always get it right every time, the perfectionist. It's called high-functioning depression. It all looks fine and dandy until one day, the person crashes and it's over with or they slowly lose things in their lives that are important to them like their relationships. I was so afraid of this happening to Tyler. I stressed myself out trying to keep things afloat. So much that I continued down my own path of destruction.

Tyler and I had breakfast the next day together before I headed out to work.

"Tyler, baby, I want you to think about what I suggested last night. I know you'll be on the road, but I think getting in contact with a therapist is going to help you out a lot, okay? Here is a list of people that do virtual sessions. Be sure to get that going for yourself." I said.

"Thank you, dear. I will check them out. I just want to thank you for being here for me. You know me better than anyone. You were right. I'm fucked up man. I miss my parents and I still feel the shame of their disapproval. I just want them to accept me. I feel like if they do, then I can live my life to the fullest."

"But what if that never happens, Tyler?"

"I don't know. That's what I am afraid of."

"Well, have you tried to make amends with them, see if they have changed their stance? I mean…it's been a few years since you first came out to them."

"I did. I just didn't tell you about it."

"Really, so tell me what happened," I said.

"I called them one day a couple of months ago. I was in Phoenix on assignment. I was feeling bad and missing them so I mustered up the courage to call them. Everything went fine but then things turned left."

"How did that happened?" I asked.

"So I called them to wish them a happy anniversary actually. It was their 40th anniversary. My mom answered. She was actually happy to hear from me. It was almost exactly like it was back when I first came out. The reaffirmation of their rejection I think just has put me in a bad headspace."

"Well what happened. You called them and what did they say?" I asked.

"They were their typical holy rolling selves. So basically I called them and the conversation was:

"Hey Tyler! It's so good to hear from you. How have you been? Why don't we hear from you?"

"I've been good. I've been busy with work. They have me on the road a lot. I'm sorry I haven't been reaching out much."

"That's too bad. You should call and visit more. We still love you, son. I'll get your dad. I'm sure he wants to hear your voice as well." She went to get my dad. He came to the phone with his serious emotionless voice as usual.

"Son, I hope you are out there taking care of yourself. I'm yet praying for you."

I already knew what he meant by that.

"Thank you, dad. I've been doing well. I'm on the road a lot for work. I'm hoping to land an opportunity that keeps me in one spot. Ultimately, I want to be a newsroom anchor. That takes a lot of work and focus to get there, but I believe I can do it." I said.

"Yes you can do anything you set your mind to," my mom said.

"Yeah but you have to be living for God to get the added favor for these grand plans to manifest you know," my dad added.

Here we go again, I thought to myself. Normally, I would have a rebuttal him, but I just didn't have the energy for it or felt that it was even necessary. I just tried to change the topic. Good thing my sister had walked into the room by then and shouted hello into the line.

"Hey Ariel," I replied. Then I continued with my responses.

"I'm up for the challenge. I wouldn't mind something that placed me in Washington, like a White House correspondent."

"That would be a good area for you to be in. I figure there are a lot of opportunities for political correspondent work there," my dad replied.

"That's a possibility. Of course it would have to be something that works with Brandon." I said.

I heard the line get quiet when I said that. Somehow, me mentioning you gets them riled up.

"Well, Tyler, you know we want you to make the most of yourself. Don't miss any opportunities because of a relationship. I mean, you both are still young. That goes for Brandon too. Focus on your careers and do what's best for yourselves." She added.

"Mom, well you know we've been together a while now.

There won't be a decision of that type that would be made without some discussion with Brandon, and I'm sure the same would be the case if he were to land an opportunity somewhere."

My mom didn't seem to like the idea of me making life decisions with you in mind.

"It's not like you guys are husband and wife. Those types of decisions are for married people."

"We could be married one day, dad."

"You do know that's wrong, son."

"It's not wrong. It's right for us if that's what we desire to do. And it is something we desire to do. We have already had the discussion and we do plan to be married one day."

The line became quiet again.

"Tyler, Tyler, Tyler. Don't do that. Listen, I know you and Brandon are together the way you are, but don't do this," my mom said. It almost sounded like a plea. I was waiting for my dad to blow his top.

"Son, I pray and ask God every day where did I go wrong. What did I do or not do to cause you to want to live your life like this? It's sad and embarrassing. You do not need to marry a man."

"I don't need to marry a man, or a woman, but I want to marry a man, and not just any man, I want to marry Brandon, and when that day comes, it's going to happen." I said. By this time, I had perked up and was amped to oppose them, like the last time.

"This is exactly what you did the last time. You drop this silly shit on us like this unsuspectingly. You know we do not support your lifestyle. We try to be Christians and treat you with some respect. We don't ask you about your sin and the filthy things you and that boy are doing."

"Dad, I already know how you really feel. Let me say that it doesn't make me feel good nor happy that I cannot get you to accept me. This is what it is. This is who I am. There really isn't a choice in the matter."

"Oh we have a choice. We don't have to accept you bringing these behaviors around. I can't stand before God and be accountable for not telling you the truth. You and Brandon are going to hell for your lifestyle."

"I'm not afraid of hell," I said.

"You better be! Hell is real!" My mom shouted.

"Mom, those are you guys' beliefs. Hell will be there waiting for those who fear it. As for me, I don't believe in Hell. I'm no longer allowing things like that to guilt me and cause me fear about wanting to have happiness."

"Son, the devil has surely deceived you. You go and get all of that education and you still don't know a thing about life. You just keep living, you hear me? It'll all come crashing down and one day, if it's not too late, you will see for yourself. Repent and be saved and put down this sin you so easily let beset you."

"I'm good with my decisions. I would love to have your support, although I already knew that I wouldn't. All I ask is for your respect. I don't want to hear the scriptures and the preaching and being told I'm going to Hell."

"We will always preach Jesus to all that need to hear about Him, and you son, need to hear about him badly. Everytime you come around and call, we will tell you the truth. we cannot let you live comfortably in your sin and think that you are getting by. You think that you are, but you are not."

"I just want to say that you'll always have my support, Tyler."

Ariel said.

"So you gonna condone this mess?" My dad asked her.

"Dad, stop. Don't throw Jesus into your bigotry. Regardless of whether you agree with him or not, it is not your place to continue to deny him and mistreat them."

"I have done nothing of the sort but tell them the truth that he needs to hear."

"No Dad, you are telling him what you want him to do."

"Okay little girl, you have stated your case. This is between Tyler and your mom and Me," my dad said.

"I'm just saying, dad. There is a better way. Alright Tyler, I have to head out to a study group. I'll be chatting with you. Tell Brandon I said hey."

I looked at Tyler as he finished recounting the conversation. I could feel the weight of his feelings without him even having to say how he felt about that whole ordeal. He stared off into the kitchen. I didn't really know what to say.

"The call pretty much ended with my parents and me disagreeing as usual. I just don't know what to do or say to get them to come around. I see how you and your parents have progressed and it used to give me hope for me and mine, but I just don't see it happening and it just hurts me to my core," Tyler said as he looked up at me. He was still sitting while I was standing next to him.

"Aww baby, I'm so sorry you had to go through that. I didn't know this happened. You should have told me. You've been carrying that all of this time. No wonder you are distant. This assures me even more now of my belief that you need to get to a therapist. Work these feelings out before they destroy you and destroy us in the process." I said.

Nine

Chapter 9

The end of the week was here and Tyler was preparing to head to DC for his next assignment. I honestly did not want him to leave. I had enjoyed the last few days of reconnecting with him. For the first time in a long time I felt like he and I had a shot. Oddly, I had not heard much from Orlando. I guess that was a good thing considering what he and I had been doing. It would seem like I was about to ghost him yet again for Tyler.

"I have an appointment on next Wednesday with a therapist. I'm looking forward to what will come of it. Thank you again baby for helping me through this. Let's go out tonight. I'll be flying out in the morning."

"Ooooh that sounds like fun. Let's go to a club. We haven't been out clubbing in a long time."

"A club? You know I'm not the club type," he said.

"Ah c'mon. Let's go have some fun, smoke a little and let

loose. You need it and I damn sure need it. Besides, we should celebrate my promotion." I said.

"Ok ok, for you, but I don't want to go to no gay clubs, okay?"

"Well where else would we go? Gay is all we know. You didn't have a problem with them before. What's changed?"

"I just don't want to be bothered with the scene," he said.

"Well I don't know any straight clubs and besides, I want to feel at ease where we go. What If I want to ride on you on the dance floor? The straights won't have it."

"I know. That's why I don't want to go," he said.

I just shook my head. The look of frustration on my face was obvious. I don't get why he has clammed up the way he has about us being together. I knew he was still sorting out his feelings, but at the expense of the relationship. I didn't like it.

"Alright," I said with disappointment. "We can find a lounge to go to. I'll call up Shawn and Lamont and have them come join us.

"Lamont? He's so loud sometimes. I don't know if I'm up for that." he said.

"What? Lamont is our friend. He was in our documentary. You've never had a problem with him before. What's the deal? Are you embarrassed by him because of his flamboyance?" I asked.

"No, it's nothing like that. He's just over the top a lot," he said.

"You know something Tyler, all of these rebuttals make me feel like you don't want to go anywhere. I think we should just not worry about it." I walked away into the closet and he followed behind.

"You don't have to stay home on the account of me. Go on out and have fun. I actually want you to. But, I'm just not in the mood for all of that."

By that time, I didn't feel like going back and forth. I was going to have to exercise some serious patience if I was going to get through this with Tyler. He found a new way to make me feel alienated. I didn't know if I could date someone who was still struggling with themselves.

* * *

I went out as planned, without Tyler. I didn't want some boring dinner at a restaurant. I wanted to turn up. I retreated to the balcony and called Lamont and Shawn and of course they were down to go out. I also invited Jamie. This was going to be interesting having him around. Jamie has never been to a black gay club. He was excited, but I didn't know how he would fit in with Lamont's straight-shooting personality. Lamont ended up moving to Atlanta since we had him in the Pulse segment of our last documentary. He still does his Podcast. He's a lot of fun to hang out with. When I called him about going out, he was ready, but we had to hassle about where.

"Lamont, I just want to go out and let my hair down."

"Girl, you ain't got no damn hair. What, you done went and got you some extensions?" He asked sarcastically.

"No, you know what I mean," I said.

"Well, where you trying to go chile?" He asked.

"I was thinking about Bulldogs."

"Bulldogs!? Chile...what you want to go there with them

old ass men honey? I'm trying to get my cherry popped by some young dick, you feel me? You don't want to go to Mixx or something?"

"No, I'm feeling grown and sexy and I don't want no youngins with milk-breath hitting on me," I said.

"Well quiet as its kept, as much as you be up under Tyler tired ass, you don't want no old men hitting on you either," he laughed.

"Now I done told you—,"

"Told me what? That your man ain't shit?"

"Yes, I told you to stop talking about Tyler like that."

"Where he at anyway, in Chicago? Phoenix? Hmph, probably playing in some trade's ass somewhere," he said.

"Ugh, why must you do that?" I asked.

"Cause it's true. I keep telling you to leave that fool alone. I mean, he's an alright guy, but you don't need nobody, man or woman who don't know what the fuck they want, and that Tyler, he don't know what the fuck he wants."

"He wants me, that's what he wants."

"Really, well is he coming out with us tonight?"

"No"

"See! Chile. Until he comes to terms with himself and stop trying to be trade dick, he might be worth your time. I don't care how many degrees that negro has, all the money and smarts in the world isn't enough to cover up this lonely shitty life he got you living, sitting at home waiting for him and stuff. But hey, if you like it I love it," he said.

"I hear you. But that's not what I called you about. Don't be fucking up my mood with this shit. Tyler and I have been talking about all of that. We are going to be alright."

"Alright if you say so girl. I don't know how you manage.

I'd be out fucking me a Falcon by now," he said.

"As if you could pull a Falcon player," I said.

"If I could? Child. You must don't know who you talking too. Hmph! If I could. You mean If I have. Don't think cause I'm a queen that I can't pull a man as masculine as a Falcon player. Don't be fooled about these so-called straight men out here."

"Now how you sitting here talking about me and Tyler and you willing to mess around with down low guys," I said.

"Bitch I said trade, not down low. There is a fucking difference. Tyler ain't hardly hardcore, but he try to be. Tyler is down low, but not nearly close to being trade material. He seems like he would prefer trade so he don't have to be out in the open holding his flower, which would be you."

"Bye boy. You just be at this club at 10pm," I said.

"I'm sorry. I think that one might have hurt your feelings. I just be trying to get you to see beyond this fantasy world you tend to build around yourself. I'm sorry. Don't be mad at me. Don't you want to go grab food before the club?"

"I'm fine. I wasn't offended. Yeah sure we can," I said.

"Cool, I'm going to come pick you up about 7, okay"

"Okay," I disconnected the line. Although I told Lamont I wasn't offended, I really was. Lamont comes on strong sometimes, and yes he is my friend and can extra sometimes, but he wasn't exactly wrong. Much of what he said was the truth. It was just taking me a while to sit in it and face it. That night, I had a really good time, despite the things that were on my mind. Lamont was the life of the party as usual and he got mind off of things. And Orlando was texting me occasionally throughout the night.

*** *** ***

"Miss thang? What you sitting over there smiling at? Who keeps texting you? Honey ya face is lighting up like one ole gay ass Christmas tree in the park," Lamont shouted.

"You mind your business," I said. The rest of the table starting cooing.

"Ooooooooweee chile. I smell some dick cooking up. Okay then honey. Listen, I ain't mad at you. If I were with…you know what nevermind. Let's just say I understand chile. We gone talk about that though girl," Lamont said.

Lamont was crazy like that. It seems he could read my mind and instantly knew the tea. There was only one person in the booth that knew the actual tea and that was Jamie. I had already told him about Orlando. He played along with the cooing as if he didn't know.

I was indeed chatting with Orlando. Orlando was trying to get me to come over after the club. I wanted to actually, but I didn't know how I would ditch the crew without them becoming suspicious, and I knew Lamont would want to drive me back home since he picked me up. I was trying to juggle all of that in my head. I'll come up with something.

"How you know I'm not talking to Tyler?" I asked peering over at Lamont who was sipping on his cocktail with a grin.

"Cause Tyler lame ass is probably reading the New York Times," he chimed.

"You ought to read it yourself, you wouldn't sound so damn dumb," Shawn said. Everyone laughed.

"Bitch, I know you ain't coming for me. I will mop this floor with you. I reads plenty, but not on no damn Saturday night,"

Lamont shouted.

I excused myself from the table. I went to the bathroom. My drinks were running through me. I was feeling good. I had a couple of gummies. I was feeling like getting banged out. I knew by the time I got home, Tyler would be asleep and in no mood to put out my fire. I definitely had to get to Orlando's place. I thought to myself, "Fuck it, Jamie already knows, Lamont seems to know, and Shawn, well he doesn't know and if he does, he wouldn't tell anyone." I was reasoning with myself in my thoughts about the dirt I was about to go and do. I just wanted to feel loved. I rushed back to the table but didn't sit down. Instead I reached over and grabbed the last of my cocktail and gulped it back.

"Alright guys, I'm about to bounce. I got an Uber coming to take me to my next destination," I said.

"Next destination?" Shawn questioned as he looked over at Lamont seemingly waiting for his reaction.

"Mind ya business," Lamont said to Shawn. He got up from the booth and faced me. "Okay let me walk you to the door," he said. He looked back at Jamie and Shawn and said, "Y'all hos watch my glass!"

I said my goodbyes to Shawn and Jamie and walked away with Lamont.

"Listen. I'm serious. You text me this address you headed to. Where does he live?" Lamont asked.

"Buckhead," I said.

"Alright so it should take you about 20 minutes to get there. You better text me as soon as you arrive. Are you staying there all night?"

"I don't plan on it. Damn mama, why you asking me all these questions," I laughed.

"Your ass laughing, but I'm for real bitch. You know we arrive together, and we leave together. I don't know who this john is you about to get with but I have to make sure you are okay. I mean I know you have good judgment, so I don't doubt that you're hooking up with some stranger, but you never know. So if you don't plan to stay there all night, then you need to text me when y'all are done. I'll come get you or if you taking Uber back, let me know you are home, ok bitch?"

"Thank you, Lamont. You give me a hard time, but I know you always have my back."

"I give you a hard time because I love you girl. Now give me a hug and remember what I said. We hugged and Lamont stood out front with me until my Uber arrived.

Ten

Chapter 10

By the time I arrived to Orlando's condo, I started sobering up. I didn't want to be sober. I wanted to let loose. I hoped he had something good to drink. I wasn't sure if a guy like Orlando smoked weed. He didn't know I would do it from time to time. Not a lot, but maybe once or twice a quarter when I just wanted to escape. I could see him being turned off by it. He's so posh, but then he's such a bad boy at the same time. I texted Lamont and let him know that I was there.

Okay Chile, <eggplant emoji>. I chuckled and knocked on the door. The door opened and there stood Orlando fine as fuck. He had on silk pajama pants with no shirt on. He has a tattoo of a long stem rose on his chest in red and green ink. He flashed me his white teeth.

"Hey sexy," Orlando reached for me and we started kissing. Before I knew it, we were rolling around on the floor.

Orlando and I fucked hard and good. We went at it three times, back to back. There was no stopping us. It was 4am as Orlando and I laid together on that same chaise we had our first experience on years ago.

"What's on your mind sir?" He asked.

"Nothing," I said.

"I don't believe you. You know I'm a therapist, right?" He said as he got up and laid across the bed.

"Yes, how can I forge? You only remind me like 100 times a week." I said.

"You hush. Seriously, though…How are you feeling about this, about us?"

I paused for a second and became quiet. He sat up in the bed and looked over into my eyes.

"I'm okay. I can't say that I don't think about where I am right now when I should be at home with Tyler," I said.

"I am wondering why you are here and not there with him. After all, you've been going on and on about how you two don't spend any time together," he said.

"Well, if I can be truthful, I'm starting to feel like Tyler doesn't do it for me anymore."

"I can see that. I think that somewhere along the line, you have fallen out of love with him or maybe not that. I take that back. I think you still love him, but I think that perhaps you two are growing apart. You are not willing to face it though and that's why you are here with me. I mean really look at it," he said. I got up from the chaise and went over and sat next to him on the bed.

"I know. I'm here in your bed at 4am and my boyfriend of several years has not texted me to find out where I am. I am here because I know that I would have gotten home and although he is there, it still would have felt like I was there by myself, and I did not want to feel that, not tonight," I said.

Orlando reached in and hugged me tight and kissed me on my neck. It felt so good, and it was so much of what I had been missing. What was I doing? It seems I was self-sabotaging an already destroyed relationship.

"Honey, I think you need to evaluate what you are doing and why you are doing it. Listen, and this is the therapist talking now, but we don't do things just because. Life is cause and effect, and if you are sitting here with me now, there is a reason for it and you need to find out what it is."

"Why can't the reason be everything you said from the start, you know…about how this is the way it goes down in your league. Why can't it be that I'm just using my power to get what I want?" I asked.

Orlando laughed. "Boy, you don't know nothing about power. You are not made for this, and I can tell. I can feel it. You are still a good boy. You keep complaining about it. It's all you talk about. Yeah you may party hard and smoke and drink, but you are still a goody goody boy. This what we are doing…nah…you are not made for this," Orlando said.

"What makes you so sure? I can handle myself just fine,". I said, annoyed and raised up from the bed to my feet.

"I'm sure," he said as he looked away into the distance.

"What was that all about?" I asked.

"What do you mean?"

"Nothing," I said.

"Spill it."

"Nothing, I just noticed you looked weird just now. So how do you feel about all of this that we are doing?" I asked.

"I'm cool. I told you. This is fun and games for me. I'm just helping you take the edge off," he said.

"Ugh!" I said. I rolled my eyes and walked away to the window. The overnight sky looked back at me. I knew he was lying. He was either lying at that moment or he lied at the Sundial.

"What now?" he asked.

"I just love how you sit here and detach yourself from this as if you and I don't have a history together," I said.

"Need I remind you it was a short-lived history, one that you broke off abruptly to get with Tyler who ironically is giving you his ass to kiss right now."

I turned around with a look of bewilderment. "You're an ass," I said.

"I'm just telling the truth, Brandon. You love to play victim sir, but that shit don't fly with me. You need to take ownership for your shit. It's not all Tyler. You contribute to the things you are going through now," he said.

"So you're saying that I'm getting what I deserve for dumping you? You know you are a trip. I'm leaving!" I shouted. I went over to collect my clothes off the floor.

"Fine leave then, it won't be the first. Until you own up to your shortcomings Brandon, and stop pretending like you have it all together, you might be able to stand in your truth a little bit better than you do. That's all I'm saying. Now if you want to leave, you can go on and get the fuck out then," he shouted back.

Looking back on this, I still don't quite understand how Orlando could switch on and off his sense of charm and evil. He carried them in a perfect balance. One moment, he was charming the shit out of me with his good sex and all, and then the next, he was brutally honest and straightforward as if he didn't care about my feelings.

"You know you can be such a rude motherfucker. I'll talk to you later," I said, still trying to find my socks.

"Yeah go on home to that man of yours," he said.

"You keep on Orlando, and I won't come back," I said. I had found my sock.

"Oh you'll be back and you know why?" I heard him say.

"And why is that exactly hmm? Because you are so wickedly suave?" I asked with sarcasm. By this time, I was facing away from the bed putting on the rest of my clothes.

"It's because you can't resist this!" I turned around and Orlando was still naked. He had thrown the cover off him and laid back on his elbows with his legs cocked and his dick sitting straight up in the air hard has a rock.

"Come get this dick baby," he said. His voice dropped several octaves lower. It sounded like the devil.

I felt something go all over me. It was like I was in a trance. I wanted it so bad, but I couldn't resist. I wanted to be mad at his rude ass, but I wanted round 4. I walked over to him and got on my knees and put his dick all the way in my mouth. I literally felt my heart expand for him in that moment. The passion that Orlando and I have is so fiery and explosive. It's why our arguments are so heated, and why our sex is so hot. Orlando and I had sex again. We set a record, six times in one night. It was 6am before I got up to leave, the sun was rising and I had finally gotten a text from Tyler, 6 orgasms too late.

"Dear, you didn't come home. I'm heading to the airport. I'm sorry I didn't get to see you before I left. Love you," he texted.

It felt devoid of emotion and almost sounded forced like it was something he had to do. Although Orlando was rude as fuck about what he said to me a few hours ago, he wasn't entirely wrong. I have to stop blaming Tyler for what is obviously my own failure to acknowledge that me and Tyler had grown apart. I felt we were no longer what each other needed.

I woke Orlando up and told him I had to go ahead and leave for home. I had broken his rule that I was not supposed to sleep overnight with him unless we were going to become more than fuck buddies. I wasn't so sure if I wanted to be more than fuck buddies with him. I mean…I am super attracted to Orlando, but I know that I love Tyler. It's just too much going on.

"It was nice having you here. I hope you consider what I said last night," he said with a yawn. I don't know how in the hell he wakes out of sleep trying to give advice.

"I will, even though it was rude as fuck," I said.

"I'm sorry sexy. Come here." He grabbed my ass and stuck his tongue in my mouth as he kissed me for about twenty seconds. I felt my dick getting hard again. I can't do round seven. I needed to leave to get my mind together.

"Apology accepted. Okay I have to go now," I said as I walked the walk of shame toward the door.

"Do you want to grab brunch later?" He asked.

"I'll let you know. You know I didn't get any sleep last night," I said.

"I know, I wore that ass out, didn't I?" He laughed.

"I wore yours out too so hush," I said. Then I walked out the door.

* * *

141

Somehow it seemed I was getting immune to the guilt. I didn't feel any actually. It could be that I'm missing so much from my relationship with Tyler, that I'm okay with fulfilling it with my relationship with Orlando. Or is it a relationship I have with Orlando? We're just having fun. That's what I told myself. Thinking back on it now, I was having a mental block, and I was not being honest with myself. Tyler and I had been talking about us until the cows came home and even still, that didn't seem like it was enough.

Okay, so yeah, I probably should have pushed the needle a little harder last night to ensure he and I spent time together, but fuck that. I'm tired of being the one to take the lead. Like his response to me this morning. I didn't come home. He didn't call me to find out if I was okay. It was in that moment that I felt unloved for the first time. All the other times, it was just loneliness, or at least I thought it was. This time, I didn't feel like Tyler really wanted to be with me. He says all the right shit, but his actions never line up. I texted Lamont while I waited in the Uber and let him know I was leaving for home.

Okay bitch. Did you get that back broken in?

I just looked away. Something about those words strung together made me flinch. This is not me. This is not who I am. I began to dial Lamont.

"Bitch what you calling me for? How you know I wasn't getting my back blown out too?" He answered.

"Lamont, you so silly." I said solemnly.

"Uh oh, what's wrong girl?" He asked.

"Nothing, I feel bad now."

"Aww, your first time cheating? It'll get easier after you do it a few times, trust me," he said.

"What?" I said.

"Yes, this is all new to you honey. And with a motherfucker like Tyler, I'm pretty sure you are good and validated on why you are doing this?" He said.

"He didn't even call to check up on me." I said.

"That's because that bitch don't give a fuck! And quiet as it's kept, he probably was digging in somebody's back himself last night," Lamont said.

"I don't think so, Lamont." I said.

"Chile, get your gullible country ass out of the clouds." Lamont said.

"Why you say I'm gullible?" I asked.

"Because you just is, Tyler," Lamont replied. "You're blonde ass fuck. You got to work on being more self-aware honey."

"I'm not stupid by a long shot. I just second guess things a lot," I said.

"Listen, Boo…I didn't want to be the one to break this to you, but I guess I need to go on and tell you the truth. Cause at the rate you going, chile, you in danger girl."

My Uber was pulling up. As I was getting out, I felt nervous. What was Lamont talking about?

"What truth?" I asked.

Lamont sighed. "Tyler isn't nearly who or what you think he is. He has a reputation out here in these streets. I didn't want to believe it, but one night, I was for sure it was real," He said.

"Ok, and…" I said.

"And…your man is a dog honey. The reason he didn't want to go out with you last night because he didn't want to face my ass. Yes honey, he tried me up at the club a couple of months ago. I don't know where you was at, but he was on the prowl that night honey, talking about, "I been checking you out, Lamont." I cussed that ass out good fashioned."

"Why didn't you tell me about this?" I asked in bewilderment.

"Because! You so in love with that man, and that's just not what we do in the culture honey."

"Fuck the culture, Lamont! I would have told you if the shoe was on the other foot. How do I know that I can trust you?" I asked.

"Wait a minute now, hold on. First of all, you and I have just begun to be close a few weeks ago, and second of all, I tend to mind my own motherfucking business. Yes his no good ass came on to me, groping my ass and shit, but I handled him, and that was it," he said.

"You still could have told me." I said.

"And what were you going to do if I did? You would not have left. So why even put you through that anguish. Sometimes there are things that you just don't need to know about unless you are ready to do something about it."

"You of all people should know how important it is to let me know. I'm not trying to turn up HIV positive because my boyfriend is out here cheating around on me. I should've known anyway. I felt it in my gut," I said.

"And you won't if you use protection. And ain't you out here cheating too? Talk about dissociative, chile," He replied.

"Don't do that. The way you talk, it sounds like Tyler is out here running around town with the community dick. I'm not doing that," I said.

"Don't do what? See this is why you need to get out of that relationship. You can't even see the cognitive dissonance that's taking place with you. You are just as much putting yourself and Tyler too, at risk for an STD as he is. You really don't have room not to be upset about a damn thing. But listen, honey, I'm not trying to have an argument with you or judge you. Now you know the truth, so what are you going to do about it?" He asked.

"I guess I need to start telling the truth myself. You think I need to break up with Tyler?" I asked.

"Baby, you are an intelligent man, you know what you have to do. And whatever that is, you make sure it's what you want to do and not what the street committee thinks you should do, okay?"

"I just feel like shit. I'm so numb, it's like I can't feel anything anymore."

"It's okay, go on and sleep off your night. You'll feel better when you wake up."

Eleven

Chapter 11

꧁ᦞꨄᦞ꧂

I did my best to sleep once I got home. Sleep didn't come easy but it came, in and out. I was still deeply troubled by the fact that Tyler didn't even see where I was the night before. For the first time ever, I started to see the writing on the wall. I could see that my relationship was falling apart and not only was Tyler not physically here, but it appeared he had checked out mentally as well. I laid in the bed, not wanting to move. I stared up at the ceiling fan moving around and around in circles. The light struggled to shine slightly around the gray blacked-out drapes on the wall. The whole room was gray. The walls, a light gray, the bedroom furniture was gray with white washed surfacing. And then, there were my feelings, gray as fuck too. Everything was simply gray. My heart was hurting because I was missing Tyler and he wasn't missing me.

I rolled over to my side and reached for my phone. It was

a Sunday. I dialed Alec hoping he would pick up. It rang a few times and just as I was about to end the call, I heard his cheery voice answer.

"Hey my friend. What's up with you. You don't normally call me on a Sunday. What's going on?" He asked.

I was quiet for a second. "Hello?" He added.

"The world is ending, Alec," I said softly.

"Oh lord. What's wrong, chile?" He asked.

"Tyler," I said.

Alec sighed a little. "What has he not done now?"

I guess Alec had gotten a little aggravated by the constant talks of Tyler and complaining. "Well, we were going to go out last night to celebrate my promotion. He changed his mind literally 2 minutes after saying he'd go. So I went on without him, and I hung out with my friends. I was feeling good, had a few drinks and an edible. I left the lounge to go meet up with Orlando. Long story-short, I didn't leave until almost 6 this morning," I said.

"You are making this up, Brandon. That's not even like you. I don't believe that for one minute," Alec said.

"I'm serious," I replied. "I didn't mean to stay over night with him but it just happened."

"Brandon, that type of thing doesn't just happen. Volcanos just happen, not random sex with a dude. Ok so what did Tyler say about you not coming home?" He asked.

I sat up in the bed. "He didn't say shit. He texted me this morning letting me know that he was at the airport heading to his next assignment. He didn't say anything to me about where I was. He didn't check on me or anything. My relationship is over," I started to cry.

"Brandon don't cry love. Listen, you know the writing

has been on the wall for a long time about you and Tyler. Sometimes God will violently show us things that shock our system so we can walk in truth," he said.

"He should have texted me or something. I just can't believe it." I said.

"Brandon, let me be straight up with you, and you know I wouldn't say anything like this if I wasn't your friend. It's time you start seeing yourself in all of this too. I mean you have been running around with this guy for months now. Are you at least using condoms with the guy? I know you have been missing Tyler and things, but when are you going to start taking some responsibility for your actions here? I don't see how you're so focused on the fact that Tyler didn't check on you last night. Honey, why wasn't you checking on yourself? Tyler can't be responsible for all of your choices, Brandon," Alec said.

"You don't understand," I said. I didn't feel like Alec understood because he is not out here in the life like I am. He is so sheltered in that church. I didn't feel he knew the dynamics well enough to call me out like that.

"There is nothing to understand. It's plain and simple," he said.

"So you're saying the breakdown of my relationshp is my fault?"

"Not directly, but a part of it is, though."

"No! I adon't agree with that at all. Tyler has never been home and—

"And what? He told you to go out with Orlando. Lay up in—wherever the hell y'all have been laying up at. Tyler hasn't done any of that. That's all on you."

"You don't know what you're talking about Alec," I said.

"There you go with that?"

"With what? It's true. You've been in that church so much, how could you possibly understand what I'm dealing with or remotely get why I did what I did?"

"I know you're upset or whatever, but I"m not about to keep listening to you diss me like I don't understand the world around me. Yes I'm celibate, and that is by choice. Yes I spend a lot of time in ministry, and that too is by choice. You hear the key word in that? Choice is the key word. I have chosen my life and everything that happens in it and everything that I'm dealing with. You could learn a little something from me," he said.

I dont' know why I said this, but I was in my feelings. I replied to him, "No one wants those boring choices you make, scared to live your fucking life. Scared to leave Mobile. You're just plain scared that's all. Has nothing to do with choices. You keep running to Jesus to solve your fear of your sexuality."

"Oh I'm scared, but yet you're the one running around town like a five dollar hoochie, cheating on your man because he isn't home to tend to you. Chile bye. You could use a little Jesus since you threw him away once you got your degrees and shit. It's good to know how you really feel about me, and regardless of what you feel about me, you still chose the shit you are dealing with, periodt! Miss me with all that bullshit, Brandon. I know you better than you probably know yourself. Like I said, the writing has been on the wall and you have refused to own it. You sit around and complain all the damn time about Tyler this and Tyler that, and look where it has you. You used to be so much better than this. I don't know what happened to you," he said. He was quiet. I couldn't tell what he was doing or where he was.

"I'm still the same person," I said.

"You're not. The Brandon I know would not be out here having sex all night while his man of five years is at home in the bed. Lately, I just feel like I don't know who you are anymore," he said.

I don't know why I was bickering with Alec. I think I took my anger with Tyler out on him and because he was saying similar things that Orlando was saying to me. The only difference with Alec is I could not hop on his dick to forgive him like I did with Orlando. Alec was striking a chord with me. He was right and I just didn't want to hear it. I knew I was acting like an ass, but in the moment it didn't seem that way. I felt I was right and he was wrong.

"Anyway, Alec. I gotta go. I'll talk to you later." After that, I rolled back over and buried my face in the pillow. I felt no remorse because I was seething in my own anger. My anger with Tyler, and what I thought was anger with Alec.

* * *

I had a meeting with Jamie later that day to lay out the first few interviews for the HIV documentary. He was to come over to my place. I wasn't feeling very engaged especially considering the fight I had with Alec. I was out behaving like a slut the night before. Who am I to do a documentary about HIV among black gay professionals and how they manage their day-to-day living and I'm out here being risky.

Thinking about that gave me some additional ideas. I began to brainstorm them out. What if I take an angle where I highlight "Freedom in HIV+ Living". I knew a few professional gay men of color who lead really great lives. I think my aim should be showcasing how HIV does not have to be the end all to be all. I felt my creative musing coming on and I was excited. For a moment, I had forgotten all about my woes with Tyler. I instantly called Jamie and invited him over early.

Once Jamie was over, I had to spill the beans about what I was thinking about.

"So I was thinking, there are so many documentaries and tropes in fiction that depict HIV as the "consequence" of a promiscuous life, but I want to tell a different story. There are so many influential and prominent men in our community who are HIV+ and doing well with their lives. Some are even married. I want to highlight that and I'll call it, Freedom: Living a Wonderful Life with HIV. What you think?"

"Umm, I like the concept. It's original and I think it fits into the timing of things. HIV is not as stigmatized as it once was and no better time than now to add to the change of conversation about HIV. I think the title needs a little work though. I'm not really feeling it," Jamie said.

"Cool! We can work on the title. We have to line up some interviews, but not before we consider what our structure will be." I walked over to my white board and started to draw up an outline. "So, we can consider focusing on one subject and tell his or her story and how they manage their day-to-day life now, or we can have multiple subjects, those who are managing the disease in varying lifestyles. Maybe some contrasting ones like a married couple, a newly dating couple, or how about hmmm, how about adding a single person who is positive."

"You still need to consider what makes this angle different from all the rest," Jamie added.

"The professional landscape. You see, I want to showcase people still having normal lives despite being HIV positive. I want to show them graduating grade school, getting married, or even owning their sexual freedom and still maintaining an active sex life. I think this will change the attitudes about HIV positive people, and then more and more of them will feel comfortable telling others about their status from a place of empowerment and not a place of shame."

"Okay, I like that. I think that has good potential. You'll need strong subjects and your questions will have to be in-depth to draw up the narrative. Who do you have in mind for this?"

"I know a couple right off the top of my head. A gay married couple. They both are doing well with life and progressing. I need to find a single guy that is positive, one who is free with his sexuality, but free responsibly. Like I want someone who isn't afraid to still go out and have sex, one-night stands, but one who does it responsibly as an HIV positive person. I think that dialogue needs to be had."

"Well alright then, let's get some interviews set up! You think Janice will go for this angle?" Jamie asked.

"I think she will. I don't know. We shall see. If not, it'll just be another independent documentary. Maybe I can shop it to Netflix or something. That'll be amazing! I have been so caught up in actually getting this thing started. Jamie, man let me tell you, I know I was drowning everyone including you in my sorrows, but I feel so alive now that I'm actually working on things that matter. I just want to thank you for being a friend an encouraging me," I said.

"Aww no worries love. I knew from the start you hand it in you. Sometimes you just need a little inspiration to push you into your destiny. I'm glad you're trusting my input to work on this with you, so no, thank you actually," he said.

"Wow, you're welcome. Amazing how so much closer we've become now, and you know something, you got a lot of wisdom to be a youngin'. Wouldn't it be great if we can remain this way forever?" I asked.

"Yeah it would be. So, not to change the topic but umm, where did you run off to last night?" He asked. He caught me in mid bend as I was reaching on the floor to pick up the white board eraser. I looked back and I stood up with a smirk.

"I was out having fun and celebrating my promotion."

"With Tyler?" He asked with his head cocked to the side. He didn't seem to believe that I would say yes to that.

"You know…" I said. Jamie just shook his head in disapproval.

"Well, how did that go? Second time ain't it?"

"More like seventh time," I said.

"What? Didn't you just get with him for the first time last week?"

"Yes but we did it six times last night until this morning." I said as I walked into the kitchen. "You want a mimosa?" I asked.

"Sure. Damn. Wow. He must be something else," Jamie said.

"He's alright. His sex is good, but his attitude is trash. He has loose morals I feel," I said.

"Then why are you messing with him? Why you feel he has loose morals?"

"You didn't hear me? His sex is bomb, both ways…good dick and ass. And it's the stuff he says sometimes that makes me think he can be a bit unscrupulous."

"What type of things does he say?" Jamie asked.

"Like last night, he pretty much told me to get out and don't come back because I told him to stop acting like he is not mutually wrong for what we are doing. I don't know. He seems to act like what we are doing is just the way it is and it's normal."

"Well, for one, it sounds like he is an abusive guy, and two, it sounds like you are feeling guilty," Jamie said.

"I don't think he is an abusive dude. He's just, different. It kinda makes it hard to trust him, but the honesty about his scruples or lack there of is enticing and for some reason I like it. I'm drawn to it." I said.

"That's probably because Tyler is the exact opposite. Tyler is withdrawn, doesn't let you in much, and not a bad boy. I think Orlando reflects the type of guy you are actually into, and Tyler ain't it." Jamie said. I looked at him for a second. He was on to something. I slid his mimosa over to him.

"Why do I feel like I've heard that before?" I said.

"Because it's true. Orlando sounds like the flame that draws you near, but to me, he sounds like trouble." Jamie took a sip of his mimosa.

"Well, Tyler isn't exactly a saint. He's been cheating on me," I said.

"How do you know?" Jamie asked as he set down his glass.

"I just know. It's been confirmed." I said.

"I'm sorry to hear that. What are you going to do about that?" Jamie asked.

"I really don't know. He's away in DC right now. I know we will need to talk. I feel like he's not present anymore. I was out until 6am this morning, he didn't call me. He sent a text to tell me he was leaving for his flight. I don't know. I know I was out doing my dirt, but I feel like he should've asked me where was I or hell, asked if I was okay. It's that type of disregard that's pissing me off." I said.

"Well, I think you need to take this time that he's away to think about what you want to do and you and him need to make a decision about the relationship." Jamie said.

"I know. So much on my mind and heart and it's making it hard for me to focus. That's why I got so excited when my thoughts about this documentary began to flow. I really can't wait to interview our first subject.

II

Part II: Take a Bow

How 'bout a round of applause...Standing Ovation.
Yea, you put on quite a show...
Really had me going.

Twelve

Chapter 12

Orlando

I sat there in silence with a stoned look on my face. The staleness of those cold hospital floor tiles staring back at me as if they were mocking this dreadful moment. It seemed they were saying to me, "I told you so! That joker didn't love you. Now look at you!" It was in that moment that I stopped living. My life paused. Sometimes I find myself thinking back on that day. Sure it's been eleven years since I discovered it, but you never quite get used to the idea of it. Even now, it still feels surreal to me. Did it really happen? Am I really HIV positive? I remember my doctor sitting in front of me on his little stool, a stoic look in his eyes like his thoughts were judging. *Here is another black boy in here who didn't give a fuck enough about himself to ensure he did not become a statistic.* He probably said that to himself. But instead, he said, "Your test came back positive." He must was a brave little man to sit in front of me on one of those rolling stools to tell me that my life was over.

"How do you feel?" He asked. I gave the religious pretend answer.

"I know Jesus and I know he got me." Or did he? The next three years of my life would prove to be so, but still, in that time I stopped living. I pretended like that young guy who I was becoming before HIV found me out no longer existed. I remember when I was about seventeen, and I felt like I would not live pass the age of twenty-one. Twenty-one is when I died. Twenty-one is when I found out I was HIV positive. I died. I stopped being me. I ran to the church trying to figure things out. I told God not to heal me because I figured He was trying to teach me something. I wanted to learn whatever that was. Maybe He *was* trying to teach me something. I acted like the disease did not exist. 'God's got me,' I would say to myself.

I'm what they call a LTNP - Long-Term Non-Progressor. That means I can fare pretty well without meds. I took that as God's grace. I would tell myself that I felt that God blessed me with a non-aggressive strand of the virus.

Did I hear myself right? *God blessed me with HIV.* You see that's the pretending shit I used to do. I spent a lot of time pretending. I pretended like I was not hurt. I pretended like I still could tolerate my ex who infected me. I still had sex with him several times after finding out. I made excuses for him. "Maybe he didn't know," I would say. I totally let my guard down with him. He was my first love, and today, a part of me still loves him. I loved him intensely without any guards, and I had sex with him the same way, without any guards. I got burned badly. Now, I'm defensive as hell. I have anger issues and I will get you off of me quickly. My therapist told me that I learned how to be guarded when I was betrayed by him. She said I learned how to stop feeling the really deep shit inside of me. Well, she didn't say *shit*, but that's how I interpreted it.

I began to tell her how I got all spiritual and what should have "been a falling out on the cold fake tile floor with sobs of despair" instead was a minister trying to be ministerial and shit. I kept up that charade for three years doing ministry until I was tired of pretending. I remember driving home from the doctor's office and a part of me felt like crying, but it just wouldn't happen. I tried to reach my ex but he wouldn't answer. Then, I told him to call me and that it was an emergency. He opted to text instead. He was evasive like that. I told him the news over text. He responded, *Are you serious*. There wasn't much of anything else said after that.

That night, I could not sleep. Tyler Perry's *I Can Do Bad By Myself* stage play was on the TV. In the bedroom, it felt like a phantom of my health was haunting my thoughts. I felt scared and alone. Hell, I was scared and alone. By the way, my ex didn't even fucking stop by and he lived in the neighborhood. I was at GA State during this time. He was older than me, more established than me. He was becoming who I am now. A powerful intelligent guy who just didn't give a damn about anyone else but himself. I texted him about how I could not sleep and how I was feeling. This came after the flood gates opened and I cried like I had never cried before. Thanks Tyler Perry. I think it was Tamela Mann screaming out one of her songs, "Step Aside". When she got to the line, "You can't fix this on your own. You're not strong enough, try Jesus, try Jesus, Try HIM." I balled like a baby. I laid in bed and it felt like a bucket splashed my face as I thought I'd drown in the amount of tears that came. The hurt I felt was deep, and I would never be able to explain it. He replied with his normal nonchalant, disconnected tone and then he told me that I was making a big deal out of it. It was at that moment I realized that it was never news to him. He knew all along. He was just waiting for me to find out on my own. I was disgusted with sex after that. The mere thought of sperm made my stomach turn. It was a month before I touched myself in that way, and several months before I let anyone else touch me in that way.

My therapist asked me once, "When did you stop allowing yourself to feel things?" It was when I found out I was HIV positive. I immediately shelved the realization and went on this journey of pretending. I used the church and spirituality to pretend until I couldn't pretend anymore, and I stopped going to church. At one point, my spirituality seemed to be fleeting and that person who was sitting in the doctor's office was still sitting there years later taking in the news as if it was his first time hearing it. I don't know how I feel about being HIV positive. What I do know is that deep down in my soul somewhere, there is a sense of sorrow about it. I went into survival mode soon after I found out. I never got any closure from it. I did not allow myself to get any closure. There is a lot that I have not allowed myself to get closure about. I have to tell myself that December day in 2009 is long gone now. I am not there anymore. I have lived beyond some of my worst fears.

I've had the virus eleven years now. I'm doing pretty well with my health. I'm surviving. But I'm surviving while still sitting there in that doctor's office emotionally. Why am I still there emotionally? I don't have to be. I should explore my feelings then and now. How did I feel then? When I was first told that I am HIV positive, I remember it feeling like the death of a family member. Sometimes, when you lose a family member unexpectedly, it feels surreal. You know it's happening, but yet you don't believe it. It's like you need time for it to settle in. That's how I felt at that moment. I needed to let it settle in.

My first response was one of strength, or what I thought to be strength. I tried to be strong for myself. I did not cry. I kept myself together in front of that doctor, in front of myself. I remember going to the lab room afterward for them to take more blood. It still felt surreal. But somehow, I was walking through the process as if I had done it a dozen times. Eventually, having blood drawn became just another thing to do. Funny, that's still how it seems whenever I have to sit and give blood for them to check how my numbers are doing. The drive home was...I don't really remember. I do remember calling my best friend. He was the first I told I believe. I don't know why my ex-boyfriend wasn't the first I called. I still talk to him today though. A part of me didn't feel like I should hold animosity as if doing that would be a waste of emotion. Or is it me shelving emotions again? I don't know. What I do know is that I was bitter towards him for a long while at one point. I finally got over it. I don't know how. Maybe all of that praying and fasting did it. Some of the pretending actually did cause me to cut some things away. Or maybe I just forgot. Is that the same thing? Probably.

Devastation had hit my life and I had to start coping. I ran to Jesus. There is nothing wrong with that actually, but I did not deal with my trauma. I just pretended like it wasn't there. Depression caught up with me and I could not pretend any longer. By that time, I was an ex-minister, sitting in a pile of my own shit, stinking up the place - smiling and pretending still and that's when I met Brandon. Before Brandon, all of my relationships failed. I was emotionally unavailable, selfish, and untrustworthy. I didn't trust them either. I figured let me fuck them up before they do it to me. But he did fuck me over first, and now he's back. This time, it feels different. We've been kicking it a few months now. Tyler still doesn't know. Or maybe he does and doesn't care. I think I'm getting myself caught up with him. With him, it feels like a relationship and I don't feel wrong about it. It feels right. I don't know why. It just does.

* * *

The parking garage to my building is always a mess in the morning. I just want to get to my office. Now that I had closed on my property, I'm back and forth, spending some nights in my condo and spending most nights now in the house.

"Good Morning, Dr. McIntyre

I nodded my head at the new security guy as I scanned my access badge. I guess he could see my name. Looks like they have a cutie pie this time. They switch these guards out a dime a dozen. I'll never forget the one that I had bent over a railing on the top-level parking deck, ahem 12:00 at night. I think someone's car got broken into that night. I don't know what he told them to explain the 45 minutes he was missing. Needless to say, he was fired. I never saw him again, but he had good booty. My day is lined up with clients. My first one will be here in a couple of hours, which will give me time to chat with Alec some. I tend to have some well-to-do people as clients, and they don't mind paying the premium price for my services. Most of them have issues with their parents. You'll get one that didn't feel loved because their dad was always at work and now, they are searching for that missed attention in their adult life. It's funny how our past can dictate what takes place in the current. This is true even for me. Some would say I'm still pretending. Maybe so.

I hope you have a good day, I texted. He usually doesn't be up this early but to my surprise he texted back.

Good Morning, <smiley face>

Wow, didn't think you would be up so early. What are you doing?

We have inventory today at the store.

Alec is this little tenderoni I had been sort of dating. He's not from around here. He kept me sane, I think. If I were to have a relationship and settle down with someone, I think it would have been with him since Brandon chose Tyler over me. I just wished he would let loose on that church stuff. I know I was a minister myself, but I was out there living life. He lived and breathed church. I think I would have gotten him to move up here with me had it not been for that church he's married to. It was all he talked about.

When I found out I was positive, it sent me into a spiral. You'd think a therapist would know how to handle trauma. No one is immune to trauma, and I was just starting out in my therapy career anyway. I wanted more than therapy. I wanted to be healed. I don't have a heart of stone, but I have gotten to a place to where I really don't give a fuck. It's about me now. I gave my all to the bastard that infected me, loving him, being everything he needed, paying his bills. That was my dumb ass fault. Yep, I take responsibility for all of that. Now, Brandon, well, that was just an old chapter that had never finished being written. Besides, that joker he's with out there playing the field. Hmmm huh, I'd heard about him in the streets. Poor Brandon. He deserved better than that. Just like I had told him before, DL guys aren't shit. I don't care what anyone says, that boy still had a little bit of DL in him. All that was on my mind was giving Brandon what he is not getting here in the A.

It was my dream to have him as my own, but Brandon loved Tyler like he loved Jesus. There's no way he would have left Tyler for me even though I wanted him to. And knowing that I am positive and I didn't tell him when we had sex, he wouldn't have gotten with me anyway I figured. The sex was fucking amazing. We had done it a few times. I guess it was too late to say something to him. There was never any risk to him because of me being undetectable, but I'm sure he wouldn't understand that at all. Anyway, he didn't know about Alec. But hell, he didn't need to know about Alec. It wasn't like Brandon and I were a couple or something, even though deep down I wanted us to be. We were only fucking. I loved to spend time with him. It's like I felt my heart grow and melt when I was with him. He warms that deep dark cold place that's there. That spot that I wouldn't even allow myself to see. HIV did that shit to me. With Brandon I could feel my emotions, when all the other times, they would evade me.

Every time I would think back on it, I felt regret. I would say to myself, "Damn, I fucked up." Let me be honest. I fucked Brandon the first time because I just wanted to get back at him and Tyler for fucking me over. But then I underestimated the chemistry we had and I was hooked like a fish. When Tyler left on those assignments, Brandon just kept texting me things like, 'What you doing? or How's your day, hon?' Admittedly, I tried to resist, but chemistry is unbeatable. It's been an ongoing affair that I just can't let go, but I needed to tell him that I was positive. I knew he would hate me for it once I did. After all the times we have had sex, telling him would be a fatal blow.

Thirteen

Chapter 13

~⚬⚬~

HIV *for me was never a death sentence.* This would be the first line of my speech I would do at the HIV event that I had invited Brandon to. That meant I definitely had to tell Brandon before the event because I invited him to attend. I'd become so casual with my status that I didn't think twice about the idea that he didn't know. This is how I learned to live with HIV. My day-to-day living was simple. I'd get up, put on my workout gear and hit the gym. I make sure to stay healthy and I try to eat healthy as well. Once I got an emotional handle on my status, I decided not to let it dictate how my life would go.

In the mornings, the gym was usually quiet. I'd often go to the one in my condo building. I'd normally walk in to dim lights and the sound of the air going. This one day I went in and there was a guy already in there running on the treadmill. He turned and looked my way. He was a nice attractive guy.

Chapter 13

I'd seen him in there a few times before. If I had to say I had a gym mate, he was it. We seldom made conversation. I think he's a lawyer. We both had our offices in the building. My condo building has offices on the first few floors with residences above. I got my suite for a steal of a price per month. I had to jump on it, and with it being just downstairs from my unit, it was perfect.

I'd see this lawyer guy passing through the halls. I'm surprised he never really talked He always seemed to be in his own thoughts. It was something I would always notice. "Maybe I'd strike up a conversation with him one day, just to see what he is all about," I thought. One day did eventually come and he and I fucked. I enjoyed having sex with powerful people. Now whether he was powerful or not, I didn't know. What I did know is he was a partner in his law firm, drove a black Porsche Panamera, and was fine as hell. His sex was good too. I guess it's true what they say that still waters run deep. He was definitely still on the outside but once I got to know him, he was pretty cool and did I mention the sex? Oh yeah, I did. We never did hit it off outside of having sex that one time. I'd still see him in the gym though from time to time.

The gym was massive. It took up what would be the equivalent of probably 4 units, most of the 23rd floor. The perimeter had a track that wrapped around the floor. That's usually how I started my routine. I wasn't much of a treadmill type of guy and being able to look out of the window as I ran was peaceful for me. Each morning, I'd run for three miles, then I'd hit the weights and do some lifting. I've been doing this for many years now, even before I became positive.

I have never really struggled with my sickness, outside of

fatigue early on before I started medication. I remember the day my doctor pretty much scolded me because I had not started meds yet. It came out of nowhere because according to him, I didn't need them. My viral load was not low, but it wasn't high either. It hung around 3,000 copies per ml of blood, which is actually decent. Well, the CDC changed direction and gave out guidance that all HIV positive people should be on treatment regardless of whether their viral load is self-maintained or not. My doctor's way of explaining this to me was emphatically telling me it was time I started to get serious about getting on medication. Honestly, in that moment, it did not bother me. I just remember sitting there listening to him and me nodding okay over and over again until he finally shut the fuck up about it. Once I got in the car, I felt like shit and the tears begin to fill the wells of my eyes. By that time, I had been living with HIV for about 5 years. In all that time, visit after visit, my doctor would give me a clean bill of health and never once mentioned that I should consider medication. His line of questioning came out of left field for me and it took me by surprise. Honestly, I think I was pissed at him as I quietly drove to work. I probably was more pissed at having to now take poison to keep me alive, but it seemed convenient to be mad at my Doctor. I mean, I didn't understand why he was talking to me like it wasn't he that kept telling me I didn't need meds. Now, according to him, some government official said, "Put them all on drugs." He said I needed to start getting serious, as if I was never serious about my health. Actually, yes I was pissed at him for that and not the idea of getting on meds.

I had to process that. The reality hit me hard. I am HIV positive, and this shit is not going anywhere. Driving slowly back to work from the appointment that day, I had a million thoughts on my mind. Cars drove past me when normally I'm the one zooming past them. I thought about all of my regret and how I didn't deserve this. I considered why me and what did I do to deserve this. It took me a long time to stop blaming myself for turning up HIV positive. I used to blame the world too, then a friend of mine got really frank with me and he said, "It's no one's fault but your own that you are positive." It was the harshest truth I'd ever received, but he was right on the money.

My journey towards being able to live with HIV has gone through little moments where I've learned new things about myself and faced the parts of HIV that scared me the most. My biggest fear was dying…sometimes it still is. When I jog, I have these types of profound thoughts with myself. It was my way of journaling. I realized that I can be a motherfucker, but I've learned that I have to be in control because of the one thing in my life that I cannot control. I can maintain it, but I have no control over it. HIV will always be in my body and that's the control it has. I do pray a cure comes in my lifetime though.

The CDC now says I'll live well into my 70s because of the drugs, but that's an uphill battle full of land mines because I'm susceptible to all types of illnesses like cancer and liver disease, heart disease, and renal failure. This shit sucks balls. My best defense is to remain healthy, limit my meat intake, and eat a whole lot of green vegetables. Oh and something about having love and support, yeah that shit. I supposed to have that shit too. I always hoped to have that one day though for real. And that's probably why I was feeling Brandon. He is the closest thing to consistency I've experienced in a long time.

Even if he wasn't mine. I've heard the saying, "Having a piece of a man is better than having no man at all." Sometimes that shit feels very real and true no matter how stupid it sounds.

Fourteen

Chapter 14

lec knew about my status and he was cool with it. I wasn't that cold-hearted. Or maybe I was. I told a guy I never met but didn't tell the guy I was actually fucking. Alec lived so far away. We hadn't even met yet, no sex or anything. I'm not sure why I disclosed it to him. I did look forward to a night with him though. Alec is tall and handsome, red skin tone. He's serious eye candy. If there were no Brandon, Alec would be my first choice. I had to be honest with myself though. I had feelings for Brandon and every time we had sex, they got deeper and deeper, but Alec was my safety. I didn't want to let that safety go, but sometimes I felt like something was there lurking. It was a weird feeling, like a shoe would drop. For that reason, sometimes I kept up a wall with Alec. I sensed not to let him get too close to me. Just when I could tell he wanted to express his devotion to me, I'd flake out or do something to make him mad on purpose. And then, there were times that I would always call him to check up on him.

"Tell me something sweet. I've had the day from hell dealing with these customers," Alec said. The sound of Alec's voice was so soothing sometimes despite the walls I put up. That damn job always stressed him out. I told him he needed to leave it and put that business degree to use somewhere else. He needed to get out of retail period because the retail market is going to shit anyway.

"Aww baby, what happened?" I asked.

"Let me tell you, I was called to the service desk, right. When I get there, there is the woman standing there with her hand on her hip. 'You the goddamn manager?' She asked me. I said, 'Yes, I am the manager. How can I help you?' Then she goes into her rant about how she's been waiting in line for thirty minutes trying to return her TV. I said well what seems to be the problem. Then she points to the customer service girl who was looking like she was about ready to quit. I walked over and asked, 'What's going on here?' She didn't say anything, she pointed at the TV and rolled her eyes. I turned to see the dustiest ass TV I'd ever seen in my life. This lady done wheeled a 90's box style TV in here talking about it quit working and she wanted a refund."

I just busted into laughter. "Well, what did you say to her, Alec?" I asked. By this time, I was done with the gym, showered, and in my office with my feet kicked up.

"The lady then commences to say, 'Sir, I want my money back for this shit. It stopped working.' I said ma'am, this TV is too old to return. She got mad and said, 'What you mean; well, what you want me to do it with' I said, 'I don't care what you do with it, but we are not taking it.' And then I walked off. I don't have time for the foolishness. These people get on my last nerves," I said.

"I told you to quit that place man. Why do you keep putting yourself though this?"

"It's beyond my control, Londell. I can't just quit my job. I have bills to pay."

"I'm not saying quit your job and don't work any place else, but you should find something else to transition into. I mean…get out of the customer service game so that you will not have people dumping on you all day."

"I'm a minister. I was made to serve people," Alec said.

"I get that, but that doesn't mean you are made to absorb their negative and toxic energy. Walmart is full of that crap, from the workers to the shoppers that come up in there," I replied.

"Ugh! I need a vacation. That's it. I'm coming up to Atlanta for a visit. I need to get away from here for a while. The holidays are coming up and I better get some time off before blackout comes."

"What's blackout?"

"We won't be able to take time off during the holidays. The schedule will be blocked off."

"Oh, never heard of that," I said.

"Well, when you are your own boss you don't have to worry about that."

"Don't be salty. Quit your job and take control of this. You don't *have* to work there. You have convinced yourself that you do, but you really don't. You don't know how many times I hear this from my sessions. People convince themselves they have to put up with negativity in their lives and they sit in bad situations. If you want out, then get out. The power is in your hands."

"Why are you always lecturing me? I'm not completely unaware of that, you know," Alec replied.

"Alright, alright, I'm sorry, love. I just want you to be happy. Is that asking too much?"

"I'm happy, I have you. I am happy. Yes these fools work my nerves sometimes, but I'm not down and out and in despair."

"Ok, I take your word for it. You sure? I know you are down there being celibate. You might have some pinned up energy going on there." I said.

"Now see, why you want to go there. I am doing quite well in that department."

"Oh, is that right?" I replied.

"Yes that's right. Don't you be worrying about my sexual energy. Focus on your own. I'm sure you are managing it."

"I might be," I said with a chuckle.

"Good, well you better get all that shit out of your system because when I get there, it's gonna be none of that going on."

"Oh, so you're not going to give me any ass?"

"Of course...NOT! I don't play about my celibacy. I'm serious. So I hope you got some good ass up there that you are using to buy you over until we are together for real."

"So we aren't together for real now?" I asked.

"You know what I mean. I don't care about you having to manage your sexual urges while I'm not living there. You just better not be catching feelings or that's ya ass."

Alec and I were in somewhat of an open dating situation. We had our ways of respecting boundaries. I respected his celibacy, and he allowed me to manage my sexual urges by allowing me to be sexual with other people. The conditions were I had to use protection and I could not catch feelings.

It has actually made me to be somewhat of a dog. Maybe I was already a dog. I'd like to think not. I actually used to be a good gentleman. The gentleman until I was jaded. Maybe that guy is still in my heart somewhere. Who knows? But I do have feelings for Brandon. I think I'm in deep with that too. I don't know what to do. I'm willing to play this game because, well…Brandon is with Tyler and I am pretty sure they will be together. This thing I have going with Brandon is temporary until he and Tyler are on more stable and consistent terms, and when Alec moves to Atlanta. In the meantime, let the sex continue.

"So Alec, what if I did catch feelings for someone. How would that make you feel?" I asked.

"I'd come up there and kick your ass," he said.

"That's not a feeling."

"Bitch it's one when you feel my foot going up side your head. I bet you feel that. And why you ask me that anyway?" He asked.

"Just asking. Just wanted to see where your mind is about that type of thing, that's all," I replied.

"My mind is where it should be as it concerns that. Now don't get me wrong. I'm not the type to get caught up in that whole montage of wanting to control a cheating man, but I'm not exactly on to the idea of some type of open relationship," he said.

"So, do you think we are in a relationship," I asked.

"I mean, somewhat. I know it's only been a while that we have been talking consistently, but I feel like you and I have a vibe going on. Yes, we do need to meet in person so we can see if what we feel from a distance is actually a real thing that's happening. Then I suppose we move from there with what we should call ourselves. So, no, we are not in a relationship per se, but we are more than friends I know that shit for a fact because I don't send nudes to friends sir," he said.

"Well you know I do," I chuckled.

"I bet you do, nasty ass. So who you up there dating. I think I have figured you out somewhat, Mr. McIntyre, and I know you don't pose questions for the hell of it."

"Don't assume you know me. It's a therapy technique. A lot of times we ask questions for the hell of it, just to get you to talk about what's in your heart or on your mind. You can find out a lot that way," I said.

"Get on somewhere with that psycho babble bullshit. You ain't fooling nobody," he said.

"What?" I laughed, attempting to be coy. I think a part of me wanted to mention Brandon to him only because despite the facade I put up, I'm not really that cold-hearted. I actually may love Brandon, although I don't think I should tell him that. I also don't want to be juggling two guys and then, shit, one of them is in a marriage, damn near.

"I'll let you slide this time, but my spidey senses are going off left and right, and I believe you got something to say to me. But I'll let it ride cause I got to get in here and start this store meeting," he said. He laughed afterwards, but I knew he was deathly serious about what he said. Alec is a prophet. He discerns easily, so I have no doubt that he is picking up on the fact that I am doing what I am doing with Brandon. Alec and I wrapped up our call. My first client would be coming in soon and I needed to prepare.

Thoughts of Brandon were on my mind as I walked over to the floor-to-ceiling windows of my office and looked over Peachtree Road up towards Lenox mall. The traffic was moving like ants. My office is on the tenth floor, not so high up as my condo. I considered myself to be a blessed individual, and I was closing on my new house soon. It's a big one and all that space and here I am, alone, and sleeping with someone else's man. A part of me feels guilty. I took a sigh and walked over to the little bar I have in my office and prepared a cappuccino. My heart began to feel heavy because of the guilt. I looked into the mirror and I begin to give myself a pep talk. "Get back in focus, Orlando. This is not the end of the world. You can't get distracted. Stay focused…stay focused," I said out loud. Then my intercom buzzed. I walked back over to my desk to answer.

"Yes, Sidney?" I said.

"You're ten o'clock is here. Should I send them in?"

"No, I'll come out and grab them. Thank you."

I finished off my cappuccino quickly and walked towards the door, stopped, and took a deep breath. Life goes on…

Fifteen

Chapter 15

❧

Later that day...

"Sidney. Did I get any calls while I was out on lunch? I'm waiting on the Mayor's office to give me a call back.

"No, no one from the Mayor's office called, but that cute guy that's on the news came by."

"Oh did he?" I asked.

"Yeah, I told him you were out."

"You didn't tell him where I was did you?"

"Of course not. Your secrets are safe with me."

"Good, let's keep them that way." I said. Sidney is my buddy from undergrad. She knows all of my business. That's not good. She could torpedo my career with a phone call and a video camera. She feels indebted to me. She went through a rough divorce and lost damn near everything. I gave her a job and paid her well. She does really well with running my office, and she keeps my covers. I don't know how many aliases she's had to remember for my sake- Johnny, Bobby, Nicholas, oh and that time I told a guy I go by R Kelly, Richard Kelly that is. Boy boy, I was a mess and a half when I first started gaining notoriety in Atlanta. By the time I became more well-known, I couldn't get away with that alias stuff like I used to. I'd like to think that I've calmed down a lot. I'm really interested in having someone to settle down with now that I'm nearing my mid-thirties. I'd love that to be Brandon. It doesn't look like that will ever happen so right now, he gets my games and not my seriousness, although deep in my heart, I want to be serious with him and not have to play games. I do have the capacity to love.

Brandon had a funny habit of popping up. For someone that is tied down to someone else, he sure is clingy to his side piece. I had a little rendezvous while at lunch. I guess Brandon thought I was still at the office. I wondered why he did not try to reach out to me. I guess he's not so clingy after all, but I was going to have to talk to him about this popping up unannounced shit. I'm a scorpion and that rattles my stinger.

I'm surprised he popped up actually. The last time we saw each other, it didn't go well. I got mad with him. Maybe it was my fault. Maybe I was being an asshole. He came to my house. We were going to watch a movie and just enjoy each other's company. It turned left. I must admit, I was in my feelings a bit. It was my fault. I'll call him this evening, maybe even pay him a visit.

As I walked up to my office, my phone began to ring. It was

my boy, Chauncey. Chauncey and I went to Georgia State together. We go way back.

"What's up, sir. You've been AWOL. How are you?" He asked.

"I've been good. You know me. It's been busy as ever work, work, and more work, and then I have ministry work too," I said.

"Hmm huh, I'm sure you've been putting in a lot of work, ahem," he clears his throat.

"What's all that shit for?" I asked.

"Nothing, you know you better than I do," he said.

"I guess. I'm for real, sir. I've been tied up with work."

"Hmm, tied up with work and probably tied up with Mr. Anchorman too I bet."

"Hush your mouth. You know you are not supposed to speak on that unless spoken to," I said.

"I'm just saying. My man, I believe you are getting caught up. You and him spend a whole lot of time together. If I didn't know any better, I would believe you and him were together for real!"

"We are together for real. I can't help his man is always on the road. I'm just the clean up woman." I laughed.

"You so silly." He replied.

"Well," I replied.

"I honestly cannot believe you are somebody's clean up woman. I just never pegged you for a homewrecker"

"Okay, I'm gonna blame that little comment on all that weed your ass smoke. Don't come for me. And I'm not a home wrecker. I don't intend to wreck his relationship," I said.

"What happened to 'This was supposed to be a one-time thing.' You and that boy have been fucking since November of last year. It's a whole new year, bruh. Shit, Valentine's Day is coming up. You know we don't be boo'd up around Valentine's day. Recipe for disaster waiting to happen," he said.

"Just make me feel bad why don't you?" I said.

"Listen I'm not one to do that, but for real, I want you to be careful. If you keep this up, you are going to get hurt, Orlando. You know you've been hurt once already by him."

"I know, but Brandon isn't really like that. If I were to get hurt, it wouldn't be because he did anything. It'll be because it ended. It would be because of me starting this foolishness in the first place. There isn't a moment I don't look at myself in the mirror and feel like shit because of this."

"Orlando? Are you in love with him?"

I got quiet for a moment. I knew the truth, but I had been avoiding saying it for some time now.

I sighed a long sigh, "Yeah…I am. I don't know how I let this happen, bro. This was not supposed to happen like this."

"Does he know?"

"Well if he didn't, I think he got an idea after the last time we were together."

"What happened?"

"Man, me being stupid. He was at my house, we were cuddling on the sofa watching a movie and then that boy of his called him. He went to smiling and shit and threw my arms from around him and went into the other room to talk to him."

"What?"

"I know, I know. I should not have cared but I think seeing that just kinda pushed me over the edge. My jealousy raged and I tried to hold it in but I couldn't. As soon as he got off, I just started to treat him cold. He came back to the sofa like nothing had happened, and I sat there hurt. Like, I was really hurting. I think it was in that moment that I realized, shit, I'm the other man and he's going home to thoughts of the man he probably intends to marry one day. He leaves me here to feel the loneliness that he comes to me to escape. It all reminded me of when he broke it off with me to be with Tyler the first time. Chauncey, how did I get myself into this?" I asked.

"I don't know, but what I do know is that you don't deserve this. Here you are again, giving yourself away to some man and you end up being the casualty in the end. The same thing happened with you and that dog you used to be with, Rodgerick. It's how you ended up positive. I know you love Brandon and he sounds like a really sweet guy, but you don't deserve this though. It's in your hands to choose better, Orlando." The line went silent for a moment as I sat without a response to what he was saying.

He continued, "We've all played the fool in love before. You just need to take some time to yourself, you know. Figure out what you want. Maybe we should take a trip to Miami. Go get some guys. You know how we used to do. I could use a good threesome," he laughed.

"I don't want to go anywhere, and my threesome days went away long time ago. I want him," I said.

"But honey, he is good and taken. The sex might be good but that's really all you are getting out of him. His heart belongs to someone else," he said.

I can't bear the thought of that. I hurried to get off the phone with Chauncey. I told him I had a client session starting soon. I didn't. The only session that was needed was one with myself. I shut myself in my office, told Sidney to hold all of my calls, shut the blinds and drowned myself in my thoughts and feelings.

* * *

The pressure of loving a man that you can't have was beginning to take its toll on me, so after my last client for the day, I decided I would go out and do some retail therapy. I found myself at Zales. I picked out a 10k gold Movado watch.

"Please gift wrap this for me."

"Sure thing, sir. That'll be $2,456.99. Will you be putting this on your account?"

"No, here." I handed him my AMEX and turned away to stare out the window. I had invited Brandon to dinner tonight. I wanted to talk to him and also apologize for my behavior. I had so much on my mind to get rid of. Chauncey was right. What was supposed to be me making a power move had turned into me being a schoolboy in love.

Somehow, I felt like this evening was special, so I got a pedicure and a manicure and a facial. I told him we were going to a fine dining restaurant, so he needed to wear a blazer. He seemed excited about it despite what happened. I wanted the evening to go well. It would really be the first time I'd actually taken him out on what I considered to be a real date to my standards. What we had been doing over the last few months had been all play, now I wanted to move in a little more seriously. That's what I had gotten out of my meditation. I had to consider the nature of his relationship with Tyler. They had a lot of problems and as a therapist, I could see the inevitable about to happen. They would split before they both realized it was happening. It had been happening already. I loved Brandon, and I wanted to have the chance to love him the way he deserved to be loved. That night, I intended to make my move in a totally new way now. I know I'm taking a hell of a risk. He could say no and break my heart, again.

In the back of my heart, there was a phantom plaguing me about HIV and the fact that I had still not told Brandon the truth. Any chances of a future with him would be wiped away once he found out. A part of me was hoping that he'd be opened-minded about it. It's very reminiscent of how I continued to entertain my ex who infected me even though until this day, we have never had a conversation about him giving me HIV. The heart is funny how it makes a person make the wrong decisions either because their traumas cloud their judgment or our unmet needs make us feel like we have to pacify some type of emptiness. Then we will pacify that emptiness with anything as long as it feels good. For me and Brandon, it's each other. He's doing the same thing I am. Deceit to pacify a feeling. How did we become these type of people? People that lie and cheat...Who are we really?

Sixteen

Chapter 16

※

A black Tahoe arrived to take me to Brandon's building. I sat in the backseat nervous as ever. The driver opened my door and I stepped out. A couple coming out of the building stopped and stared. I wore a black suit with a crisp ivory shirt, no tie. I approached his building with a single long-stem rose in my hand. I waited in his foyer as he made his way down. I heard the elevator ding and there he was, as beautiful as ever. He was magnificent. He had on a cream suit with a similar white shirt, no tie. He quickly smiled at me and it seemed like the smile brightened the dimly lit vestibule. We meet up close and I embraced him softly. He was a little hesitant as he nodded over to the security booth.

"The guard shouldn't see this," he said as he quickly urged me closer to the exit.

"Oh I forgot," I said. I actually did. I was caught up in the moment but I did forget I was picking him up in his territory where he and Tyler live together. I probably should have left the rose in the car. We walked out to the SUV and the driver let us in and closed the door. I then handed him the rose. "You look amazing."

"Merci beaucoup monsieur. Tu n'as pas l'air trop mal toi-même," he replied.

"Listen at you. I didn't know you know French."

Brandon's smile became full as he winked at me and then looked back out the window, staring at his apartment building as we drove off.

"You are so full of surprises. That's what I love about you."

"Oh you love things about me?" He asked.

I grinned and chuckled, blushed actually.

"Perhaps, I'll talk about that some later. In the meantime, let's head on to dinner. This rose reminded me of you. It pales in comparison to your beauty."

"Oh stop it will you. You Scorpios are so slick."

"I'm just me and you tend to bring the best out of anybody."

"Umm hmm. So what is all this pomp and circumstance about? The last I saw you, you were being rather bitchy."

"I know. You'll see," I said.

Brandon and I were both looking out of our own windows as silence fell over the car ride. The space between our seats seemed to house an elephant.

We cruised back through Midtown toward downtown to dine at the Sundial. I reserved a room at the Westin and a table at the restaurant. I intended to wine and dine that night. As we approached the building, the driver let us out and he and I both stepped out looking exquisite. I was caught up in the moment and onlookers stared our way, partly because they recognized him from TV and they just know me from being a bit of a celebrity. I didn't feel the need to be incognito. If Brandon was my man for real, this is the type of life he could expect.

I looked over at Brandon who actually seemed to be eating the moment up. He was poised. He was confident. He fits this well. His gorgeous smile outshined the streetlights as he walked through the small crowd. I don't know why it was so busy tonight. We made our way into the lobby and took our elevator ride to the 73rd floor where the iconic Sundial restaurant sat atop the Westin Tower. The maître d welcomed us and seated us at our table. The view was stunning. We were 723 feet in the air and we could see over all of downtown, Midtown, and Buckhead off in the distance.

"Here are our list of wines and cocktails. Is there anything I can start you off with tonight?" The waiter asked.

"Yes, thank you. Please bring a bottle of Marchesi di Barolo," I said.

"Excellent choice. Coming right up."

"You are trying to get me tipsy tonight I see," Brandon chimed.

"No, I'm not," I laughed. "It's a good wine, fitting for the quality of the meal we are about to have. I promise you it'll be the best red you've ever tried."

"I know the best red I've ever tried," He said. He stared intently into my eyes. It didn't take me long to figure out what he meant. I almost peed my pants. That was the slickest and sweetest, sexiest line ever. I'm not accustomed to him actually talking in that way. It sounds more like something I should say.

"Look at you, flirting. When did you learn those type of

lines?" I asked, trying to pretend like I was not turning flips in my heart over it.

"I'm glad to see you tonight. I'm hoping we have a wonderful meal and then afterwards, spend some intimate time together. No phones, no computers, no nothing. Just you and me," I said and pulled out a room key to one of the Westin suites a few floors beneath us.

"I knew my bells were going off. You're up to something. I could feel it. What's going on?" He asked.

"Don't ruin the evening with your suspicions. In due time, we will...talk...about some things. Hopefully our discussion goes well and we can end the night on a nice note," I said.

"You know you can't do that to me?"

"Do what?" I asked.

"That what you're doing. Dropping me these little hints like I have something that I should be anticipating. I hate that. Now, I'll spend all this time trying to outsmart you and figure you out," he said. He was rubbing his hands one over the other. I could see his brow bent slightly as fold lines appeared on his forehead.

"Well just be cool and don't worry about it, and you won't be under any type of stress, OK?" I said.

"I guess. Where's that damn waiter with that bottle? I swear you keep me on edge," he stated.

"That's a good thing."

"Yeah that's why I'm here with you now, when I'm not supposed to be."

"I thought you were pass that," I said.

"I talk to him every day. You never get pass cheating on your boyfriend when he has no clue it's happening," he said.

"I suppose you are right," I said.

I'm fighting the urge to want to probe him to see where his head and heart is but I won't do that. It'll mess up my plans. I need to follow through with the purpose of tonight and then let that conversation and feelings come out naturally from him.

By this time, the waiter was back and opened our bottle. We placed our order. I ordered the rack of lamb and he got the halibut. As we waited for our food to come out, I decided to start the conversation.

"So, Brandon, I wanted to have a bit of a serious conversation with you tonight. Let me start by first apologizing to you for my behavior the other day. I was upset and in my feelings."

"But why?"

"Do you remember the day we met for the first time?"

"Yes I do. I remember you being the debonair and polite speaking guy that you still are today. You were absolutely handsome. I had never really seen anyone so umm…pretty, not a man I mean. Honestly, I was immediately attracted to you and shortly after, I realized that not only were you physically attractive, but you were attractive in a whole other dimension. It's like your energy and your aura was so strong. I didn't really stand a chance."

"Well, I get that lot. I don't know what it is. Some say it's the Scorpio trait that makes me that way. I am not that way on purpose. I just have a natural seduction about me. The first day I saw you Brandon, I knew that you were the one I wanted. There is no mistake in my mind about it. When I saw you, I saw myself. I saw the missing part of myself. It was like the world around us faded away and all I cared about in that moment was getting to know you, even though you were the one asking all of the questions," I laughed.

"Yeah I was, but it was really easy to talk to you. You made it easy to talk to you. You always have actually," Brandon said.

"I'm not one to talk to people easily. If I vibe with a person really well, then I am able to open up to them and talk to them and share parts of myself with them. I'm usually quicker to do that with people I like. When I first met you, you made an imprint on my heart that day that I have never really been able to move past. I mean…I've always had a soft spot for you. When we departed that day, I walked back to my car with what felt like a flame burning in my soul for you. It hasn't gone out since that day. I'm reminded of when David saw Jonathan for the first time in the Bible and how the scripture says that when they saw each other, their souls were knitted together. That's how I felt about you. Engaging you, word for word, felt like little stitches of thread tying my spirit to yours."

"That's a sweet analogy Orlando. What does this mean about how you acted the other day?" Brandon asked.

"Isn't it obvious? Brandon, I started out being really into you. When you chose Tyler over me, that broke my heart into pieces. I never told you that, but it did. When you came back, I must be honest, I wanted to sleep with you to pay you back for what you two did me. Well, how you did me. This was supposed to be just sex between you and me. I caught feelings. I have stronger feelings for you now, and I just don't know how to handle seeing you actually be excited and happy to talk to Tyler. I guess I had gotten used to you moping and complaining about how he was not fulfilling your needs. I was in my feelings and I'm sorry about that. I'm not sorry about how I feel about you. When I think of you, I think of the man I want to be with forever. I think of the guy I want to be on my arms when I walk into events. I think of the picture-perfect life," I said.

"Wow. I mean…just…wow. I was not expecting that. I mean I could tell that you were getting a bit clingy but damn, I didn't know it was this much."

"I know, and I'm sorry."

"It's okay. So, what are you looking for out of this now?"

"What do you mean when you say that?" I asked.

"I'm talking about us, your feelings, and what we are doing," he said.

"I don't know. I still have not been completely honest with you about everything," I said.

"Oh, really. So what else do you want to share with me?"

I took a deep sigh. This is where the night might actually end on a sour note.

"Okay, well first before I tell you, here is the room key in case you storm off. I understand completely if you get totally pissed with me. I would want you to gather yourself and then let's have a discussion about it," I said.

"Okay, you are freaking me out now. What could you possibly tell me that would make me that upset? Did you have sex with Tyler before?" He asked.

"What? No! Hell no! Eww. Only you want that man," I said.

"Don't come for my boyfriend. I'm serious; what is it?" He asked. His eyes were sincere and the hazel shimmer they have were mesmerizing even more. I looked away, and then continued.

"Okay, I'm sorry. No it's not that, but it's pretty bad though, maybe worse. Listen, I'm telling you this now because I do love you. I should've told you from the start, but I was being selfish and in my feelings and to be honest, I just was not thinking about it."

"Okay, well what is it then?"

"I'm…ummm…" I sighed again. "I'm…"

"Okay you're what…?"

I signed once more.

"Brandon…"

I began to tear up. I've been positive for 9 years and I've never felt this hurt to have to share my status with someone. It's a shameful feeling when you have to tell someone you care about. I always share my status before engaging in sex. I was afraid of losing Brandon.

"Oh my God, Orlando, what is it? You are scaring me now. What's wrong?" He said frantically.

Through my tears, I just said the three words. "I am HIV+."

Brandon sat silently. He was holding my hand and I felt his grip loosen a little bit.

"You're what? Wait wait wait wait wait wait wait…You're HIV+! And when were you going to tell me this? How long have you known?"

"I've known for nearly ten years. I found out in 2011. Please let me explain," I pleaded.

"The only reason I don't cuss your ass out right now is because we are in this restaurant and people know me in here. You're lucky I don't slap the shit out of you right now," he said under his breath through his teeth. By this time, he had let my hand go and he was gathering himself as if he was about to leave me there. He did not take the room key though, but I could tell he was trying to keep his composure as to not cause a scene.

Luckily for me, that gave me the opportunity to explain

something that had no explanation to begin with. I'd decided to just tell the truth and hopefully that would be enough. I was done playing games and lying, and when you finally meet someone that you care about and you discover is worth getting your truth, then the truth is what you always should give them. I actually wasn't planning on telling him about HIV, but after realizing how in love I was with him, hiding that from him was no longer acceptable.

Seventeen

Chapter 17

Brandon

Orlando's eyes were dark and full like a startled cat. We sat in silence as the chatter of the other patrons overpowered our tension. There I was, sitting across the table from Orlando. I really just wanted to punch him in the face. I should have walked out and left him here once he told me, but a part of me wouldn't let me. It's like I cared to hear what he had to say. Or maybe, a part of me didn't want to believe that he would intentionally hurt me.

"I have never lied to anyone before about my status. I've never withheld that from anyone that I remotely gave a damn about. I don't know. The first time we had sex, I was drunk and I honestly was not thinking about it. That does not make it right because I could have shared it with you the next day. I thought about it, but I just couldn't. I was afraid you were going to drop me and stop talking to me. It was selfish and cowardly, but you must believe me when I say I had no intentions of hiding this from you on purpose. There were so many times I wanted to share it with you, but I felt so ashamed of myself for being so stupid to allow HIV to happen to me in the first place. It's a tough battle that I have to live with daily." He said.

"Okay. I hear you. You're not going to play victim with me right now, though. And yes I'm so sorry that you are HIV positive, really I am. But your behavior with me in that regard has been beyond egregious. How can I trust you after this? I mean, did you not think about my health? or Tyler's health? You are not the only victim here sir." I folded my arms and looked intently at him. He dropped his head.

"I know. Well, I'm undetectable. I take my meds daily, I get checked on every three months. I'm good. My health is stellar. My CD4 count is 1100. All of my vitals are good." He stretched his arm across the table towards me. "Listen, Brandon, I know I did not tell you but I always had you in mind," he said.

"Getting physical with me was a line that you should not have crossed knowing you have HIV regardless of whether or not you are undetectable," I said.

"I know you are upset and you have every right to be. I don't want to give out any excuses nor do I want to play the victim. I accept full responsibility for my actions. If it means you walk out of my life for good, then I'm prepared to deal with that consequence," Orlando said.

I just didn't know what to do or think at that moment.

When Orlando was bearing his heart out to me, I found myself smiling inside because I could remember all of that stuff he was saying about how we met and the chemistry that was there. I never forgot it, and when things between Tyler and me had become stale, I would remember back on the last time someone actually made me feel electrified inside. I had to weigh whether Orlando meant to deceive me on purpose or was he just dealing with his own psychological trauma that prevented him from telling me the truth. I know many would think that's absurd, but the heart wants what it wants.

"I have to go get tested now. I could be sitting here HIV positive right now because of your negligence. My boyfriend could likewise be HIV positive right now because of your negligence. Well, I should not have been fucking you in the first place so that would be all my fault." I sighed. That last line made me realize that while I'm berating Orlando for being deceptive, I'm no better than he is. Perhaps it took this to make me see myself. Now I must decide what I want to do.

"I'm sorry, Brandon. That's all I can say right now," Orlando said. He could barely look me in the face. His tears were there and his eyes were red, and so was his skin. He was obviously worked up.

"I'm not going to berate you, and I hear your apology. If anything, this has caused me to see how careless and reckless I have been with my own relationship. Yes, I still do love Tyler very much. What we have been doing is the result of me not having Tyler around. There is no excuse for it, but I'm not going to pretend like what I'm facing now is all of your fault. Yes, your ass should have told me the truth about this from day one. It's a fucking felony for a reason. Two wrongs don't make a right," I said.

"So, what does all of that mean exactly?" Orlando asked.

"It means that I see myself and my shit and it stinks. I need to rectify this. It also means that I can no longer have sex with you. First because you lied to me and betrayed my trust, and two because I am with Tyler and I should not be having sex with anyone but him," I said. I wouldn't look him in the eyes as I said my words. Instead, I looked past him and focused on the waiter walking with a platter of wine glasses on a tray.

"That means we are over?" He asked.

"Yes, it does. I cannot live this lie. Look at the circumstance it has brought to me. I cannot have that type of blood on my hands if Tyler or even I turn up positive."

"I understand," he said.

Orlando had a disappointed look in his eye. I wanted to have compassion for him but I was still ticked off. He lied to me. He was deceptive. There is no excuse for it.

"I'm sorry, Orlando." I was preparing myself to get up from the table to leave.

"Wait, before you leave. I want to give you this. I bought it yesterday for you. I honestly did not know I would share this information with you tonight, but I also realized that I'm in love with you. I could not continue to hide the secret from you knowing that. But anyway, here. This is a gift from me to you. If we never speak or see each other again, at least you'll have something to remember me by," he said.

I looked at the gift. It was wrapped in metallic blue paper with a silver bow. I grabbed the box and put it in my pocket of my coat. I gathered my things and I got up from the table. "Bye Orlando." I walked away from the table towards the door. As I stood and waited for the elevator, I looked back across the room to see Orlando with his face buried in the palm of his hands as if he was sobbing. I hate I saw that. The elevator dinged and rode away from the restaurant. Luckily, I was the only one in the elevator at the time. The image of him crying at the table weighed on my heart. I felt a rush of water come to the forefront of my eyes in the form of tears. I cried. My heart hurt. I don't know why. I know a lot about HIV because of the stories I've been working on about it for my show. I honestly was not at all concerned that I could be positive, as long as he is undetectable like he says he is.

What I realized as I rode 72 stories down to ground-level is that I have deep feelings for Orlando and I was crying about losing him. He made me feel alive. He gave me something that I was not able to get from Tyler. He gave me openness, passion and fire. My relationship with him was not just one that was moving alone day by day in a boring routine. He was giving me the excitement that I never really got with Tyler. I had come to realize that Tyler had given me camaraderie and safety. He gave me friendship and solidarity. Orlando gave me those things too, but he also gave me electrifying chemistry. I had much to think about. For the first time ever, truth seeking had led me to consider if Tyler and I were no longer what we needed out of each other. Why does he stay gone so much? What is he running from? Does he even want this relationship? Does he want to still be incognito? I have so many questions with no answers in sight. The only answer I did have was that Orlando put a move on my heart and I couldn't seem to shake it even knowing what I know now.

* * *

The last time Orlando and I had sex was 2 weeks ago. I sat in the clinic to get my rapid HIV test done. It may show negative, but I'll have to continue to be tested over the next 2 months or so to ensure that I'm actually not positive. Orlando and I did use condoms except the first time, and that combined with him being undetectable effectively means no real chance that I could contract the virus from him. The science has come a long way with the treatment and prevention of the spread of HIV. I didn't think that I would be sitting here having this test done after all of the research that I had been immersing myself in over the last few weeks with it. I thought to do this test with cameras and make it a part of the documentary for the show, but I didn't want to do that. A part of me felt like what if it does come back positive. That's not something I'd want on TV, although I wouldn't actually have to show that part though.

"Mr. Chambers? Yes the nurse is ready to see you?"

"Thank you," I said. I got up and walked with her to the back and met with the nurse. First she wanted to take my vitals and take my weight. I had gained 10lbs since I first started up with Orlando. All of the eating out we do had added on the weight. We walked to an exam room where she commenced her spill about the process. "So we will do a rapid test. I'll just swab your cheek with a cotton swab and run the test. We should have you out of here in no time with your results. Have you ever been tested before?" She asked.

"I have, a couple of months ago," I said.

"We recommend you to be tested every six months and if you are sexually active in risky behavior, then you should be tested every 3 months. Are there any other STDs you'd like to be screened for?" she asked.

"Umm, well, I guess so. Might as well get the whole shebang."

"I must let you know that some of the results are not rapid and will take a week or two to return from the lab. We will call you with the results, but you'll get your HIV results today."

"Okay great," I said. By now, I was a little nervous. What if it comes back with something bad, and if it did, how would I have that conversation with Tyler?

She began to swab my cheek and then placed the specimen in a tube.

"Now we must wait 20 minutes, okay? In the meantime, I will take some blood for your other tests."

In that moment, I felt like I needed Tyler. It is in those moments where I would have needed him the most. I couldn't call him while sitting in a clinic getting an HIV test done because the guy I was cheating on him with lied to me. On top of that, the guy is Orlando. I just couldn't bear myself to be that unscrupulous. I am one to talk about scruples now. Where were they when I was fucking Orlando? I closed out of my text thread with Tyler. There is no use in contacting him. As I sat and waited, I begin strolling through my messages with Orlando. I found myself crack a little smile because there was so much flirting happening between me and him. Our chemistry is something else. I begin to wonder if I could actually stay mad at him. I have not heard from him since the night at the restaurant. It's not like him. I'm hoping he is okay.

Sitting in that sterile room had my mind going and my heart racing. I paced back and forth in front of the examination table. Then I read a poster about kidney disease and HIV and another about HIV medications and a new drug they were releasing. I noticed how much advertising for medication was posted everywhere. Whether I end up positive or not, I hope that a cure is on the horizon.

"Okay Brandon, I have your results."

I felt a jolt go through me. I don't want to turn up positive. I should have been more careful.

"Sir, your results came back negative."

I felt a sigh of relief. No matter how calm I was trying to be, you never feel easy about an HIV test especially when there is a chance that you could be infected. I'm considering my situation now. I should not be here. The bigger picture is that I am here because I fucked Orlando, but I fucked Orlando because I wanted to. But why did I want to? I can't say I don't know because, actually, I think I do know. Even from the start, when I first met Orlando, he and I had such a strong chemistry. It was different. Not like how Tyler and I were. I can't keep pretending like I am no longer getting the things that I need out of Tyler. I can't keep complaining about it either. I believe I complained about it instead of talking it out with him because deep down, I was getting to a resolution of realizing we were done. Maybe the relationship had run its course.

Eighteen

Chapter 18

❧❧❧

"I think we should redo that shot, Brandon."

"I thought it was pretty good, what's wrong with it?" I looked at Jamie with some confusion and my hand on my hip.

"Ehh, the lighting was off, the sun was behind you and it just made the shit look amateur. I'm canning it." Jamie said.

"You're what?" I said with a smile and jabbed him on his shoulder. "You do know that I am in charge here."

"Yessir Mr. Executive Producer. I know you are in charge, and I'm just your lead camera man, I mean what the fuck do I know, huh?" Jamie said sarcastically.

"Ugh I hate your smart-ass mouth."

"No you don't." he said with a smile. "You love it and you know it. If you could live off banter you would. At least your ass will get smaller. Child your appetite done picked up lately. Shit we scared to eat around you," he laughed.

"I know I've picked up a few pounds, but I'm gonna take care of that." I said.

"You better. Tyler ain't trying come home to an extra person boo. You need to stop fucking that man you are fucking. I know sex weight when I see it."

"Boy, you are still wet behind the ears. You don't know what you're talking about," I said.

"Yes huh. I do know. You've been having sex on the regular and I know Tyler hadn't been here lately for it to be him. You still fucking that guy? What's his name anyway?"

I've been holding so much in and I really do need to just let it out to someone. I guess I'll give him a little bit more of my business. I sighed, "His name is Orlando."

"Ummm Orlando. He sounds like he can fuck."

"Please stop," I said.

"What? I'm just saying. Okay so...where you meet him. Grindr? Jack'd? Give me some backstory. You haven't really told me much about him and it's been two months now since I first found out."

"What? No! I would never take a man off those apps."

"Look bougie bitch, don't get beside yourself now. Some of us depend on those apps to get our regular dick appointments in. Don't be judging."

"I'm not judging, I'm just saying they aren't for me. And you know something, you have become the regular queen now. Since when you talk like this?"

"Honey, I was just keeping it professional with you, but now that you know what I am, It's free game baby. You gonna see and hear all of me. Now I'm trying to catch these Ts cause I know you have plenty of them. So spill it. We got time."

"Well, we sorta aren't talking anymore."

"Damn child, now how the hell you run the side piece off," Jamie laughed. "I have never in my life heard of someone running their damn side piece off.

"He ran himself off with his lies."

"Well you know these men lie. What's new?"

"About being positive, yeah that shit is what's new."

"Whuuuuuut? For real?"

"Yes, he is positive and did not tell me."

"I know you fucked his ass up, right?"

"I don't have time to be doing all of that."

"Oh I forgot you Miss America. I would've given him the business."

"I told him how I felt and I haven't spoken to him since."

"Well how long ago has that been? You know when that heat turn on you will have to let up a window?"

"Say what?"

"I'm saying, your man at these rallies and stuff, you will turn up horny sooner than later, and you gone call that man to come bang you out."

"First of all, he wasn't banging me out. Secondly, I can handle myself if I get to that point. I dunno. I do think about him a lot, though."

"Wait, do you have feelings for him?"

"I don't know. He has them for me for sure."

"It's been five days, and this is the longest I've gone without talking to him since we started back up a couple of months ago."

"Started back up? So you have fucked him before?"

"Not exactly. So long story, I met him when I was still in school -when Tyler and I were down here filming the documentary. He is the owner of the string of Rainbow

Houses for Homeless LGBT Youth here."t

"You mean that fine ass light-skinned dude you interviewed in *The Bow* documentary? Bittttttch!"

"Chile. Anyway. So we hit it off instantly. We called ourselves deciding to date. Tyler was not out the closet yet. I didn't even know for sure he was gay at the time. Well Tyler eventually came out, told me how he felt about me. I felt the same and I chose Tyler over Orlando. Orlando was crushed and well, we lost contact for about 5 years. I saw him a few months ago and we have been talking to each other since then. It didn't start out as anything when we reconnected but one night, I was feeling some type of way after Tyler cancelled another night he was supposed to be home. So Orlando and I met up for dinner, afterwards, he was drunk, I was tipsy, and we ended up having sex. It was the best I've ever had. I've been hooked since. And then, the other night, he took me to the Sundial, and he told me he was HIV+. I didn't hang around long enough to ask many questions. I don't really know how long he has had it or where he got it from. I think he may have mentioned it but I was so shocked and pissed, I really kinda zoned out. He did say he was undetectable. I just know that we have been physical numerous times and he didn't find it necessary to tell me."

"Can I play devil's advocate?"

"I guess," I said.

"Do you think he didn't tell you on purpose? Maybe he didn't know how to tell you. Or maybe he felt ashamed. I'm not making excuses for him, but I dunno. I sit here and listen to some of our subjects being interviewed, and I can see why a person would really struggle to reveal that about themselves, especially if they are undetectable. In their mind, it's no harm no foul."

"That's bullshit, Jamie. You don't take away a person's right to choose whether they want to take that risk with you."

"That's true, but considering we are not in 1995 anymore, the CDC has confirmed that a person who is undetectable cannot and will not infect someone they are having sex with. So where's the risk? I'm just saying, at what point do we begin to decry the stigma about HIV? It's not what it used to be. Treatment makes it virtually impossible now to spread the virus so if a person is on their meds and is undetectable and they know they are and are committed to that, then should they really have to disclose their status now?"

"Listen, I get the point you are trying to make, but in my mind, I just don't see it that way. And maybe, just maybe, the idea is too new, too fresh. I don't think this notion of undetectable equals untransmittable has been out long enough for us to start really using it to change attitudes?"

"But isn't that the point though?"

"What?"

"I mean…isn't it the point now that HIV is a chronic illness, it's not what it used to be. It's no longer a death sentence for those who are positive. Wouldn't it be the point to stop treating it like we always have treated it? So okay, what if there was a cure out. What if people were being cured of HIV. Would you think it be proper or mandatory even, that a person still have to tell you that they were or are HIV+ if they have been functionally cured? Do you think if you are having random sex with someone, or even a fuck buddy, that they should automatically tell you their status. Isn't the point of telling you their status, like you said, to give you the choice about risk?

"Yes…"

"OK then, if there is no longer a risk, why be so pressed because you did not know at first?"

"It's the dishonesty."

"Okay so you feel he lied to you. Did he or did he just struggle to tell you a simple truth about himself at first. I mean…he did tell you on his own eventually. I don't know. I think I just see this differently. I think if he was infectious and having sex with you without you knowing his status would be very problematic. But undetectable equals untranmittable. There was no risk. In fact, I'm sure if you have or have not taken an HIV test yet, your results will unequivocally be negative given the circumstances. Listen, friend, I'm not suggesting your reaction to this is invalid, but I'm inviting you into an opportunity to see it a different way so that you are not so hurt about it."

"I can consider that. I mean…I dunno. I came up in a time where HIV awareness was drilled into our heads like avoiding the plague and now they want us to just pretend like it's no longer a threat. I struggle with that. Yes, my educated ass struggles with that. I know its fear and maybe a little of my own ignorance, but I must admit, I'm not there yet.

"Maybe this is an opportunity for you to get there. I mean as much as you are learning and about to share about HIV through this project, I think this has to be a part of the conversation. Destigmatizing the disease. It's not what it used to be now. As a matter of fact, a person might die of high blood pressure before they die of HIV/AIDS in this day now. People sitting here mad at a man for being undetectable and not saying anything but didn't say shit when that same man took them to the Juicy Crab for dinner, all that damn fried food. I'm just saying that maybe we should challenge our own prejudices and fears sometimes to better deal with the people in our lives."

"You know something, I underestimated you. You are quite wise. I'm glad to have you in my life, Jamie."

"Aww, give me a hug."

"What you think I should do now?"

"What you mean, about Orlando? Chile, leave that man where he at!"

"Wait a minute. Wasn't you just saying to see things from his experience?" I asked.

"Yes, about HIV, but honey you have a whole man. I don't care if he was HIV positive, negative, plutonium, you still need to leave him alone. But, it's obvious that you have a strong affinity for him though. I think you owe it to yourself to consider if maybe he's your one. He just may be. But you need to go about it the right way. Stop with this cheating and sleeping around shit. It's just trashy. And you don't want that juju coming back on you.

"Jamie, what the hell do you know about juju. You're a white boy."

"Umm I'm sure I didn't miss that when I looked in the mirror this morning. Here we go with that white people don't know black shit again, ahem, black lives matter, I mean."

"Don't even play about that," I said.

"I'm sorry…"

Nineteen

Chapter 19

" Jamie, I hear you. We better get going and head over to Donald's place.

Donald was participating in the documentary. Donald was a nice guy who had a house near Alpharetta. He was the Director of Asset Management for an investment firm. He was willing to have us do the interview with him and have us show us his life living with HIV. He also had a 4-year old daughter. I had so many questions for him.

"I'm excited for this one, Jamie. I think he is going to be one of the anchor faces of our theme. He exemplifies someone managing a normal life as a gay man with HIV."

"Yeah, I think it'll be a great anchor for the story," Jamie said.

When we arrived, Donald invited us in. He had a very nice house which seemed to have three floors. It was nicely decorated. He had two dogs and a cat but somehow the home didn't seem to be lived in, which is one of the hallmarks of gay men, fabulous homes. He led us to his office which was massive with wall-to-wall bookshelves and a large oak desk facing a bay window that overlooked a rose garden.

"You guys can set up right here," he said.

"Donald, thank you for letting us into your life. This is a brave thing," I said.

"I don't mean to sound curt, but no, this is not a brave thing for me. Living with HIV is my life, my daily experience. It's not brave, it's just me living. I want you to consider me no differently than you consider anyone else you are interviewing for any other story," Donald said.

"I see," I said. "I hope I didn't offend you. I didn't mean to sound patronizing," I replied.

"You didn't. Most people carry the stigma of HIV etched into their brains and so they assume that I should be treated a special way because of it. I didn't mean to be so direct," he said.

"No, I certainly understand. Well, we are ready to get started. So, I'll start off with some questions and basically we will just flow into a natural conversation," I said.

"Sounds good to me," he said.

"Have you ever felt like you were different because of HIV?" I asked.

"All the time, which is why now I speak up when I feel like someone is placing me back into that "special" category, whether they are doing it consciously or unconsciously. I was 19 when I found I was HIV+, on my death bed. I nearly died. My t-cell count was 40, and I had double pneumonia. I had full blown AIDS. I was a fast tail. I was out having sex at 14 years old with 30-year old men," he said.

"Your story is different from others in the documentary so far. So far, most of my subjects speak about how HIV found them in what they thought was a monogamous relationship. Do you ever have any regret about becoming HIV positive?"

"You always have regret. No one turns up positive and thinks it's a good thing. You always have regret. I definitely had regrets. I regretted not knowing about it. Honestly, I didn't know much about it. Growing up down here in the south, they didn't' teach us about sex and they damn sure wasn't going to teach us about gay sex," Donald laughed. "I had no reason to think I needed to protect myself. Shit got real in that hospital bed. I had a lot of time to think. My life, the little that I had experienced, was flashing before me, and it was then I decided that if God allowed me to get up out of that bed and get well, I was going to show up for myself, and that's what I did. I enrolled into school and I got my Bachelors in Finance and then I got my MBA. Living with HIV, I had to struggle a lot. I came along during the era when AZT was going out and HAART was starting. I was onboarded with HAART medications. Oh my god, it was the devil."

"Tell me more about that," I asked.

"AZT was the very first drug used to treat HIV in the late 80s. Then around the mid-90s, HAART came, which people referred to as the AIDS cocktail. It was nothing to take several pills a day to maintain. The side effects were something else, too. The first night I took that shit, I dreamed I was jumping off of a bridge. My doctor didn't tell me that the side effects were so wild. The drugs did become better over time. I eventually got on Atripla and that shit would cause me to wake up vomiting and nauseous. It was interfering with my ability to work. I ended up on disability which didn't pay much. I had it hard. That's why now, I look around and I feel how blessed I am to have made it through that," Donald said.

"You know something, Donald, our angle for having you in the documentary was to show how people can thrive with the disease, but I see you've had your share of down moments with HIV. What would you say has been your source of strength," I asked.

"I would be cliché and say God," he chuckled. "But, no, it was more than just God. It was God within me, giving me vision and a will to live. God has blessed me with so much now, and I'm grateful for it all. It was my drive that gave me the strength, even on days where I was too weak to get out of bed. Man you don't know how many odd-end jobs I have blown through."

"So once you were on the HIV cocktail drugs, did it ever get to a place where it became bearable for you to take it?"

"Yes, it did eventually. Also eventually, I was able to switch to Atripla once it came out which made keeping up with the regime much more effective. The wild dreams never stopped though. They were wild. Many times, I'd wake up out of my sleep screaming or attempting to run out of the room because of some gory dream I was having. Atripla interferes with the mind and that's how it causes those types of dreams. Thank God more and more classes of drugs have since come along and I was able to get on something that didn't affect me that way. It's been smooth for a while now. Life feels somewhat normal."

"Why do you say somewhat?" I asked.

"What I mean is you still never quite forget you have HIV. Sometimes you really do forget about it with the way these drugs today are, but none of the drugs are without side effects not to mention HIV makes me more susceptive to having vitamin D deficiency and low testosterone. Both of those deficiencies mess with my quality of life a little. HIV makes the body age faster than normal."

"How to do you manage the low T?" I asked.

"Exercise. It does wonders for that. What I've learned is the key to living well with HIV is paying close attention to your daily habits, eat well, and stay active. Hmm, I suspect I should at least live through my 60s."

"That's a great outlook. I studied that now with the advanced HIV treatments, many people can live a normal lifespan, well into their 70s and even 80s with HIV now, and that's just in 2020, Imagine how that will look 10 years from now," I said.

"That's true and I'm happy about those type of advancements. It gives me hope that we are on our way to a cure. However for me, because HIV damaged my immune system, it created challenges for me that I'll likely have to deal with as I transition into older age. This is why now the guidelines are to treat all people who are positive. It's found that the best pathway to a long healthy life is early treatment. The drugs now are safer and their side effects are minimal. People are truly living normal lives now. HIV is no longer a death sentence. It's considered a chronic condition, no different than diabetes. To be honest, I'd rather have HIV than be a diabetic. The maintenance for HIV is easier, just a pill a day and eat a lean, healthy diet with minimal sweets and cholesterol," he said.

After the interview, Donald showed us more of his home. We met his little girl, Alexa. She was a doll. We got to showcase just how normal his life is. Donald was not living a lonely shut away life. He had endured early struggles in life, just like many people do whether they are positive or not, and landed on his feet. He has built a great life for himself and his daughter. I asked him about how love goes for him and this is what happened:

"So how is dating for you?" I asked.

"Tuh, the same way it is for the rest of these guys out here. No one wants to be serious about a relationship and being HIV+ has nothing to do with that actually. Guys are just jerks. I casually date here and there, but mostly, I have my daughter to think about."

"When it comes to sharing your status, how do you feel that should go?"

"I come from an era where sharing your status was the ethical thing to do. I know nowadays undetectable equals untransmittable, but that's just not how I'm programmed. I grew up in the 80s and I contracted HIV in the 90s and there was still a very heavy stigma about being positive in the 90s. I think a part of me still believes that it can be passed along. No one understands that really until it's them that has contracted HIV and so you have a sort of anxiety or fear that you'll pass it on to someone else. And then, there is that thing about rejection."

"Have you ever been rejected by someone for being positive?" I asked.

"Absolutely many times. After a while you just get used to it and then you start to lead the conversation with, 'hey, I'm positive so let me know now if you can handle that before I waste my time.'"

"What's the worse response you've ever gotten?"

"Hmmm, it's been so many harsh ones, let me think. Oh

yeah, I know. Once, a guy frowned up at me so badly like he had smelled a skunk, and he got up and walked out of the restaurant that we were at. Now that would normally not bother me but it bothered me because we were really connecting. We had great conversation all evening, we were obviously vibing with one another. I never heard from him again. I think HIV+ people were probably the first group of people to ever experience what you young guys today call ghosting."

"What is your outlook on dating? Do you believe there is a soul mate out there for you?" I asked.

"Yes, I do. HIV is so common now that I've actually dated a few guys that are positive. But they were all not ready for a relationship so they didn't work out. But yeah, sure…I feel like when the right one comes along, he will be everything I desire for him to be."

"Do you think many guys who are not positive miss out on their prince or princess charming because of ignorance," I asked.

"Oh yeah, most definitely, I do think that. Actually, there are people you probably know, work with and talk to on a regular basis that are HIV+ and you have no idea that they are. This is because HIV is not a label like society has made it be all of these years," Donald said.

"Lastly, and we are going to close with this: What advice would you give to a guy who has just found out he is HIV+?"

"Live your life. That's my best advice. Another thing is to be willing to feel the disappointment, the hurt, the pain, all of it. You have to understand that contracting HIV feels like death and you will go through the grieving process, and you must allow yourself to grieve. You've lost a special part of your make-up. Something your parents gave you, clean blood. So yes, it'll feel like a separation from the very nature of your being, but it doesn't have to become that. There is life on the other side of the plus sign. Sometimes, the trauma is deep and it can carry on or years. I have a friend who is positive and 15 years after he found out, he started developing depression and outburst of anger. He started therapy and his therapy work lead him back to that lonely day in the doctors office. He had been carrying the hurt and the trauma for many years, telling himself that he was okay and he really wasn't. Listen, HIV positive people can teach college courses on the effects of unmanaged trauma because for the most part, none of us dealt with that shit the right way starting out. Like I said, there is life on the other side of the plus sign, and I hope you and everyone who reads and hears this knows it.

Twenty

Chapter 20

⚬⚬⚬

"Donald, I just want to say thank you. Listening to you talk about your experience has helped me more than you know. If you don't mind, I want to get your advice on something personal, and this is strictly off the record," I said.

"Sure Brandon, I'll be glad to talk with you. Is this private?" He asked as he glanced over at Jamie who was putting away his equipment.

"No, I've already talked with him about this, so he knows," I said.

"Okay, well let's go into the kitchen and sit around the bar area. We can have a couple of cocktails while we chat. Ask your friend here what is his favorite drink once he's back inside."

Jamie had walked out to the car to load it up. He was walking back inside to find us waiting in the kitchen.

"Jamie, what do you want Donald to mix you up to drink. We are going to hang out a little and chit-chat. You don't have anywhere to be do you?" I asked.

"No I don't. I don't mind it. I actually have a hankering for a lemon drop if he can make it."

"A lemon drop and a margarita for me," I said to Donald as Jamie and I walked into the kitchen.

"I didn't tell you guys one of my many jobs back in the day was bartending. I could fuck up a good night with my drinks. One lemon drop and one house special margarita coming right up," he said.

Donald was a tall older guy. When I say older I mean forty-five, compared to my twenty-eight years. That's older for sure and definitely older than Jamie. He looked well for his age. He had a nice milk chocolate complexion with shoulder length locs and a nice build. You could tell he worked out often. I was surprised he was single. He is a nice catch. I'd date him actually.

"So what you have on your mind to talk about?" He said to me with his big black shimmering eyes. They almost caught me off guard a little.

"I have a dilemma. You may want to sit down because this one may take a while..."

The three of us got settled around the island in Donald's kitchen. He was busy scrambling with mixing drinks. His kitchen was also nicely decorated. It had a very airy feel to it. The cabinets were antiqued, white finished with aluminum door handles. His counters were marble. You could tell he was very well off. His furnishings were neo-Italian. I thought to myself how this is something Orlando would do with his house. At any rate, Orlando, Donald - it was refreshing to see how hard work could pay off in this way and that POZ men can lead a happy life. Now I know material things don't make the man. I consider Donald is here single, but he has his daughter, so he's not exactly alone.

"Here you go guys, two lemon drops and one margarita," Donald said.

"What are you having," I asked.

"I'm going to have some Weller on the rocks. I'm a bourbon kinda guy. Y'all can have those mixed drinks. At my age, I've earned the ability to drink darks liquors right out the bottle," he said with a laugh. The he commenced to pour himself a serving.

"My dad loves bourbon. I've had it a couple of times. Not really my speed, but I guess it's a mature taste," Jamie added.

"It is a mature taste, and once you get accustomed to it, you begin to appreciate drinking quality dark liquor. You won't touch that white shit again, no pun intended" Donald laughed as he looked at Jamie who slowly caught on to the joke and then he laughed.

"See this is what I'm talking about. I can imagine a world where I have a clique of well-to-do friends and we don't have to go to the clubs to have a good time. We can chill at each other's massive ass houses, watch movies, talk about all types of things and just enjoy life," I said.

"You're right about that! So cheers, to life, to friends, and to success however it comes," Donald said as he raised his glass for a toast. Then came the clinking of our glasses as we toasted to the moment.

"Now, what's the boy trouble you got going on," Donald asked.

"What makes you think it's boy trouble?" I asked.

"Because it's always boy trouble with us."

"So what's his name?"

"I can't' say his name, you may know him," I said.

"I probably don't," Donald replied.

"He's a bit of an Atlanta celebrity so I think you likely will," I said.

"You swear that man is a celebrity Chile," Jamie said.

"You shut the hell up." My sarcasm slipped.

"Ooh girl you so rude. You see how he talks to me, Donald? It's a mess," Jamie said with a laugh.

"I see," Donald said with a chuckle as he sipped on his bourbon.

"So…here's the tea. Well first, this is a no judgment zone right?" I asked as I slid my glass to indicate I was done.

"Absolutely sir! Listen I don't have a heaven or a hell to put you in, and I'm sure what you are about to tell me, I've done way worse. I take it you want another drink?"

"If you don't mind," I said.

"Well, while I fix your refill, give me some background," Donald said.

"I'm in a relationship with a guy that I've been with for a very long time."

"What's a long time," Donald asked.

"About 10 years now," I said.

"Damn, that's a long time in our world."

"Well, it's weirdly complicated. We didn't start out together but we were together during colleg. Ugh, that's another story. But anyway, driving to the right now, I've been—,"

"He's been cheating honey…" Jamie interrupted.

"Oh my," Donald replied.

"Judgment free remember," I said

"No Judgment, just wasn't expecting *that* to come out. I have questions, but I'll let you continue," Donald said.

"Okay so I know I'm wrong for cheating, but like I said, it's complicated, but that's not what I want advice on. The guy I've been seeing just revealed to me that he is HIV+ after he and I have slept together several times. He knows I have a boyfriend. I just don't get why he would not tell me, but claims he loves he."

"Whoa, love? So this sounds serious on his part. I mean... how do you feel about this?" Donald asked.

"I don't know. There is something there I do know, but I can't determine if that's because it's for him or because it's just a convenient escape from the troubles I have in my actual relationship with Tyler," I said.

"Well, I told Brandon to consider why Orlando did not tell him at first. I don't think it's that bad. Don't get me wrong, I get it. I totally get it to be upset about not being told, but like I told him, times are different and I believe if a person is undetectable, it changes the game a little or a lot," Jamie added.

"You just said his name, chile!" I grunted at Jamie

"Oh shit!" He clasped his hand over his mouth. "I'm sorry."

"Well you didn't say his last name, and I don't know any Orlando's so carry on," Donald interjected.

I was still looking at Jamie with a look of death. Then I continued. "Anyway, so yeah...I'm not trying to hear that shit about modern times, but maybe I need to. So that's where I need the advice," I said.

"So, let me make sure I am clear here. You want to be in relationship with this guy? And although you are with someone else and have been for a long time now, you need to understand how to move forward about him having HIV and not telling you?" Donald asked with legitmatic confusion on his face and in his tone.

"Yes basically," I replied.

"Okay, so…first thing is first. I think your bigger concern here is why you are cheating. HIV is a big fucking deal, but so is cheating on your man of 10 years, regardless of what you and him have going on at home. I can't seem to wrap my mind around that. Now, Jamie, I get your point, but even though I am HIV+ myself and undetectable at that, I don't know how I sit with the notion that I am not responsible to disclose my status to anyone simply because I don't pose a risk to them. Like I said before, I guess the reason I feel that way is because of the era I come out of. Many people got infected because of lies and secrets such as what this joker right here is doing. I carry a different awareness about it," Donald said.

"I agree with that as well, but I must add that my reasoning is not as nurtured as yours. And what I mean by that is my reason is one of fear maybe, or perhaps some type of ignorance. Because Jamie's point is very valid I feel, and I can actually understand his aim. But I don't know, I don't think society is ready for that. Or maybe I just want to be mad at him for not telling me that he was positive while we were continually having sex," I said.

"If I can offer some fatherly advice here, and I don't mean to cut you - but like I led with, I think your focus is in the wrong place. Cheating on someone you've been with for so long is an extreme red flag that suggests there are some things either you are going through or that the both of you are going through as a unit, and you need to figure out what that is. So what are you really mad at? Is it fact that he lied to you or is it that what he did forces you to see how reckless you have been? You've been wreckless with noot only with your life, but with your boyfriend's life. That's why the bigger issue is not even about this mystery guy you're fucking. It's about the reason why you are fucking him to begin with. You should ask yourself if you are happy in your current relationship," Donald said.

"I know I'm not happy. I think that's been established a few times already, and my boyfriend knows this. We've talked about it too much now for him not to know," I said.

"Then it sounds like to me you know what you need to do but you are afraid to do it. Instead, you are out here having sex with another dude. That's no way to confront the issue. You need to sit your boyfriend down and tell him the truth, all of it. Then from there you need to decide whether you two want to try to build or rebuild, that is, or if you just need to let it burn in words of our friend Usher," he said.

I just sat silently because he was right, so very right. It's like when I think about making that decision to walk away from Tyler, my heart freezes up. We've been with each other for so long.

"How do I decide to leave someone I've been with for so long?" I asked.

"You do it because you love him, that's how. But see, Brandon, that type of thing requires a lot of self-awareness and accountability. It's the HIV thing all over again. You're so focused on this guy sleeping with you without telling you he was undetectable, which carries no risk at all. I'm not saying that he's right for doing so, but what I am saying is that is small compared to the fact that you are cheating. You're making the smaller issue the bigger issue because you don't want to hold yourself accountable to the bigger issue. Just say it. You're being selfish."

"How am I being selfish," I asked and looked him in his eyes intently.

"Because...you know in your heart you are not happy with your relationship and I suspect it's probably been that way for a very long time now. But instead of making the proper decision, you make the wrong decision because you want to keep what's comfortable to you. What's comfortable to you is the 10 years you've spent with this guy, so much in fact that you are telling yourself that you don't even know how to decide to let it go for the sake of your own integrity. See how the heart can make you play yourself? Especially when you don't hold yourself accountable to what it feels," Donald concluded.

"I never thought about it all that way. I'm going to talk to Tyler. I had plans to do so anyway," I said. By this time, I had completed the second drink and was feeling a little buzzed, but my mind was on my problems. Jamie sat next to me quietly. He didn't have much to say. There was such a weight in the room, all coming from my feelings of despair. It's so tempting to want to blame the world for my problems and my actions when really I need to take accountability. If things are not seemingly working out with Tyler and me, then we need to be responsible about it and put it to an end or take a break or something.

"I hope it works out for you. I really do. You seem like a decent young guy who has his head on pretty straight. I'm not impressed with the cheating thing but you're finding yourself and that type of thing happens at your age, but that still doesn't make it right though. I just want you to learn from it. Don't let any of this be in vain. And for the record, I absolutely think your friend should have told you he was HIV+. You are right to feel some type of way about it and you should definitely hold him accountable for it because it's definitely not cool. However, in doing that, don't make it the big issue in this outfit because it pales in comparison."

"I don't know. I just can't shake how mad I was about him not telling me, and I think it's more so because I was building something with this guy. I think I do have feelings for him like he has for me. Ok, so perhaps we were having a full-on relationship on the side. It just feels like such a betrayal," I said.

"Then it sounds like you're stuck in a dilemma. You should evaluate that for real. Are you mad about HIV or is it something bigger? Just some stuff to ask yourself," Donald said.

"I have a lot to think about. Listen, thank you for your advice. You have given me something to think about. I'm still uncertain how I feel about being lied to about HIV like that though," I said.

Janine came out of his quiet, "Chile, let that shit go."

Twenty-One

Chapter 21

Donald and Jamie helped me to see a different side of things. Another thing that helped was that same day after my conversation with them, we had an another interview with one of the subjects in the documentary who was positive and he talked about the anxiety he feels when he has to share his status. He talked about it being a mounting load of pressure and although he has never not told anyone, there were times where he considered not sharing his status. He also said now that undetectable equals no transmission, he has now started to think twice about sharing his status on random one-nighters.

I guess I can see the other perspective a little bit, but Orlando and I have not been one-night stands. We had been building a twisted connection, and yes I was wrong for cheating on Tyler the way I was doing, but that did not mean that I deserved to be exposed to HIV, whether there was a risk there or not. I felt and still feel I should have had the say so on how that went down, period! Tyler was scheduled to be home in a few days. I had talked to him earlier that day. He shared with me he had started going to therapy and he was learning a lot. I could only hope that meant that our relationship would get better, but I didn't think it would. I needed to share with him that I felt the relationship had gone its course and neither of us were willing to own it and we both were acting out as a result.

My lonely drives home after work were normally when I got to dwell on the things that bothered me or the things that were making me happy. That day, I felt extra weighed down. I knew that if I didn't talk to someone and soon, I was going to have a breakdown. As I sat at the red light in a little town south of Atlanta called Stockbridge, on my way from my last interview, my phone rang and like magic, my bestie always knew when to call me.

"Hey friend! You okay, I was feeling you."

"You always know when to call."

"What's going on with you?" Alec asked.

I took a sigh and was quiet for a second.

"Hello…?"

"Yeah I'm here," I said. "Alec I swear I think you have a crystal ball or something. You always know when to call me," I said.

"That's just because I'm your best friend and I got a crystal ball alright. Now what's up?"

"Everything, chile," I said.

"Well why don't you tell me what's on your mind right now," he said.

"Everything. Like I said. Tyler, Orlando, life…just a lot

man."

"Things between you and Tyler still not getting any better?"

"No. They are not. And I've come to the realization that it's not him or me, it's us. I think we are just done with our relationship. It has run its course."

"How do you feel about that, Brandon?" Alec asked.

"I don't know."

"So what does Orlando have to do with all of this?" He asked.

"I've been sleeping with Orlando for a while now. It started out as a fun thing and now it's all serious and shit. He has HIV and didn't' tell me. Now I think he done caught feelings too. And here I am sitting here with all of this drama surrounding me and it's wearing me out. I don't know what to do," I said.

"Ahhh, I see. Okay, well let's deal with one thing at a time. Wow. I'm so sorry that you were exposed to HIV. That's grimy as fuck. But I'll come back to that. I know Tyler means the world to you and I am sure that's at the forefront of your heart. Why do you think your relationship has run its course?"

"Because, I don't feel the excitement anymore. I'm changing, Alec. Orlando has helped me to see that I'm not the person I have always presented myself as. I've been living a boxed life. Tyler has been my one and only. Yeah, I've had little run-ins here and there but Tyler is my first love and I shudder to think that I may have settled for him and that he is really not the one for me, and that hurts," I said.

"That's a harsh reality. It really is. Life is funny like that. It wishes to teach us profound lessons in the most absurd ways, in ways that seem to hurt the most."

"Yeah, I guess that's one way to look at it," I said.

"It sounds like you really like Orlando too," Alec said.

"Yes, I do. He makes me feel alive, but I can't trust him really."

"Why do you feel like you can't trust him,

"Because, I just don't. You know how you feel something weird sometimes about someone and you just can't put your finger on it. That's him. And even though now I know that he is HIV+ and he didn't tell me, I still feel like there is another shoe to drop and when it does, it's going to be devastating."

Alec was quiet after that. I know him. He was discerning and listening, and I was intrigued to know what it was that he was discerning.

"What do you think?" I asked him.

"Hmmm, I don't know actually. I can feel what you are saying and I definitely do believe Orlando is hiding something else from you. I think there is another shoe to drop. Man, you can't trust these men out here sometimes. Makes me glad that I don't deal with that right now."

"What happened to ol' dude you were talking to?" I asked.

"We still talk. He's okay. I'm not in love though. But he's fine as hell. I'm thinking about coming up that way so he can break by back in. It's been a minute as you know."

"You'd give up your celibacy for him?"

"Yeah, I think I would. But I shouldn't because, I don't think he is as one hundred like he claims. He seems hidden, and like when I asked him about stuff that doesn't sound right to me, he gets really evasive. I know he's a Scorpio and that's just the shit they like to do, but no, with him it seemed extra. I think in my mind, I've decided that I'm just going to go fuck him and let it be that."

"I can't even be mad at you for seeing it that way. We have to learn to take our power back with these guys for real. Stop letting them do us in the way they do. And you know, I think that's what my escapades with Orlando have been all about. I was just trying to take my power back from how Tyler was doing me, and still does me," I said.

"You mean to tell me Tyler is that bad?" Alec asked.

"You don't know a person until you know them. I mean the streets are buzzing too talking about how he is running around sleeping with people."

"Well, have you asked him about that?"

"No, I don't want to start any trouble so I just keep it to myself."

"But that's the problem, Brandon, you keep it to yourself and then it festers and now its oozing out in the form of you running around with Orlando. You need to take your power back by telling Tyler the truth and setting the boundaries with Orlando. You are in control here," Alec said.

"So you saying this has changed me?"

"I didn't say that, but I mean, unhealed trauma will change how you choose to respond to situations. That's all I'm saying. That's why I never say what I'll never do because you just never know what life will deal to you to make you change how you would otherwise respond to a situation. You need to talk to Tyler and you should do it sooner than later while things are fresh on your mind and heart."

"You are right. I'll call him tomorrow. I don't want to do it tonight. I have to edit these videos to present to my boss lady in the morning and I need to focus."

"That's good. Get this shit off your chest so you can take control of your life. You owe that to yourself. Listen, I got to go back out on the floor, I'll be checking on you soon," Alec said.

"Thank you so much, Alec. I don't know what I'd do without a friend like you."

"I don't know what you would do either," Alec laughed.

"You so damn shady. Bye."

Alec is always right. Even when we were in school and he'd tell me to not be afraid to explore new things that interest me. He was just always right. I only hope he's surely right about this too. I'm not going to wait until Tyler gets home. I'll call him tomorrow and have this very hard discussion with him.

III

Part III – Burn

When the feeling ain't the same and your body don't
want to—
But you know... gotta let it go 'cause the party ain't
Jumpin' like it used to, even though this might bruise
you
Let it burn
Let it burn, gotta let it burn

Twenty-Two

Chapter 22

I decided I'd give Tyler a call first thing this morning. I told him already that I wanted to have a serious conversation with him. He said he'll be able to after his morning jog to the coffee shop.

"There is this little coffee shop in the business district of DC right around the corner from the White House. I just love to come here and people watch. I like to watch the people come and go with their cell phones glued to the sides of their faces. You can see one who appears to be cursing out his secretary. *I told you to order five of those goddamn things, Annie! Now what am I supposed to do now? I have to meet with Senator Sons. I oughta fire your ass.* Now you don't hear colorful language like that around here often but I mean …this is the capital." Tyler chimed on and on. Whenever I ask him about his day, he goes on a tangent.

"So why do you opt to go sit at that coffee house if it's so disruptive," I asked.

"I tune that type of stuff out. I come here to write in my journal. I've been pretty consistent with it, and it helps me to get my feelings together. My therapist insists that I shouldn't keep them bottled up inside. I'm so used to doing that. I come here daily, get a bowl of fruit and a caramel macchiato. I sit in my favorite spot back here in the corner. It's usually available. I normally don't have to come stalk someone for the spot, but the rare occasion I do, I pace back and forth until they get up and leave. I know that's some passive-aggressive shit. My therapist only can work on one issue at a time with me."

"It sounds like your therapy is doing you well. What do you guys talk about or do you mind telling me?" I asked.

"A little of this and a little of that. Mainly about my feelings. She's trying to get me to tap into the wells as she calls it. It's been helpful, I'll say. You don't normally call me to chit-chat like this. What's on your mind?" He asked.

"We need to talk, Tyler."

"Well I know that much. I mean you did start the call off with that, no hello or anything. That's not like you either.

"There is a lot that I don't normally do. Things change."

"Well, you sound aggravated. What's up?"

"You. Us, We, all of this that we have not been doing?"

"Oh so you want to talk about the relationship? Don't you think we should do this in person?" He asked.

"No, we need to talk now. I don't want to wait until you get home."

"Okay, well...let's talk. I already know what you want to say. I know that you feel like I am not around enough and have not been paying you any attention. Well, I'm not there to pay you any attention and—"

"And when you are here you don't pay me any attention."

"Okay, I can take that too."

"It's the truth. I think we should talk about that."

"That's what we are doing now, right?" He said.

"What's up, man? You don't want to be with me anymore? Is that what it is?" I asked.

"Brandon, listen…I have a lot going on right now. I think I do, but umm, I dunno. Look, it's nothing about you personally," he said.

"So, you don't want to be with me, or with anyone at all?"

"Brandon, it's more me not ready to go all in with someone just yet."

"What the fuck does that mean, Tyler? We have been together almost five years plus another five years of toying around before that. When were you going to tell me that you didn't want to be with someone?"

"I just came to this conclusion through therapy. You're the one told me I needed to see one. This is what came of it."

"How long have you known or been *aware* of this?"

"Just a couple of weeks or so. It hasn't been that long. My therapist helped me see that I have repressed fears. I thought I had dealt with my anxiety about being out of the closet. Somehow, that shit is still there. Brandon, I love you so much, but I don't think I can give you what you need right now. I need to heal. I wanted to be sure before I told you. I was just literally writing about you in my journal. I don't want to hurt you baby."

"But you've been hurting me for a long time now. Broken promises here and there. you've made me make some terrible decisions around here."

"What do you mean?"

"Nothing. I'm just saying, I haven't been in a good space here lately. It's been hard concentrating on work and things."

"I don't mean to put you in a bad head space," he said.

"Do you think we can work this out, Tyler?" I asked.

He sighed. "Brandon, I have something I need to tell you."

"What is it?" I asked

"I slept with someone last month. It was a one-time thing. One thing led to another and, man I'm so sorry. I never want to be that guy that cheats and it's not in my heart to do you that way. I would just as much leave you alone before I do that to you, even if it was a mistake."

I was silent. I had to process what he had just said to me. He was telling me that he cheated on me, but then it sounded like he had only done it once and not a million times like the street had been reporting. I was conflicted on how I felt I should respond because I had pretty much done the same thing.

"Hello, baby, are you there? Did you hear me?"

"Yeah, I heard you," I said.

"So...how do you feel about what I just said? I mean I should know how you feel, but I mean...say something," he said.

"I don't have much to say. It is what it is, but I understand though."

"Why do you understand? I wouldn't want someone I'm with to just understand that I've cheated on them. It makes me wonder if you care or not. Shit, do you care?" He asked.

"I care, you know I care."

"So say something more than that."

"What do you want me to say?" I asked.

"I want you to tell me the truth."

"I can't do that. You can't handle it. If I told you the real truth, it'd kill you."

"Then so be it. At least I will die with no barriers between you and me," he said.

"Why do you make things so hard, Tyler?"

"I'm not—I am just saying. You know me, Brandon. Everything has to make sense and everything has to have real meaning to it. I need to understand why you are not upset or at least not showing it."

"I want to tell you the truth, Tyler, but it would hurt you too much."

"If you love me, you'd tell me how you are feeling. Tell me your truth," he said.

"It's not that truth I'm talking about," I replied.

"So what is it then?"

"Baby…I slept with someone too."

"Wait, what? When did this happen? Why?"

"You know why! Your ass is never here…I mean NEVER HERE!" I shouted. By this time, I was crying. All of the feelings that I had been holding and hiding from him and my lies and deceit were all bubbling out into a frenzy in that moment.

"I've been gone for a long time so are you saying you've been sleeping around with multiple people to get your fix?"

"No, it has happened multiple times, but it's not with multiple people."

"Okay so, it's one person a few times. Okay."

I heard the phone get quiet. It sounded like he was processing what I had said. I was unsure if he was mad or if he was shocked or what.

"Okay. Okay. I got it. I understand. Do I like the idea of you with someone else, no. But given the fact that I haven't been around for you, I understand that you have your needs still. Even though I would have held out," he said.

"But you didn't either," I snapped back. The nerve of him playing tick for tack.

"No, I'm not going to say that. What happened with me was a mistake from me letting my guard down. I wasn't out fishing for dick and ass," he said.

"I wasn't either."

"Okay, so mine happened with a colleague. How did yours happen?"

"Tyler, I do not want to go down this hole with you, okay? You know how you get trying to be investigative and shit. Let's just leave it here."

"I think I'd feel better if I knew you just had some random hook up with someone. So is that what it was?"

"No."

"*No?*"

"Yes that's what I said, no. It was not some random hookup," I said.

"Wait so are you telling me you've had an affair with someone. You're dating someone else?"

"No. That's enough questioning, Tyler. We both know that we've stepped out on each other, now let's decide how we want to move forward."

"Ummm, no, I can't do that. I feel funny about this. I know I cheated, but I get the feeling you have done more than just had sex. I know you. You like the whole package. You've been seeing someone for more than sex. Tell me I'm wrong."

"You're wrong, but not entirely."

"What does that mean?" He asked.

"Okay, so we had sex, it turned into a repeat thing. The guy caught feelings, I broke it off. So no, I was not dating him. He was dating me though."

"How do I know you broke it off. And who was it with?"

"I can't tell you that."

"So that means it's someone that I know. Now I'm getting pissed," he said.

"Why? I mean you fucked someone else too. Why you getting mad for?" I asked.

"You don't cheat with someone that I know. It's rude as fuck."

"What? Are you for real?" I asked.

"Who the fuck is it?" He shouted.

"You need to calm your nerves."

"Brandon…!"

"Well I guess I may as well tell you since you're already mad. If you're around your colleagues, I suggest you get up and walk off."

"I'm not. Tell me the fucking truth, now!"

"Orlando."

"Are you fucking kidding me? You know what? You are full of shit. You are sitting your ass on this motherfucking phone talking about *he was dating me and I wasn't into him*. You are a lying bitch. You have had googly eyes for that bastard since you two met. You must think I'm a fool if you think for one minute I believe your ass when you say you wasn't into him. I don't fucking believe it. You are a trip."

"You need to stop all that cursing at me."

"Fuck you, Brandon. How about that?"

"Someone has been and very well, might I add."

"You are a slut for this shit. I'm so fucking mad at you I can't see."

"If you are going to be talking to me like you are crazy then we can just end this right here."

"As far as I'm concerned Brandon, the shit ended the first time you put his dick in your mouth. I gotta go. I can't with you."

Tyler hung up the phone on me. I was utterly dumbfounded. I mean…I can't blame him for being upset. He's right. Of all the people, Orlando should have been the last I chose to cheat on him with. I was shaking by the time I disconnected the line. After all of these years and this is what he does. By now, I was headed to my car. I could not allow my colleagues to see me like this. I got inside and shut the door. I grabbed the steering wheel and screamed into a fit of sobs. My heart was broken. My relationship was over and I didn't think it would happen like this. It's funny how the universe tries to tell you something and you spend weeks and months trying to ignore and resist it, and then she forces the destiny on you violently and abruptly.

Twenty-Three

Chapter 23

A few days later, I found myself in deep thought as I sat in the afternoon rush hour. I had so much to consider. Orlando stayed on my mind a lot and I found myself missing him greatly. I couldn't believe how badly Tyler blew up on me. He said some pretty harsh things. I didn't know if I could forgive him and the cheating. We were so fucked up. I wanted to work it out, but Tyler hadn't spoken to me since the fight. It had been days since it happened. He was supposed to come home and he didn't. I sat there and waited for him to show up. I felt too ashamed to text him to make sure he was alright. His ass was alright because I saw him updating that raggedy-ass Facebook page of his. I guess he felt he was some type of big shot now with his 100,000 followers. I really missed him. My heart hurt as I sat and thought about how in one swoop, I had lost everything that I ever cared about.

I sat at a stoplight, pondering my problems and mulling over my feelings. I heard a honk behind me as I looked up and realized the light was green and I'd been sitting there in my thoughts. I was trying to resist the urge to call Orlando. I considered what Jamie had said. I really did like Orlando and perhaps I needed to decide what was best for me. I mean I could try to work things out with Tyler and end up much lonelier than I was. Even though we had everything out in the open, he and his career was going to always come before me. He had such big aspirations and his time away from me would only become more and more. Instead of it being days at a time that he was gone, it'd become weeks at a time that he was gone. I didn't want to deal with that, but then I considered that we had been together for so long. He was my first friend away from home. He became my lover and he had always been by my side. I failed to believe that we could not work through our problems. He was so angry with me. Then I had Orlando to consider. That dude really cared for me but Orlando was HIV positive. I didn't know what I should know about HIV. I did know that it was not a death sentence anymore, but the fact that he didn't tell me still did not sit too well with me, at all. If I do want to build something with him, I'd have to get over that for sure.

Traffic was still moving slowly, inching on up interstate 75. The congestion by the downtown connector seemed to get worse and worse every week. The good thing about it was I get to think. I wondered what Orlando was doing. Was he thinking about me? He hadn't called me and I hadn't called him. I should not have been so cold. In my heart of hearts, I did believe he meant well. I started to consider calling him. There was no sense in things not being resolved. I should not have walked out the way I did, but I was mad. Hell, it probably was best that way.

* * *

"Hey Siri, call Orlando Cell."

"Okay, dialing Orlando." The phone rang and for a second. I thought it would not pick up, but it did.

"Hello," I heard over my speakers.

"Hi. Umm, hey I was just calling. We need to talk. Can you meet me in an hour or so?"

"What is this about?"

"Orlando, come on. You know what this is about. We need to talk," I said.

"I'm really busy. I'll have to check my schedule. I'll get back to you."

"Okay," I said, and then the call disconnected. I guess Orlando had had time to seethe about me walking out on him, but I didn't see what for. He was the one that did the dirt. Why did I feel hurt by that though? I had two men that I cared about, and neither one of them wanted to have anything to do with me. I had really fucked up big time. I could've really used a friend at that moment.

I had made my way home and into our parking garage. You never quite get used to coming home to a lonely place. I mean Tyler was hardly home so it already felt lonely, but knowing that we were probably good and over with made it feel worse. The sounds of loneliness were everywhere. The way my shoes tapped against the floor and the sounds that echoed down the corridors as I made my way to the elevator. The elevator creaked and croaked as it took me up to the seventh floor to my lonely apartment. There I'd face my lonely bed and a lonely turkey sandwich for dinner. I got to our unit and the steel gray painted door seemed cold as I faced it and dropped my head. I just felt lonely as hell. Although I had been feeling lonely for months, the feeling was extra heavy that time. As I walked in, the place was dark, only a fade of the setting sun shined through. I could smell the scent of familiarity. I smelled Tyler. Damn, was I missing him that much? I turned on the lights and quickly realized that wasn't it. He had been there. Not only could I smell him as if he was in the apartment, but I could also see traces of his presence. There was a Starbucks cup on the counter and I know I didn't drink any damn Starbucks. I actually found myself feeling a little excited. My baby had come home. Maybe he was in the bedroom sleeping or showering. I put down my bag and made my way to the bedroom. I turned on the light to see no Tyler. As a matter of fact, I saw no trace of him or his things. I ran to the closet and my heart sank in the seat of my pants. I just fell on the floor and sobbed uncontrollably holding myself for dear life.

The left side of the closet was bare. All of Tyler's clothes and shoes were gone. He had come and got everything that was his and left. I felt like I'd been hit by a Mack 10 truck. What did that mean now? Were we over? Would I ever see him again? I felt so lost. I slowly got up from the carpet, my face sticky from the tears. I walked into the bathroom hoping to find a note or some words from him with an explanation, but I found nothing. I slung back drawers, peeked in the medicine cabinet. Surely he wouldn't leave me like this. His name was on that goddamn lease too. I found myself getting a bit angry. I sat back in the. middle of the closet floor like a kid playing with blocks, but instead there were no blocks and no fun happening at that moment. I couldn't believe it. I pulled my phone from my pocket and began to dial. I needed some support. I heard ringing and ringing and finally, the ringing stopped and a *hello* sounded from the speaker.

"Alec. Please tell me you can talk. I need you," I said.

"Hey, friend. Yeah, I can. I ain't doing nothing but chilling. I just got off the phone with my boo. What's up. What's going on?"

"Tyler broke up with me. He moved out," I said sobbing.

"What! When? Whah…how…I'm so sorry to hear that! What happened?"

"We had a fight a few days ago when he was in DC. You know I said I'd call him after I got off the phone with you. Well, I did the next day. The conversation went entirely left field. We had a huge blow-up and I think it's over," I said sobbing.

"So you mean to tell me that bastard left you over an argument. That sounds like he wanted to break up anyway. I say good riddance."

"It's not that simple, Alec."

"Don't tell me you about to sit here and defend his ass. You have been moping around here for months complaining and talking about how he does not show you any attention. Sometimes God is really trying to move things out of our lives that have been hurting us all along."

"It's not that simple. Trust me on that."

"Then why ain't it that simple?"

"This is not just his fault. I have to take some of the blame too," I said. I was still sitting on the floor sobbing.

"What happened? You still haven't given me any details."

"I told him about Orlando after he told me that he had cheated on me. He got extremely upset with me when he found out that it was Orlando that I had been messing around with."

"So wait? He was out cheating and is saying your cheating is worse than his? That's just like a man for ya."

"Mine was definitely worse in comparison."

"See what we not going to do is sit here and take the blame for this relationship falling apart. Tyler should have had his ass at home more often tending to you and you would not have to go out and get wooed and swayed by another man. How about I come up there and visit you over the weekend. It's about time I did anyway."

"You just want to see that man of yours," I said drying my eyes.

"So. Maybe I do and maybe I will. You can finally meet him too. I think you are going to like him."

"We will see. If he anything like that last one you were with then I don't know. Listen, thank you. I don't know what I would do if I didn't have a friend like you to talk to me during the hardest moments of my life. You were there for me when my parents threw me out of the house. I am forever grateful for our friendship."

"It's no biggie. That's what friends are for. You know I will always choose you just like I am sure you will always choose me no matter what."

"Well let me pay for your flight. Let me know when you want to take off and I'll get a ticket for you."

"You don't have to do that. I'll be fine," Alec said.

"Well, okay. Oh my, I'm so excited. I can really use the visit."

"I know, honey. Okay, let me go. I got some greens on the

stove."

"Greens?"

"Look here, don't act like you too good for a pot of greens and some fried porkchop…"

"Keep on eating that shit, hear? That's why you got high blood pressure now at 28."

"A pig ain't never gave me high blood pressure."

"If you say so, eat for me then, I guess. Yuck."

"Man, as much country food your mama used to cook and you sitting there acting like you ain't from around here."

Alec was right, I used to love soul food, but I couldn't get down with that artery-clogging food anymore. I didn't want to insult Alec, so I just said okay and I held the phone thinking about Tyler. I didn't really care about those greens. I cared about the barren closet that I was staring at. I got up and walked from one end of it to the next, running my hand across the dusty shelves remembering the spot where he kept his gym clothes. He was so neat. They would be folded up so perfectly, almost like he didn't work out in them. It was little quirks like that about Tyler that made me love him so much.

"I know, I'm just saying. We have to do better is all. Speaking of food, I got a sandwich in here that's probably good and soggy by now. Thank you for listening to me. You're the best friend a guy could ask for."

"No problem, shugs. I'll touch base with you a little later this week, okay. I'll let you know what time my flight will arrive," he said.

We disconnected the line and I set the phone down on my nightstand. The walk to the bed felt drafty. I was alone. I stared at the bed, neatly made up. I looked over at his side. I couldn't believe he was gone. I just couldn't believe it. My heart hurt like it had been shot. He took everything. I walked out of the bedroom. He took his books from the bookshelf. I noticed the record player he said belonged to his granddaddy was gone. His favorite vinyl albums were gone too. All of him was gone. In the midst of all of that, I didn't think to text or call him. I went back into the room. The cool draft met me again. It was like the bedroom knew that night would be the loneliest night of my life.

I reached for my phone to see if Tyler would pick up a call from me but was interrupted by a text from Orlando.

I'm sorry about earlier. I had a client to take care of. Do you still want to talk?

I didn't know whether I should respond or not. I'm was a vulnerable space. Anything Orlando said to me would probably all make sense and I'd forgive him and be riding his dick soon after. I found myself feeling how I used to feel months ago when I was trying to resist him from the start. I wanted to ignore him then and didn't. I wanted to ignore him at that current moment and couldn't.

Where are you? I texted back.

I'm at my office. If you want to come here, I'll be here a while. The day is over so no one is here except my admin. She is leaving soon. We can talk candidly.

Okay, I'll be there shortly.

Twenty-Four

Chapter 24

⟨⟩

Orlando was wrapping up a call when his receptionist let me in. She always looked at me like she knew what he and I were up to. I wondered why he had her here so late. I'm sure she had a life to get to. I guess that was all of our stories—always at work.

"Thank you, Sidney, you can go ahead and head home. I'm done here. Thank you for staying over to help me with the Centennial Park project. It's gonna be epic," Orlando said to her.

"It's my pleasure. I'll see you in the morning. And nice to see you again, Brandon."

She walked out and Orlando motioned me over to one of his offices. I must say, he had a nice suite in this building. He was always so posh. His suite was a few floors up and the view of the city was amazing, but not nearly as good as his condo which was several floors up. It was dusk so the city lights were shimmering. Orlando walked over to his desk to clear away some papers. I took time to walk around examining the space. He had his degree from Emory University on the wall. It read Doctor of Counseling Psychology: Orlando Londell McIntyre. I believe I had heard that name Londell before. I couldn't remember if he told me once that's his middle name.

"Wow, smart guy. I didn't know you got your Ph.D from Emory. You never told me that," I said.

"No, I don't think so. I worked hard for that sucker too. That allows me to up my prices and brand myself as one of the best LGBTQ counselors out there. I built this practice from the ground up, with the help of my parents' wealth of course. I'm glad to be doing well with it all. I have a few LPC's under me and a couple of interns. I enjoy what I do. Isn't that great?"

"Absolutely, it is! I'm proud of you for this. Well listen, I wanted us to talk. I know it's been a few weeks since the last time we saw each other. We didn't really leave on a good note," I said.

"No we didn't," he replied.

"I've had some time to think in between that time. I think I may have overreacted. Sure, I think you should have been honest with me about being HIV positive and having sex with me and not telling me. That was foul as fuck, but I've had time to sit in it, and I don't believe you were malicious in not telling me. I honestly believe it just wasn't something that was on your mind. It took me a while to get to that place, so I'm not 100% on board with that idea, but I'm getting there," I said.

"I wish you had not walked out on me that night. I could have explained that to you. Brandon, I've had HIV for a very long time now, and with the way the drugs are now, I literally go on about my day-to-day life and it just is never something I think about. So when I say that first night I was seriously not thinking about it, I'm for real when I say that. I was drunk too, and it just wasn't on my mind. The next day, I was too afraid to tell you. Then all the time after that, I just could never resist the chemistry we have and sex with you has always felt good so I bargained in my mind that since I'm undetectable that you are not at risk. It was that which helped to try to deal with not telling you right away. However, I always knew that I had to tell you eventually. That's why I did. I'm so sorry it took me so long. I hope that gives you the closure you need. You really did deserve an explanation," Orlando concluded as he rose up from his desk.

"No, it's not about closure. I can't say that I want that like you're thinking."

"What do you mean?" Orlando walked over to the window and stared out of it as if there was something to see from way up where we were.

"I mean…I don't know what I mean. I mean yeah, I raked my brain for days trying to understand why you did not tell me. But as I worked with subjects in the documentary, I came across some varying perspectives. Ultimately, I understand now that the bigger issue is why you and I were having sex in the first place and not so much about the HIV," I said.

"Truth is Brandon, HIV destroyed my life. When it happened, I did such a good job with pretending like it wasn't something that was happening to me. I shouted and praised to Jesus for a healing that had not come and may not come ever. One day, I woke up and realized that I was in a state of PTSD with having lost my health. I was jaded. I was hurt.

You never think about how something like this would happen to a guy like me. I wasn't always this calculating. I was a nice guy..."

"You still are a nice guy, Orlando," I interrupted. He still had his back to me looking out the window.

"Yeah, but I hurt you. I know that's only because I'm still hurting. You never get used to having to take pills every day. When you realize your body is aging faster than it should be because your immune system is always active as they say, the hurt always remains. The void is always there. I could go on and ride off into the sunset with a husband one day, and riding behind me will always be this ghost. So, that's why I didn't tell you. It hurts too much," he said.

I walked up behind him and put my arms around his waist. He laid his head back on my shoulder like he had done the first night we had sex. I felt all the feelings I had been trying to suppress over the last few weeks come rushing back.

"Listen, Orlando, don't beat yourself up about being HIV positive. Life happens to all of us, and let's face it, one out of two black gay men will contract HIV. That's an ugly statistic, but it's our reality. HIV is unfortunately a normalcy for us now. It does not make you less than the person you are. Look around you, I mean, just look. You have this wonderful practice, you are closing on your second house at what, age thirty-three? You are an entrepreneur, a true boss. Look at it this way: You took HIV by the balls and you made life manifest for yourself anyway. Now that's a triumph. You have to stop feeling sorry for yourself about it. Listen, I know I don't know what it feels like so I can't tell you not to beat yourself up, but I want you to not beat yourself up. Instead of that one mistake, see all of the accomplishments you've made. You're concerning yourself with the life you think you destroyed, and you are at the same time not paying attention to the life that you are creating. It's one that's worth relishing in. Don't you think?" I said.

"I know, but I should not have lied to you for so long," he said.

"Yeah, about that…like I said, I'm not saying that I'm just all the way okay with that yet. It's not the HIV thing that bothers me, ahem, anymore, it's the dishonesty. And had you not been dishonest with me, I dunno, I think we would be talking about something differently right now," I said.

"I get it. I'm sorry. I mean I don't like how you dropped me like that. It's not something I like to go through, but I get it. Honestly, I don't know where your head is as it concerns us, and because I find myself wanting you and that makes me uneasy because you are taken," Orlando said.

"I do know that what we had been doing is more than what it has looked like," I said.

"What has it looked like to you? I know what it has looked like to me," Orlando said. By this time, he had disengaged from my grip and sat back behind his desk. He looked like the executive that he touted himself as. He looked intimidating, and I felt like I was supposed to explain myself like an intern afraid of being fired.

"Well…," I paused. "Can I sit?"

"Sure, I'm sorry. Yes, have a seat. You don't have to be formal with me. I mean I know I look like I'm about to hire you for something, but no, I'm sorry, go ahead."

"Well. I have to be honest, Orlando. I have been trying to pretend like all we were doing was having sex. I didn't want to acknowledge that we were becoming a lot more than that.

For me, I wanted it to look like a fling, and that when Tyler and I got back on track, you and I would stop. Then when you told me about HIV, that shined a light on me and I have to admit, I was mad as hell. I thought it was all about you not telling me, but then I realized that it's deeper than that," I said.

Orlando leaned forward in his chair, "Well, I guess that is what we discussed at the table that time, how you would end up using me as an escape. It just sounds like you didn't realize how far you had escaped to," Orlando said.

"Yes," I said.

"I know this is a fucked-up situation. I wasn't intending it to get like this. And I sure wasn't intending on getting caught up," he said.

"How are you caught up? I mean, I think I heard you say at the Sundial that you were catching feelings, right?" I asked.

"Something like that," he said.

"I mean…you either are or you are not."

Orlando swayed from side to side in his gray executive chair as he tapped his fingers on his pristine desk fit for the Oval Office.

"I don't know what I feel honestly, Brandon. I just know that I have enjoyed what we have been doing, whatever you want to call it. Is it a relationship or are we just fucking? I really don't know the answer to that. I just know that I think I'm in love with you," he said.

"I know I have something for you, I can't say that I'm in love with you, though. Even if I—"

"I know, if you did, you won't be able to admit to it because of Tyler," He said as he fiddled with the pens on his desk. He wouldn't look at me when he said it.

"No, I mean yes, but no too." I didn't know if I should tell him right then that Tyler left me. I feel he would pounce all over that.

"Well, what do you want? What do you want from me?" He asked.

I sighed and walked over to the windows and gazed out into the skyline with Lenox Mall in the distance and the W hotel nearby. I wasn't really sure what to do or say to that question. I don't really know what I want. I do know that I don't want this uncertainty that has been taking place with me over the last couple of months. I don't want to continue to have a ghostly relationship where I only get to see my man 3 or 4 times out of the month. No matter how much I love him, I know I don't want that. I'd rather be single. I broke my silence. "I want…" I continued to stare out the window, afraid to face him. "I want you." I can't believe my lips. I could see the reflection of the office in the floor-to-ceiling window. Orlando was rising out of his chair and began to walk over toward me. I still did not turn around. If I did, I knew what would happen. I swore I would not do that again.

He came up from behind me and held me with his hands softly around my waist.

"I want you to, and not just in the way that I've had you," he said into my ear. He turned me around. "Listen, I think we have done this all wrong. We started wrong and this is why the lies have happened like they have. I don't want to push you into making decisions that you will regret later. If you want to be with Tyler and work on your relationship with him, then I can respect that and give you the space and respect for that. If you don't want Tyler anymore and you want us to build something, then I am ready for that as well. It's your call."

"Well…about Tyler," I said.

"Yeah, what about him?" He asked.

"Tyler cheated. We had a talk that turned into a major blow up shortly after you and I stopped messing around. He confessed it to me on his own and then I ended up telling him about my indiscretions, but when he found out it was with you, he got really mad. He cursed me out and called me a slut. I haven't spoken with or seen him since. He has blocked me on Facebook and Instagram. Today, he moved his things out of the apartment. I found out when I got home today and saw his stuff was gone," I started to cry. It is so heavy on me. I could not hold it in while talking about it.

"Oh my god. Baby, I'm so sorry. He is dead wrong to do you like this no matter what has gone down with you two or who has done what. You don't deserve to be treated this way. Listen, I know you. You are a good guy. I've sat here and watched you love him and hurt for him and miss him and he does you like none of that even matters to him. Everyone makes mistakes, you made a mistake and so did he. Who gives a fuck about who it was with? Two wrongs don't make a right and he is an asshole for doing you like this. I wish I could kick his ass right now."

"Thank you, Orlando. I don't need you to do that. I just want to feel okay with myself. I still love him. This hurts like hell."

"I know you still love him. Are you going to try and get back with him?"

"I don't know if I want that. I don't think we would ever be the same. Tyler is a man's man. You don't bruise the ego of a man's man and think they will return to the same guy as before. If we decided to work things out, he would never be the same to me again. He would treat me differently. I don't want that."

"That's actually quite insightful of you to see that."

"Yeah. I just know him well, that's all."

Orlando wiped away the tear lines on my face. He is always so careful with me. Having him here is just what I needed because I felt like shit and what I was about to do next was a matter between me and God. I just wanted to feel loved. I looked into his eyes and I leaned in to kiss him.

"Woah, wait. What are you doing? You are not in a head space to be doing this. You'll regret it in the morning."

"I don't care, Orlando. We've done this a dozen times already. I am clear on my intentions," I began to unbuckle his pants and they dropped to the floor, so did I.

"Brandon…don't…Bran…ahh…shit."

Soft moans flowed from Orlando as I felt his passion increase and his hand rake through my scalp. In that moment, my hurt seemed to evaporate and what remained was my raging hormones needing a fix that I hadn't gotten in a while, one that Orlando hadn't particularly been privy to either. I pushed him back on the sofa. Yes, that one his clients lied down on. The clock had started for my session and I was going to get some therapy that night.

By this time, Orlando had given in to my spell and his will to finally be the moral guy had gone away. He flipped me around and his hands pinned my arms down like a cop does a suspect. My neck trembled with the wetness of his language. Orlando is like a sexual drug, one that I can't ever seem to get enough of. His sex is one I'll never forget and I'm sure of it. I surrendered my body to him and looked him in his eyes with a daring come hither stare. He undressed me with his eyes while his hands assisted. His hands were everywhere and by the time he got my clothes off and his, we were making passionate fire all over the plush sofa where no doubt many people have shared their most intimate parts.

That night, I shared my most intimate part with him, one that he's never gotten a chance to have. Tonight, I wanted him to have it. I needed to have him have it.

Twenty-Five

Chapter 25

The morning after, I still woke up with a hole in my heart. I was in my bed without Tyler and that was actually something I was used to, but it felt different this time. Although I had feelings for Orlando, I still loved Tyler. Submitting my body to Orlando the night before did nothing for me but give me a good time. I didn't think I was looking for him to make me feel good. It honestly was one thing that led to another type of thing. I still didn't even know where we stood. We didn't talk about what we would do next. I think he didn't want to bring it up since I had just broken up with Tyler. I guess I can't blame him. I didn't know how I let all that shit happen. How did I get to that place? The bedroom felt cold still as I got up. It was full of sunlight but the light cast shadows that matched my despair. My heart hurt at the thought of my love not wanting to have anything to do with me. "I got to get myself together. I cannot keep dwelling on him," I said aloud. My phone rang. I walked over to grab it. It was my mom.

"Hi Mom."

"Hey sweetie, I just wanted to call and check up on you. How is everything going up there?" She asked.

"It's...umm...it's going." I wasn't sure if I wanted to tell her that Tyler and I were not together anymore. I didn't want to go into the questions of why.

"What's wrong?" she asked. Mom was not one to play coy.

"Nothing, I just woke up."

"At 1:30 in the afternoon? What time did you go to bed?"

"It was late. I can't remember. Where's Dad?"

"He's at church which is where you should've been this morning."

"Yeah, you know me and the church don't get along."

"That's cause you don't make it get along. You better keep some type of faith in your reach honey. You can't make it in this world without some higher direction. One day, you will understand. You used to understand. I don't know what happened to you. Once you start struggling to keep above water, you will surely learn. You cannot live without God, son."

"What does the church have to do with that, though?" I was starting to get irritated. I can't deal with the Bible thumpers even if it is my mom.

"It has plenty to do with it. You used to be very mindful of it."

"Well, listen, mom, you know what my stance is on the church and gay people. I did a whole documentary on it. When I find a church that isn't hell-bent on being puppets then I'll attend it, until then, I'm perfectly fine with how I choose to abide by my spiritual principles. Just because I don't go to a church on Sundays doesn't mean that I don't have a spirituality that leads and guides me from day to day."

"Okay, son. I hear you. I'm just saying when trouble comes, you know what has always kept you. I don't know what you do now, but I know what has always worked. Don't forget that. I can sense you've been dealing with a lot and sometimes prayer and meditation can go a long way. Sometimes sitting and listening to the Word be taught can go even further. Just keep that in mind. How are things with you and Tyler? The last you were here, you didn't sound too happy. Have things gotten better?"

"No, they haven't. Tyler and I have taken a break. We are separated," I said.

"Separated. You guys are not married. What do you mean separate? Are you guys planning to work things out?"

"I don't know. I don't know anything right now. I'm just trying to make it from day to day."

"I'm sorry to hear that, baby. Relationships are hard. I think you and Tyler need to talk it out if that's an option. You have been together for far too long to not at least talk it out."

"Yeah, but both parties have to be willing to talk. He won't talk to me," I said.

"Why not? What happened?"

"Nothing, we had an argument after I tried to talk to him about how I have been feeling. Some things were said and revealed and…well…here we are."

"Take it for me, Brandon, even when the other person doesn't want to talk, sometimes you have to make them talk. You must remember where your power lies. Never let anyone one-up you. Just like how you came back and made us talk about what we went through in the past with you, I need you to take that same courage and do the same with Tyler. You have to make it mandatory for him. He will listen. If he loves you like he has said he does, he will listen. Trust your mama, ok?"

"Thank you, I'll try to get him to talk. You know my stubbornness doesn't want to."

"Honey, true love is not stubborn. It is patient and kind. You know that. I tell you what to do now, go pray. I'm serious, go and pray and I promise you once you are done, you will feel all the power to move forward with your life, whether it's with Tyler or not."

"Okay, I will." Somehow, I felt like God was using my mom to really get something to me. It was the strength that I have needed the last few days. I haven't prayed in a long time. I used to do so often. I don't know what happened. How did I become this person, someone that cheats and lies? I started to feel bad about myself. I ended the call with mom and went into the living area. I dropped to my knees and propped my elbows on the seat of the sofa. I started to call out to God to ask for His help and His guidance. It felt foreign at first because it had been a while since I'd prayed like that. I guess it'd been a while since I felt like I needed His help. I like to pray to music so I played one of my favorite artists, Maranda Curtis. She sang fill me up on a YouTube video and then segued into a hymn. *Fill my cup, Lord. I lift it up, Lord. Come and quench this thirsting of my soul. Bread of heaven...feed me 'til I want no more.*

There was once a time when I knew how to pray myself out of tough situations. There was a time where this type of dilemma would not have affected me as it had. Sometimes, the thirsting of our souls will lead us on a ramage to find solace in things that keep us in trouble. Our power is in God. Once I was done, I did feel empowered, just like Mom said. I felt like I could confront anything. I sent Tyler a long text and I pretty much told him that we needed to talk and that we had to handle our affairs like adults. I don't know what it was, but he replied back almost immediately and said he would be back in town tomorrow and that we should meet to tie up our loose ends. I guess I can take that, even though tie-up loose ends sounded like we are confirming the breakup and making plans to go our separate ways. Earlier that would have stung a bit, but right now, I felt empowered to face it.

Twenty-Six

Chapter 26

Tyler and I scheduled to meet at a nearby Starbucks. I guess meeting in public meant we would have no choice but to act cordially with each other. Tyler said this meeting would be strictly to handle business with the apartment and sever any other financial ties we still had together which were a savings account and a few high-priced electronics we bought together. I got there first. I chose a spot that was a bit away from the entrance. I was nervous. I hadn't seen him in so long, a few weeks now, and it had been a few days since he got his stuff out of the apartment. I just sat and did what I always do, people watch. I saw one guy to my left, buried into his laptop, typing away. He seemed to be writing something. I wondered if it was a book or something. Was he telling a story? If so, does he ever get writer's block? I wondered if I walked over to him and said, "Hey, you need some content about a broken heart? I'm your man if you do."

I should write that tale myself actually. I looked up and saw a guy and a girl, the girl seemed agitated and the guy looked apologetic like he had just said something wrong to her. I wonder what other people-watchers are in here today. Are they looking around the room like I am, and have they spotted me out and made up a story in their minds about why I'm here or what I'm going through? I wonder if I am wearing my pain on my face, and can anyone guess it?

I looked down at my watch. Tyler was late. He was always late. I guess some things never change. Well, it's only been a week. It's not like it's been two years or something. Just as my agitation of his tardiness began to arise, I saw him enter. I felt my heart flutter. He was nicely dressed in a burnt orange cardigan, navy blue chinos and camel-colored boots. I love how he is so preppy in his appearance but has this street aura about himself. He stood and looked around the café in an attempt to find me. I threw my arms up to get his attention in my direction. Once he saw me, he slid his sunglasses back on and headed my way. There was a time that he would have flashed me his beautiful smile. That time, I just got nothing.

"Hi," he said as he sat down.

"Hello, thank you for coming."

"It's nothing. We have to tie these loose ends up."

"Okay, well let's jump right in. We have 4 months left on the lease. I cannot afford to buy you out of it. It's a one-bedroom so I don't have the option to sublet your half to anyone else," I said

"Well, I didn't think you'd stay in it."

"What did you think I'd do?"

"I thought you'd just move out. I suggest we break the lease and move out."

"Well, *we* could have done that but you moved out last week, remember?"

"I know, and with good reason, but I didn't think you would want to stay either."

"Tyler, you don't leave me a choice but to stay. We can't just abandon the place and end up messing up both of our credits."

"I don't plan to just abandon it. I think we should put in a notice to break the lease."

"Tyler, that's going to be a waste of money. We may as well stay until the lease ends," I said.

"Stay? I'm not staying there anymore. Why would I pay on a place I'm not living in?"

"You didn't *have* to move out, you know. We could have worked this out," I said.

"There is nothing to work out. I think the ship has sailed on working the relationship out."

"I was referring to our living arrangement. You are always on the road anyway. I mean how much time would you have been here anyway? You are here maybe one week out of a month if that. I could've slept on the sofa if you needed the bed or vice versa. It could have been worked out, and still can actually."

"Nah, I'm good." He looked out the window like he didn't feel the need to talk about it more.

"No, you're not. But I digress. So here are the numbers because I figured you'd come wanting to break the lease, and I actually gave that some thought, but the numbers just don't make sense to do that. So breaking the lease will cost just about as much to do as staying in it. The lease says we have to pay twice the rent amount at move out plus give a 60-day notice. We would have to keep the place for two months and then at move out, pay two more months of rent. It'll literally be the same cost to just not break the lease."

"Okay then, there is no difference in either one then if we will pay the same amount either way, so I say we break the lease," he replied.

"No, you're missing it. If we break the lease early, we still pay the same amount, but then we will be paying someone else rent for two months that we could have saved by just staying here. Breaking the lease is more, dear," I said. I didn't mean to add the dear part on. It's a habit. Tyler sighed, but at what, I could not tell.

"Okay, let me think about it. I just want to be done with it all."

"Well, we have the joint account and our savings account, and you know we bought that vacation club thing together."

"We can go to the bank to dissolve the accounts," he said.

"We need to keep the joint active until we have moved out. Bills are still set up to come out of there." He didn't say anything. I caught him staring off again. I turned to look to see what he was staring at. It was too young guys, maybe about 20 years old, sitting together studying. It was obvious they had strong chemistry. Their body language said they were probably more than friends. I used that as an opportunity to get Tyler to talk about us. "One thing that has always worked with us is our ability to collaborate. We produced a really good documentary because of our ability to work well together, no matter the chaos and no matter the friction. You and I, we were always something else together. I've been raking my brain to try and figure out how we got here. Why does it feel like I'm sitting in arbitration for a divorce with the man I so desperately love? Tyler, why are we not talking about our problems? The elephant has taking up all the space in the room, and yet you and I are sitting here pretending like our backs are not pressed up against the wall due to its overwhelming presence.

Tyler looked at me. I could see the deep well of his emotions in his eyes. He is deep in that way. His passion was always a deep one. You never could really tell what he was feeling or thinking, but you always knew that whatever it was, it was deep and profound and passionate. That's my Tyler. The man I fell in love with.

"You hurt me, Brandon. I never thought in a million years that you would do what you did to me. I mean, shit, I know I messed up too, but you, no you messing up means something different. It meant you stop caring as much. That hurt me. You know, Brandon, you were always one that I could depend on. I had you figured out. *Not my baby, I'd think.* How could you do that to me? You should have sat me down and made me understand the gravity of the situation and how you were feeling. I would have done whatever I needed to do to save us, to save you. It makes my heart hurt to know that someone like Orlando got his hands on you. He is so fucking manipulative. I blamed myself so hard for this. I should have been home more," he said.

I could feel Tyler shaking the table with the vibration of his leg. He was either very nervous or very stressed or a combination of both. What it told me is that he really, really cares about me. He was holding back tears, I could tell. He would not look me in the face but kept staring beyond my shoulder.

"Thank you for sharing your heart with me. I'm so sorry for

hurting you. It was never my intention to hurt you. I love you more than words could ever say. I think I made the mistake of making you my everything. When my parents put me out, I went off to college and found you. You became my day and night, my everything. When you started being away so much, I didn't know how to handle that. I was using you to fill my empty places, things that have been empty since the night I sat on my parent's porch, locked and kicked out for being gay. I thought then that I knew no hurt bigger than what that felt like, but no, this has hurt far worse. I'm not even caught up on you cheating actually. I haven't thought about it much. I'm sure I feel something for it though. I've been more caught up on the idea that you were abandoning me. That hurt me to my soul. All I could think about is when my mom would not defend me when my dad put me out. How they stopped talking to me for years because they could not handle that I am gay. You took me back to that type of hurt. You made me feel abandoned. You were supposed to love me," I said with tears in my eyes.

"All I can say to that is that I'm sorry. It has never been my intent to make you feel what you felt from your parents. I know how it took you years of therapy to get through that. I hate myself for taking you back to that place. I was just so hurt. I wanted you to feel the same hurt that I felt. I should not have abandoned you. For that, I am deeply and truly sorry. I love you. I know that things are different, now. I don't want to keep hurting you. I have to be honest with you, Brandon. I am not what you need right now. I'm still working on trying to be okay with myself, my sexuality, my parents... it's just a whole lot that I am dealing with. I think the reason why I stayed away on so many assignments was that I was so disconnected from myself that I could not give you what I did not have access to. You wanted me and I don't even know who that person is. We both are wrestling with our traumas and they are stopping us from showing up in the way we need to," he said.

"I understand. I wish you would have talked to me about how you were feeling. It would have not made me feel so alone so much. You know of all people that I understand what you are going through. I was there for you when you first started going through this. Honestly, I thought you had gotten over it once we finished shooting *The Bow*. How naive of me to assume that it was over with just like that. I should have paid more attention to you. Here I am being selfish because I'm thinking you aren't paying me enough attention," I said.

"I don't think it's anyone's fault. I think we are facing what we are supposed to face right now in our journey together. This is supposed to make us grow." Tyler looked me in the eyes and I could see his sincerity. I loved to see these vulnerable moments with him because oftentimes, he was so guarded and kept with his emotions. He was finally letting me in again like he used to do when we were in college.

"What does this mean for us?" I asked. I looked down as if I was afraid of what his answer would end up being.

"I don't know, Brandon. What I do know is that I need to get myself together. It has been proven that I am not in a place to give you the type of affection that you need. I can be selfless and mature enough to admit that to you, even if it means losing you," he said.

I found myself frozen and I tried to hold back the emptiness I felt in the pit of my stomach from hearing him reaffirm again that he thinks we should end the relationship. A tear rolled down my face.

"I'm sorry, Brandon."

I rubbed my face. "It's okay, Tyler. I think I understand. I mean, I guess I have no choice but to understand," I said with a little laugh. "I will always, always love you." He began to cry. It looked like it hit him like a ton of bricks. I reached over to grab his hand and there we sat, both crying, our hearts shattering into the pieces that we struggled to put together when we first met. Oh, how we had spent years gluing each other's brokenness only to discover that we had both been living a lie. I guess we're down to our last cry. That would be the way Brian McKnight would capitalize off of our despair if he were there to witness our broken hearts.

Twenty-Seven

Chapter 27

W e decided to keep the apartment until the lease ended since Tyler was on a ridged assignment schedule in DC to cover presidential hopefuls, he would hardly be home. It just didn't make sense to go through the rigmarole of breaking the lease and finding someplace else to go. It'd been a waste of money. He said he had moved his stuff into storage. He moved a few of his clothes back in. It was a little hard having him around knowing that we were broken up, but I did appreciate us being able to be friends at that moment. After all, that was how we started out. We agreed to not date around each other. The hurt to see him dating someone would be real for me. I'm sure the same for him as well especially if it was Orlando that I chose to date officially. He would want to hear or see nothing of it. Tyler was flying back out in the afternoon and Alec was to be land the next day. I couldn't wait to see my best friend. That night,

I had a date with Orlando. I only told Tyler I was going out. He need not know the details.

Orlando told me he was cooking up one of his fancy meals. I took an Uber to his house. I was astonished at how big the house he bought is. I had been to it a couple of times already. I bet he thought he was going to get me to come live in it with him, but he had another thing coming. I didn't want to be tied down like that. I needed to get Tyler out of my system and after 5 years of dating and 5 years of friendship where I secretly dated him in my head, it was going to take a while to get over him.

Orlando's community had a guard at the front that. The community was so guarded it would appear as if you had to give a blood sample to get access to it, and then, Orlando's property also had a gate on it. All of that damn security. It usually took ten minutes to get to his door when anyone came to visit him due to all of the security checkpoints. The Uber pulled up and he was amazed at the neighborhood.

"Man you must be coming to visit a ballplayer or something. This shit is dope."

"Nah, just my stupid boyfriend," I said as I cut my eyes and got out.

Did I call Orlando my boyfriend? I guess he was becoming something of the sort. He may as well be. The sex with him hadn't really stopped. He had become my regular since we first started months ago. His house definitely proved Orlando was doing well for himself. The house was quaint, outside of the city but close enough to get to the main action if need be. It had an old country feel to it, but it wasn't old. It sat on a rather large lot with plenty of trees and a roundabout driveway. I wondered how could a therapist afford such lavish things but I remembered he came from wealth and he was a smart businessman. I guess he could afford it. I shouldn't count his money.

"I'm going to have to give you a key," Orlando said when he opened the door.

"Well hello to you too," I said walking in.

"Why you want to give me a key all of a sudden?"

"Because this house is too damn big to be getting up out of my seat and shit to come open the door for you."

"I don't want your house key. I don't need that. The Uber driver thinks your house is dope. I guess you're a ballplayer in his eyes."

"What did you tell him?" Orlando asked.

"Nothing, Just that you're my stupid boyfriend and no ballplayer."

"Boyfriend, hmmm." He was all over me by that point.

"Enough of that, I came to eat. What did you cook?" I asked. I put my jacket down in the study and followed behind him to the kitchen.

"It's a surprise. Come. I want to show you something."

We walked up the stairs which were grandiose and long, extending nearly 30ft up to the second floor of his monstrous palace.

"I figured with all of the stress you've been under that you could use some relaxation so I arranged a little something-something for us." He took me into one of the guest suites, one that he had not been furnished yet.

"So I was up here one day and I got to thinking that I wouldn't mind having a spa, sooo…here's what I did. I ordered some massage tables and set up a little spa ambiance here. I'm testing it out, but tonight, I want you to be the first to try it."

"You don't give good massages, Orlando."

"I know, I know, don't worry, I got that taken care of," he said. We walked into the room and there were blue lights, candles lit, and the sound of a violin. I was shocked to see he had hired a masseuse and a violinist.

"Take off your clothes and put on the robe. You will be treated well. Just relax and enjoy the moment."

"Whatever you say, sir." I was all smiles and I couldn't hide my excitement. I felt myself falling for Orlando. It wasn't just because he was doing what he was doing that night with the dinner and the massage, but it was just the last few months with him, outside of the drama, had actually been really fun and nice and enjoyable.

This was exactly what I needed. I wanted them to relax me well.

"Bring me some Moscato please," I said.

"Sure thing, baby. Is there anything else you need?" He stood with his hands behind his back like a butler, his smile shining.

"No, not right now. I'll be sure to let you know when I want what I came here for."

"The food will be ready by the time they're done."

"I wasn't talking about the food," I said with a smile. Orlando blushed and walked away. He seems to be so different now. I liked seeing him in love. It's like he becomes this vulnerable sweet guy and that tough macho man that he likes to display on the outside becomes no more. At any rate, I'm glad to be here with him in spite of my broken heart. I do consider that I am probably on the rebound big time. But does it mean I'm on the rebound if Orlando and I have a history? Hmmm, that's a story for another interview.

I laid on my stomach on the massage table with my face down looking at the floor. I could smell the sweet aroma of lavender, rose, and jasmine. The violinist was playing a calming tune. The masseuse began to massage my back. It felt so good and was so needed. I found my mind drifting away as I thought about Tyler and all of the good times we had shared. I thought about that time we took a road trip to Montana, just for the hell of it. We were always venturing off to unknown places. That was the explorer in us. We were always venturing off together. Ever since our first road trip to shoot our documentary, we had been growing in our love nonstop. I don't know how we ended up as we had become. We were such good friends. I'd like to believe that beyond the heartbreak and disappointments that we've experienced, we were still good friends.

The masseuse rubbed my temples and then the base of my neck. It felt really good. My thoughts took me off into a relaxing sleep. The next thing I remembered is being awakened by Orlando announcing that dinner was ready and we needed to move down to the dining room. I was still laying on the table with nothing but my towel wrapped around me. It was just us in the room.

"Where is the masseuse?" I asked.

"He left a little while ago. You were resting so peacefully, I didn't want to wake you."

"How long was I asleep?"

"Just a half an hour after he was done," Orlando said. "Let's go eat. He has good hands doesn't he?"

"Yes, he does."

"I should know" Orlando had a sly smile on his face

"Did you sleep with him already? You are just too much," I

said.

"Of course not! What kind of whore do you take me to be? He laughed.

"Never know with you." The massage really hit the spot for me because I had been so tense lately. I had to be honest with myself about how I've been feeling. I didn't feel like I had any resolve as it concerned Tyler. I understood that we were broken up, but it just didn't seem real to me.

We made it down the massive spiraled stairs. I was still amazed at how lovely his house was. I'd never been in anything like it.

"Did you decorate this yourself?" I asked.

"That's so funny because I think you asked me that when we first met when you saw my condo for the first time. No, this time I didn't do the decorating. I don't have time for that. It's so much planning that goes into it. I hired someone to stage the place for me. How do you like it?" He asked.

"It looks really good. It's so proper and elegant. It's so… you."

"Thank you, babe. That reminds me…I wanted to show you something."

Orlando led me by the hand to a room that seemed to be tucked away out of plain sight.

"I told you that this is a home that I want to be in with the one that I want to spend my life with. Look in here."

He turned on the lights and to my surprise, it was a writer's room, complete with a desk, bookshelves filled with books, and all types of neat things pertaining to journalism.

"I did this for you."

I cupped my hand over my mouth. I was speechless. I slowly walked in and stood in the middle and turned around in circles.

"Wow, I don't know what to say."

"Well, please say you like it."

"I do. I really do. I think we should talk about something." I looked at him.

"Oh boy. What did I do wrong? Is it too much?"

"No nothing like that. I think it's a nice gesture, but it makes me realize we need to have a conversation about us."

"Okay, we can do that. Let's go do that over dinner. It's getting cold."

"Okay," I said. I could feel my heart warming up and I was really feeling this experience with Orlando. I had not thought about his HIV status or the things that happened with us, and for the first time that day, I was not thinking about Tyler.

Twenty-Eight

Chapter 28

"I had the chef throw some pork chops on the grill. I hope you like them," Orlando said.

We took our seats in the dining room. It was much bigger than the one from his condo. I remembered wondering why he needed a table that seated eight people at the condo five years ago and yet again, I still didn't see why he needed all those seats like he had the Brady Bunch living with him. Not to mention, I couldn't see how he could afford a chef either.

"I'm sure I will enjoy them." We said grace and begin to eat. It was silent at first as I looked around the room while eating. The room was oval-shaped and it had large floor-to-ceiling windows. The ceilings were maybe about 20ft tall in the shape of a dome. He had ivory drapes that swept the floor with little accents of baby blue here and there. It was a lovely room, as much of the rest of the massive house.

"Orlando, this house is fucking huge. How can you afford

something like this, plus that high-end condo?" I asked. So much for me not counting his money, but I really did want to know. In my limited exposure to people that are doing well financially, I just couldn't fathom how he could afford that type of stuff.

"I sell weed," he said. He didn't laugh or flinch. I almost took him seriously until he finally busted out into laughter.

"I'm just playing. I do well with my practice. But also, Brandon, my mom and dad are high-end realtors and that's how the condo comes into play. They also taught me early on how to invest. So I have dabbled with my money in the stock market and cryptocurrency. Let's just say I've struck out lucky in the past couple of years with that. I'm no Trumper, but I have to say I appreciate that stock market though," he said.

"You mean the one President Obama left him?" I asked rhetorically. He just looked at me and continued as if I didn't say anything.

"As for my condo, my parents bought it in hopes of flipping it back in 2013. It hit the market for $755,000. Today it would sell for twice that. I was so in love with that apartment when I first saw the views from it. I begged and begged them to let me stay in it. I argued they wouldn't have to pay room and board with Georgia State, but they would never do it. When I graduated with my master's, they gifted it to me by letting me live in it and pay half of the mortgage in the form of rent while they pay the other half. So I understand your suspicion because I would wonder the same thing, how could anyone who isn't a baller afford that condo on a professional salary."

"I see now. Not everyone comes from wealth. Must be nice," I said sarcastically, although he glazed over my comments as if he didn't hear me and continued with his spill again. He was off on a tangent and I wondered if the disinterested look on my face gave him the hint.

"So you don't own the condo, your parents do?" I added with a humdrum voice.

"No, I don't," he said.

"Well, why not? I mean you obviously can afford it now, and then you wouldn't have to go buy a house somewhere else, right?" I asked.

"Not exactly. It's a business reason behind it. My mom and dad would have otherwise rented that condo to someone else which allows them to do some write-offs and things. If I became part owner and then paid the mortgage as an owner then that would have changed the game a little. It's better I pay them rent, which actually is just paying the mortgage on a home that I'm going to inherit anyway, but for them, they can take advantage of the business things that come with that arrangement." Orlando continued on his tangent.

"So now, I want a house. I actually wanted to live in Sandy Springs, you know, get a house there, but a house like this there would have easily been over a million dollars on its own, and I can't afford that and keep the condo. I wanted a single-family house but to my liking. I wanted one similar to what I grew up in. I grew up in Alpharetta, north of Atlanta. So I wanted to live close enough to the city, but far enough away to enjoy a quiet suburban feel. This does it for me. Any type of condo with a couple of bedrooms and baths in the city is going to pretty much cost way more than a much larger house that's outside of the perimeter. We could have sold the condo in Buckhead and used the equity as a down payment for a house in Sandy Springs for myself, but I like the convenience of having living space in the same building as my practice. Besides that, now we can put it on Airbnb and make money off it, possibly pay most of the mortgage by doing that," he said.

"Sounds like you have a strong strategy as it concerns the two living spaces. I guess from the outside it just looks like you are rolling in money, but I see the investment strategy behind it. It makes good sense," I said. I looked down at my plate and stirred over my food with my fork, hoping he'd change the subject or something. He was starting to ramble on and on and my attention span was fleeting. Although I know I was the one that incited it.

"You look like you have a whole lot on your mind? Let's talk about it." Orlando said.

"Yeah, I'd be lying if I said I didn't have a whole lot on my mind."

"You still thinking about Tyler, huh?" He asked.

"Yeah, I have been a lot lately. It's like I just can't get past how we are now. It seems surreal."

"You're grieving the loss. You're in a state of shock and it's probably heading on into some denial really soon," he said. Now that he wasn't talking about that damn condo, he had begun to focus on finishing his food.

"I don't want to be consumed by any of this," I said.

"You don't have to be. You can manage this."

"Thanks. How do I do that?"

"You do that by moving on with your life. You allow yourself to feel the hurt when you need to, but don't dwell on it. Also, allow yourself to rediscover yourself," he said.

"I just don't know. Tyler has been my life for so long now. Even you said you knew we were meant for each other. If that's the case, then why are we broken up. I just don't understand it," I said looking off into the distance behind Orlando. I felt like breaking down into tears, but I fought it.

"This happens all the time. You did nothing wrong. And yes, at the time, I did believe you two were meant to be together, and you two got together. Nothing went wrong. It went just as planned, but you have to be able to know when to move on if it's meant to move on," he said. I didn't respond. I just looked away.

"I suppose so. I wonder what would be today if I had chosen you back then instead of Tyler?" I said.

"You'd probably end up cheating on me with Tyler," he said.

"I don't know about that. I don't know if you would have become so disassociated with me the way he has," I replied. He looked puzzled. For a moment I did consider the what-ifs. Why didn't I choose Orlando? I never had really given that much thought. If I had to think of a reason why I'd say it was because Tyler was familiar. Taking on Orlando would have meant new things that perhaps I was not ready to manage.

"Why do you look puzzled?" I asked.

"I was wondering, do you ever regret not picking me over Tyler?" He asked.

"I wouldn't say I regret it. I appreciate all that I've shared with Tyler up until this moment. Even the bad parts. But I do consider why I chose him and not you. Tyler was DL at the moment. It was a gamble choosing him. You were already out. I don't know why I did not choose you," I replied. He looked at me intently like he does when he's in his therapist zone.

"You want to know what I think? Of course, you do. So here's what I think," He proceeded without waiting for an answer. I smiled a little because that was just how his personality was.

"I think Tyler represented something for you. Sure, it was a gamble at the time, and you put all of your trust into Tyler because he was so familiar. You've been hurt a lot since you were a kid by your peers. You've been hurt by people that weren't close to you but you, because of how you are, still expect the best out of people. When they didn't give you that, and I'm talking about your peers in grade school, you stop trusting. But, at the same time, you still looked for ways for people to love you anyway. You chose Tyler because he was safe. I wasn't a safe option. I could hurt you. You could not predict me. You could predict Tyler. Not only that, Tyler, being the trade that he was at the time, represented the straight boys that you were afraid of getting close to because it was straight boys that always made you feel less than a man yourself. And lastly…Are you ready?" He asked.

"Yes," I replied.

"Being with me meant fully embracing your sexuality without looking back. Don't get me wrong, at the time I met you, you were definitely way more comfortable with your sexuality than Tyler was. Being with me would have meant finally facing it head-on and for years, you had not wanted to do that. You were using ministry to not have to do that. Then you chose Tyler so you could ease into who you are today. You have a lot of traumas to work through or your next relationship is going to fall apart. Relationships come to show us our shit."

He concluded by picking up his fork and taking a bit out of his food. He ate as if he didn't just read me like Iyanla Vanzant. He made some valid points, many that I'd have to go and meditate on my own about and see if I could come to the same conclusion.

"You're right, I need to focus on myself for a while. That makes me want to talk about you and me. I don't know if we should be building out a relationship like it seems we have been doing lately."

"Oh, you think we are building out a relationship?" He asked with potatoes in his mouth.

"Yes, don't you?" I asked.

"I feel like we are just being natural with each other. You know I have been sweet on you since the first day I met you. Nothing has changed for me. Are we in a relationship right now, I don't know? I don't really think about it that much. I just enjoy our time together and let us happen organically. I'd say let's not confuse things with expectations and titles. Because like I just said, you need to heal some of your past still. Hell, we both do," he said.

"So you're saying we should have an open relationship?" I asked. He put down his fork and knife and looked at me in the eyes. It felt like time stood still and if there were people in the room, they would have stopped and looked our way to hear what he was about to say. I noticed how he was able to shift the energy in a room like that often. His presence was just that powerful.

"No, I'm not saying anything like that. I'm saying why have so many expectations of what we should be or are right now especially with what you are going through. You need time to heal and time to manage your break-up." After he said that, it seemed like time picked back up and everything began moving around again even though no one else was in the room with us.

"I'm just all confused. I want to be with you, and yes I still love Tyler and I know that's problematic. I can't help but think you want to be able to date other people. And what about your HIV status. I don't feel like you truly understand how I felt about you lying to me about that," I said. He paused his eating again with a look of dismay. Then he smiled at me.

"You showed me quite well enough how you felt about that, and I believed it."

"Well as long as you know." I smiled with a look of contentment. Somehow, that's what I needed from him all along.

"I know and again, I'm sorry. I should not have hidden that from you."

"That honestly made me feel like I don't know you at all. I don't know how to feel about you hiding something so intimate about yourself from me, but yet say you have feelings for me."

"Sharing your status is not something that really comes easy. I was afraid to tell you but I must make you understand that I had no ill-will towards you about that. I've become quite used to being positive and being healthy on my meds. I really don't think about it at all. It's something that has never been a problem for me, so it's easy for me not to think about it," he said.

"How many people have you not disclosed it to?" I asked.

"I don't know. I mean...ok...so before I got on meds, I would. When I became undetectable, I begin to rethink it. I don't normally share it because I'm undetectable. I can't transmit it to anyone. There is no risk. I figure why complicate things with someone that's just a one-night stand."

I put my head in my hands and said, "Oh this is so much

to deal with. That's the part I'm struggling with about that whole HIV thing, the idea that you are okay with sleeping with someone and not telling them your status."

"I get your concern, really, I do. But it's not so black and white like you are seeing it. People are so ignorant about HIV nowadays that as soon as you say you have it, they start to treat you very differently. If I just want to get some good sex because I'm horny, I don't have time or the energy to deal with all of the back and forth and having to educate someone from the gay community who should already know for themselves what HIV is about and the risk or lack thereof for those who are on treatment."

"Wow," I said with an aggravated tone.

"C'mon babe. Listen, I don't want to argue about this. I do understand how you feel about it. It was not my intention to hide that from you. Honestly, it's just the behavior I was accustomed to because I'm single, and yes I have encounters with people that I don't have any other type of relationship with outside of sex. I don't owe them my HIV status when I'm maintaining my undetectable viral load. If they are having hookups and one-night stands, it's more on them to take responsibility for their own health. They have prep and condoms to protect them from HIV.

"So you're saying because I am more than sex to you, you felt I should know the truth?"

"Yes which is why I told you the truth, albeit two months later," he said.

"That's still some bullshit and you were wrong," I replied.

"And I agree with you. I've said that countless times. I'm not sure what more you want me to say, Brandon."

"Okay, so it sounds like you have sexual encounters here

and there, which I guess I understand by you being a single man. Are you on Jack'd or Grindr or any other apps like that?"

"Yes I am," he replied.

"How often are you meeting up with people from there?" I asked.

"Not often. I work too much for hookups and honestly since you've been in the picture, you've been my regular sexual partner," he said.

"Have there been others while you and I have been sexual?"

"Yes, I have one guy that was a bit of a regular for me," he said.

"Will he remain a regular?" I asked.

"If you don't want him to be then, no," he answered.

"Hmm. Okay, well…what about the long-distance guy that you told me about? Are you still talking to him?" I think I can deal with you getting your rocks off with randoms here and there since we are not making this exclusive, but I don't think I want you building something meaningful with someone else," I said.

"I can respect that, but you must know that he and I were already building for quite some time before you came back into the picture. We haven't met in person yet. He is actually coming to town this weekend."

"Oh really, so you two could actually end up hitting it off, and boom you blow me off right along with it," I said. I sighed in more aggravation. This shit just gets richer and richer with him. I don't know if I have the mental headspace to deal with casually dating a guy who is also casually dating someone else and sleeping around.

"It's a possibility that we would have ended up in a relation-ship," he replied.

"Would have?" I asked.

"Yes, we have been steady for a while. He's consistent and you know I like that, but I am not really into him like I am into you. I mean he's a cute guy, nice - but the chemistry with him is not the same. It's something I tolerate but it's not something I gravitate towards either," he said.

"Sooo, let's say he were to move here? Who would you try to woo the most?" I asked.

"That sounds like you think I'd woo you and him at the same time," Orlando said.

"Well, isn't that what you have been doing lately? You know you are a sweet-talking player. You said so yourself. I shouldn't even believe much of your promises right now. I can really believe that you have been laying it on thick with him all the while doing the same with me."

"I suppose that is what I have been doing, but not in the way you are painting it though, Brandon."

"Right," I said. "So what's his name, where is he from?"

"He's from Mobile. He is supposed to be here tomorrow," Orlando said.

I felt my heart skip a beat. It couldn't be, it wouldn't be... Oh God I hoped it wasn't...

Twenty-Nine

Chapter 29

I peeped my eyes up at him from looking down at my plate with a piece of pork chop in my mouth. He looked confused a little as he gazed into my eyes. He was so perceptive so he was able to instantly tell that my vibe had changed.

"What's wrong, boo?"

"Nothing at all," I lied. I didn't know how to respond to what I was thinking could be the case that Orlando had been dating Alec. Shit! It all makes sense now. Alec has been raving and going on and on about his well-to-do fancy beau from Atlanta. It has to be Orlando. Shit, shit shit shit shit shit!

"Nah, you feeling some type of way about me dating someone else for more than sex aren't you?" He asked. Now he was twirling his fork around in his potatoes.

"Now did I say that, Orlando? I could care less about you dating someone else. We aren't together, remember?" I was really trying to play it off that I was suspicious about him possibly dating Alec. Who the fuck was I kidding? It had to be Alec. It's too obvious. My dilemma was not knowing how I want to handle it. Alec is my best friend, but Orlando had been a love interest of mine for many years. Would it be selfish for me to want him because I had him first?

"Lies you tell," he said.

I needed to find out for sure who this guy from Mobile was that he had been dating. I wondered should I ask him what is his name? That would have been the best way to know for sure. I was afraid the name Alec will come out and I'd have to try to pretend like I wasn't feeling some serious internal conflict about it. And then, if I told him that Alec was my best friend, what would Orlando do? Would he cut it off with Alec and hurt him? I didn't want that for Alec. Oh boy, it was a fucked-up situation. It seems like fucked-up situations had just been following me around a lot.

"How did you meet him?" I asked. I was truly interested, but I wanted to get this guy's name in a roundabout way, or at minimal find out more about him.

"I met him at a convention for a church that I went to in Mobile. He was there. He was quite charismatic with his preaching gift. I must admit I was attracted to that. So later, I saw him in a Facebook group and we connected from there," he said.

"So he's a preacher?" I asked.

"Yeah but he works a regular job."

"A regular job? What does that mean? He's beneath you because he works a regular job?"

"That is not what I said, mister. I mean he doesn't do ministry full-time. He's a manager at Walmart," Orlando replied.

Oh, shit shit shit shit shit shit. It is Alec! I screamed inside.

"You sure are asking a lot of questions for somebody that doesn't care," he added. That was my perfect opportunity to be honest about my suspicion which seemingly had just been confirmed, but I guess I couldn't quite do that. I didn't know why. I really liked Orlando. It was like one thing after another continued to make it seem like being with him was so forbidden. First I started off cheating on Tyler with him and now staying with him meant betraying my best friend.

"It's nothing, honestly," I lied. I felt a bit of shame and I tried my best to hide the energy of it. He seemed to not really believe me much.

"Hmmm. Okay, well if you say so. You sure you are okay. You seem preoccupied all of a sudden." He stared at me like he was trying to read my body language. I know that's a thing therapists do. I tried to through him off my scent though. It wasn't working.

"I'm not. It's just..." I took a sigh and looked up at the dome ceiling where I noticed he had a mural of angels painted. It was beautiful and they looked so innocent and pure. It was at that moment I felt my conscience get the best of me. I can't lie to him about this. It would surely destroy any changes that I would have had with him later, and there would be no way that I could hide my friendship with Alec away from him forever. He would have definitely found out eventually.

"It's just what?" Orlando asked. He seemed concerned. He has a way where he peers over the rim of his glasses to focus on his subject. It's so shrink-like of him.

"Let me be honest. I know this is going to be a bombshell for you, well for us. I don't know how we will need to handle it. I do believe I know who you are talking about. His name is Alec, isn't it? He's my best friend. He and his family took me in when my dad put me out the house in high school." Orlando had a blank look on his face. He didn't say anything for a short while. I could not tell if he was upset, shocked, sad, or what. "Well, what do you have to say?" I asked.

"I'm just…wow…I'm completely lost for words right now. I can't believe this. What are the odds…I mean…oh my god… this is not good. What do we do?" He asked.

"I don't know. It's not really anything for you to do or decide on. I'm the one that has to make the decision on what to do. He's *my* best friend."

"Yes, but he's my friend too, well a little more."

"How do you feel about him, then?"

"Does that really matter? You should tell him the truth, Brandon. I mean…you *are* going to tell him the truth, right?"

"I dunno, I—"

"Brandon?" Orlando said with a look of concern on his face. "This is not like you. I mean I get it. I know that we have invested a lot of time in each other, but c'mon now. This is not right and definitely not like you to want to hide this from him," Orlando said.

"I've been cheating on the love of my life, well who I thought was the love of my life, for months with you. Don't purport to know what I'm capable of," I said. I threw my napkin on the table and turned towards the window. I was frustrated by now, but not at him, at the situation.

"I'm sorry. I'm just saying. The Brandon I met would never have cheated with me and he would have never considered trading his best friend for a fling," he said. I turned back to face him with a look of anger.

"You are a piece of work, Orlando. In one sentence you get all self-righteous on me and then turn around and degrade what we have become at the same time. I gotta go. Whatever happened to, *this is how we do it at my level*" I proceeded to get up from the table. I tried to avoid looking at Orlando. Deep down I knew he was probably right. He seemed worried that I was getting up to leave. He quickly got up to grab my hand.

"No, don't. Listen, you can't keep running away every time we have to talk about something difficult," he said.

"That's because this particular issue is very difficult. I actually think I love you, Orlando. But, I love Alec too. He was there for me during the lowest place of my life," I said and started to cry.

"Then sit him down and tell him the truth. Yes, it may hurt him, but it'd be better than him finding out that you knew and did not tell him," He said.

"You don't know Alec as I do. He is going to cuss me slam out, and besides, we have already had a heated discussion once recently. It's one of those things friends do, We just needed space but I don't think we are necessarily in a bad place because we've since talked and he's planning to visit. Once he finds this out though, we for sure will be on ice," I said amidst the tears.

"He won't be mad, not if you be honest with him. How about we tell him together."

"So what does that mean? How is that going to look? *Oh hey, Alec, I think you're dating the guy I've been screwing around with, oh and by the way, he's in the other room. Here he is, he now wants to break up with you.* Yeah, that shit will go really smooth," I said. I was pacing around the room at this point. My appetite was gone and our half-eaten plates sat listening in on the conversation as if they couldn't wait to hear what our plan would end up becoming.

"I am sure there is a tactful way to do this. Do you think this should be done before he even gets here? I think I'd be pretty pissed if I knew that you knew a whole day prior and waited until I got here to say something. I say give him the option to cancel his trip if that's what he wants to do for his own emotional sake," Orlando said.

"I guess this is why you are the psychologist in this outfit," I said. I walked over to him and hugged him and kissed him. I felt myself falling in love, and I knew that was a bad thing. It's too soon and I shouldn't be. Orlando sat quietly. He stared out into the open of the dining room.

"What are you thinking about?" I asked.

"Alec," he said. I could feel somberness in the room. Is it bad that it seemed he was more troubled than I was at that moment? Sure I was worried about hurting Alec, but it seemed Orlando was more worried than he initially showed. I thought for a moment if perhaps he did have some feelings for Alec.

Thirty

Chapter 30

I stayed over at Orlando's house that night. I didn't sleep too well. Orlando told me the next morning that I tossed and turned the whole night. I had so much on my mind. Alec was expected to fly in that evening. I needed to call him and let him know the truth. I didn't know why I was so nervous to do this. It's wasn't like I actually knew. I just found out myself. I know what the conflict is. I am not sure how to tell Alec that I wanted to continue seeing Orlando. I took a deep breath. On my drive back to my apartment, I thought back on how Alec's face seemed to light up when he first told me about his relationship. I could tell that he was in love or close to it. Orlando said to just tell him the truth. I don't know if I can do that. I knew it would devastate Alec. All of these thoughts raced through my thoughts as I took an Uber back home. By the time I got back home to my apartment, I was expecting to walk in to see Tyler packing up to leave out for DC. He wasn't there. I wondered had he left already. I thought maybe he would have let me know before he left, but I quickly remembered that he didn't have a reason to do that now. The thought of that hurt a little. I was an emotional mess. I braced myself to call Alec. I walked to the bedroom and shut the door. I don't know why when there was no one else with me. I guess the horror and anxiety on what I was about to do was that bad.

I sat on the edge of the bed. I had my phone open with Alec's contact positioned to dial. "Here goes nothing," I said aloud. I started the call. The ringing seemed like the longest ever. A part of me wished he wouldn't pick up, but the gravity of this situation needed for him to pick up. This conversation would be ten times worse if I had to have it after he got to Atlanta.

"Hello," I heard his cheery voice.

"Hey friend. What are you up to?"

"Just running some last-minute errands before I leave for my flight. I was going to call you later this afternoon just to make sure we are still good for our visit," he said.

"Of course, we are. I'm excited to see you too."

"How is it going for you up there? How you hanging?"

"Well, I do have a lot to catch you up with as it concerns Tyler and me, but first I have something to discuss with you."

"Okay, what about?" He asked.

"It's deep. I think you better take a seat for this one."

"Oh…okay. Now you have me worried."

"I don't want you to be, but this is serious though. So, I found out something last night. The guy that I was seeing behind Tyler's back is the guy you have been talking to. I had no idea until last night when he was talking about you. I just feel awful about this." I heard the line get silent. I wondered what was running through his mind after hearing that. I got up from the bed and began to pace the floor in front of the bed.

"This can't be the case. Are you sure?"

"Yes, Alec, I am sure. He and I were having dinner last night and that's how I found out. I had no idea he was even dating someone long-distance," I said.

"Wait, this doesn't make any sense. I thought that dude's name was Orlando. My dude's name is Londell, Brandon," Alec said.

"Yes, but turns out Londell is Orlando's middle name. He goes by Orlando up here in Atlanta. You mean you never knew what his full name is?" I asked.

"He never told me his full name. I just assumed it was just Londell McIntyre," he said.

"How could you not know his full name? You mean you never looked him up online, looked at his website? What the hell, Alec? We could have pieced this together long before now," I said. Alec sucked his teeth and responded sharply.

"First off, it doesn't seem like you were all that aware of his full name either. And besides, I don't be thinking about all of that. This job works me 50-plus hours a week and I have church. I don't chase after no man like that and you know that," he said.

I took a seat on my bed again. I couldn't tell yet how he was really taking the news. I think he was still in a state of shock. "So, how you feel about this?" I asked.

"I don't know. This is a lot, but thank you for saying something to me so I don't come up there looking like an ass. To think his ass didn't even tell me. And you said y'all found this out last night?" He asked.

"Yes, at dinner."

"Wait! So both of you knew and neither one of you told me soon after? Brandon…what the fuck man?" He shouted.

"I know…I know. I wrestled with how to tell you this," I said.

"Nah, I believe I know exactly why. You probably fucked him last night after you knew he was talking to me, didn't you?" He asked.

"Does that really matter, Alex?" I replied.

"Yes, the fuck it does matter. It matters a lot. You should have called and told me immediately! And Londell doesn't even suppose to be dating other people. He's only allowed to have sex so you see, he could not possibly be taking you serious at all. You're nothing but a lay for him. I'm the one he wants!" Alec shouted.

"Seriously, Alec. Are you really going to do that? Are you going to be that guy to fight over a man? Look, let's not do fighting again," I said.

"I'm not fighting. I'm just telling you what's real. I'll deal with Londell, oh I mean Orlando as you call him, when I talk to him. The truth is he and I are together. I don't know what it is that you and him got going on but it's nothing, I'm sure of it. It won't be a fight if you just walk it back," he said.

I didn't know how to respond to Alec I was really trying not to get into a fight with him, but I do need to assert myself and let him know Orlando and I are not what he thinks we are. We are way more than that. Honestly, I'm not that prepared to just walk away from him and just let Alec have him. I don't know what Orlando tells him, but I don't get the vibe that he is all that into Alec, at least not the way that he's into me.

"Alec, I'm really not interested in having a big back and forth. I called you because I felt you should know the truth especially with you coming up here tonight. Now the slick comments are really not called for. We can talk about this like the friends that we are and come to an understanding about what is going on, other than that, I'm not interested in anything else." I said.

"You are interested in my man, sis! How else am I supposed to feel right now, Brandon? You are sitting here telling me that you've been fucking the man I'm in love with and have been for some time now. Have you forgotten he and I have been talking for months now?"

"Alec! I didn't know he was the guy you were talking to!" I said.

"But you knew last night and just now telling me today after you done probably had his dick in your mouth. As far as I'm concerned that's gritty, grimy shit! Now I see why Tyler left your ass. You have become an old dirty dusty ho! Just sleep with whoever because, 'oh my man ain't home enough, he's this he's that.' If Tyler did cheat on you it's probably because you pushed him to do it!" He shouted.

Okay, Alec had gone too far. Friend or no friend- he crossed the line with that.

"You know what Alec, I'm going to let you have that. I just thought to tell you the truth. I could've kept the shit quiet and not told you a damn thing. I could've let you come up here and have you sitting around thinking Orlando is just yours only. I'm done with it. You do what you want with the truth you now know. I'll talk to you later," I said.

I hung up the phone and let out a loud scream. I can't believe he reacted like that. And to say the things he said. I was speechless. I felt like he had better not bring his ass up to Atlanta if he knew what was good for him. Admittedly, I was in my feelings and didn't mean any of my aggression, but he was out of line with his attacks.

I went out on the balcony and got fresh air. The wind was breezy and the birds were chirping. At least there was happiness in something living. I wanted to call Orlando and let him know what happened, but I figured he may be with a client. I was still holding my phone from the interaction with Alec. "I need someone to talk to," I said. Tyler would normally be the one that I'd call and get advice from on something as serious as this, but I couldn't call him and tell him that Orlando of all people was seeing Alec and now Alec was pissed with me about it. Which I didn't really understand why. I mean...it's not like I did anything. And from the way it sounds, Orlando had free reign to have sex with other people. My plans for today were all jacked up now. I was supposed to go do some shopping and prepare for Alec's arrival. I didn't even know if he was still coming, and as mad as he was, I don't even think it'd been a good idea for him to still come.

I leaned on the balcony and stared down. My balcony faced W Peachtree Street. At the time of day it was, there was nothing but bumper-to-bumper traffic, which actually occurred all times of the day. My phone began to buzz and it startled me because I was so lost in my thoughts. It was Orlando.

"Hey, what are you doing? Are you good?" He asked.

"I take it you've heard from Alec today," I said.

"Yeah, he called me. He was pretty mad and he's mad at you, but not as mad as he is at me. I think he's mad at me the most and he took it out on you. He's heartbroken."

"He said horrible things to me. I was shocked. He ticked me off so I just cut the call short because he wasn't trying to hear rationality," I said.

"Well can you blame him? He's hurt. I think he will be fine. I don't think he was mad at you, just mad at the situation," Orlando said.

"Fuck that. You didn't hear what he said to me. It was not called for. He hit below the belt, talking about Tyler cheating on me was my fault. That shit hurt," I said.

"He will apologize," Orlando said.

"He thinks that you only want me for sex and that he is your real choice. You sure seem calm about this as if he didn't give you the business too. How did your conversation with him go? What was your response to him?" I asked.

"I told him I knew he was going to call. He immediately hurled some insults to me which included you. Once I got him to calm down, we were able to talk amicably. I told him I was sorry this happened. He now knows that you and I have a history together. I owned my part in it and I was not supposed to catch feelings, which I did tell you that this was really just supposed to be sex for me, but you know, things happen," he said.

I rolled my eyes. He always has some smooth shit to say. I didn't have the energy to sort through it.

"Okay, so what's the outcome?" I asked.

"What do you mean?"

"I mean what is his expectation. Did you promise him the world and shit or did you tell him the whole truth?"

"What's the whole truth, Brandon?" Orlando asked.

"Look, don't fuck with me! You know what I'm talking about. Listen, Alec isn't the only one hurt in this situation. I am too. I was just as hurt finding all of this out last night," I said.

"You don't have anything to worry about. Alec said he would make this easy for all of us by just stepping back. He said he doesn't feel he can compete with you. That's why I think he sees that you and I have a deeper history than he and I do," Orlando said.

"To me, that sounds like he's ending his friendship with me too," I said. I felt my eyes tear up. I just continued to look over the balcony at the cars driving by down below as I put my head down on the balcony railing with my face buried into the angle of my elbow.

"I know baby, I'm so sorry this is happening. I wish I could change it. I honestly had no idea he was your best friend. Funny how the universe is," he said.

"Did he say he was still coming to visit?" I asked.

"I took what he said about stepping back to mean that he would not come to Atlanta tonight," Orlando said.

"Do you think I should reach back out to him?" I asked.

"I don't know. You did say you ended the call on him. I think you both definitely should talk. You are his friend and he is yours. You are both going through a tough ordeal, and I think you could use each other right now," Orlando said.

"Why do you seem so damn calm about all of this?" I asked.

"What is there for me to be upset about? You're the one I want," he replied.

"Did you tell him that?" I asked.

"In so many words, I did. Listen, I wasn't trying to make him feel worse. I didn't lay it out in those terms, but he left the conversation knowing that you and I have a deeper history than he and I have and that it's you I'd want to pursue. That's when he said he would step back," he said.

"I guess I need to reach out to him."

"You should. I have a client about to come in. I'll check in with you a little later, okay?"

"Okay, I'll talk to you later."

I kept my head buried in my arms and I cried some. My heart was hurting at the thought of losing my best friend, the one who had been by my side since that dreadful day in middle school. I loved him like the brother I never had. It seemed like this thing with Orlando has cost me everything that is dear to me, Tyler, and now Alec. I lifted my head and dried my eyes. I dialed Alec to only get his voicemail. I left him a long message. I hope he hears it and wants to talk. I can't take all of this heartbreak that's happening to me all at once.

Thirty-One

Chapter 31

I left the balcony and eventually left the apartment. I brought my sorrows down to the street level with the cars driving by my building. I needed to go for a jog around the block. The wind was still up. I plugged up my ears and turned on some Beyoncé and hit the pavement. The sun was out bright and beautiful. I took off and headed west. Atlanta's West Peachtree Street was all the buzz with cars honking and traffic still bumper-to-bumper. I made it a couple of blocks down the road only to run into the perfect stranger who was out for a jog as well.

"I thought you were gone," I said.

"No, I leave this evening," Tyler said.

"It's good to see you still do your jogging."

"Yeah, I have to stay fit. If I had known you planned to jog, then I would have waited for you. I know you just started. Do you mind coming with me over to the Which Wich shop?"

"Umm, I guess so, but I haven't jogged as much as I need to. I don't need to be eating."

"C'mon, for old times' sake," he said.

"Well…OK, I guess so." It was so good to see a friendly face after what I'd been through, but I couldn't talk to him about what I'm dealing with. We jogged to the sandwich shop. He opened the door for me as we walked in.

"Want to sit in our usual spot?"

"Sure," I said. It was starting to feel a bit awkward for me. The sandwich shop was breezy, and the patrons coming in and out were steady. We stood in line behind a white girl who was chatting away on her phone. Being here with Tyler reminded me of the simpler times we had before we got all educated and estranged.

"Yeah, let me have a Philly. Do you want your usual?" He turned to me and asked.

"Yes, please," I said.

"And please add a meatball hero."

I felt special when he ordered my food for me and remembered what my favorite was. Tyler and I would come to this shop every Saturday after we did our morning jog together. I missed those times. I bet he did too. As we stood and waited for our spot to open up, we exchanged niceties. He pretended to be interested in how work was going. Then he talked about the apartment and how he hated moving. Turned out he was definitely going to move to D.C. CNN had promoted him again! He was so fucking lucky. He was going to be a White House reporter. It was step two in his aspirations for White House correspondent. So this meant more airtime on the national platform. He was getting closer to meeting Don and Wolf and boy oh boy, Chris Cuomo. He's so cute.

I congratulated him and told him I think D.C. is the perfect spot for him. All the while we were talking, Tyler played with the napkin holder, tossed ketchup packages. He just couldn't keep still. I wondered if he was nervous or something.

"Order for Hunter is ready," a girl shouted.

I made my way to our spot which was conveniently available. I sat and watched Tyler from behind as he grabbed our food from the counter. He was in grey jogging shorts with black tights that extended down to cover half of his calves and then I saw his very beautiful, dark skin. His ass was firm. Wow. I had forgotten how attractive he is. I couldn't remember the last time we had sex. It had been a minute. He made his way to the table with our food.

"Here you go. This looks good. Let's eat, shall we?" He said.

I begin to unwrap my sandwich and he unwrapped his and immediately took a bite then he looked up at me while chewing to find me looking at him.

"What?" He said.

"This feels…I don't know…weird. Don't you think?"

"Why? It feels fine to me," he replied.

"Tyler, come on. We are broken up. Some bad things have gone down between us. Why are we sitting here like Opie and Andy at the jailhouse? Just best of friends now huh?" I said.

"Brandon, I know a lot of shit has gone down with us, but that doesn't erase the years of friendship we had underneath the relationship. Listen, I have come to realize that we probably have just outgrown each other as far as a relationship is concerned. My cheating and yours were just the symptoms of it. You and I were afraid to tell each other the truth about how we have grown apart. I am okay with that now and I have come to peace with it. Does that mean I don't miss you? No, it doesn't. I love you and I always will, but sometimes loving someone means you have to love them enough to let them go. Now eat your damn sandwich and stop being fucking mushy," he smiled. I hated him so much and loved him even more!

"Well, I guess I have nothing to say to that then."

"You shouldn't. You know I'm right as usual," he said.

I rolled my eyes. "Yes, Tyler. What would the world do without your wisdom? Sarcasm intended."

"Don't get your ass slapped," he said.

"Well...I mean...you always did slap it well," I said with a grin.

"Anyway, boy. I meant what I said though, for real. I'm okay with us. I want you to be happy. If Orlando is who you want to pursue, then I can support that. Don't invite me to the wedding, though."

"Who says I want him?" I said. Tyler just looked at me with a side-eye and then continued to eat his sandwich. "So you think I want him?" I asked.

"Listen, Brandon, no one knows you as I do. So I know that if he is the one you were cheating on me with, then it was not just because you needed sex. As I said, I'm good with it now. Yeah, at first I was pissed off, but I worked through that."

"Wow, I don't know what to say. I didn't think you and I would ever get past what happened. I didn't think we would ever talk about him like this."

"Well, I didn't say I wanted to talk about him and you like that either," he said.

Tyler balled up his wrapper and took a sip out of his drink. He was done with his sandwich.

"Well, let's find something else to talk about as it concerns me," I chuckled.

"Always about you, huh? Ok, well, whatcha got—How's the documentary coming along?" He asked.

"Umm, it's going. I got a good mix of participants in it. It's been good so far, but I do feel like it's dragging and I don't know how to fix that," I said. I was still eating on my sandwich. I had half left to go. I was eating slowly. Whether I was doing it on purpose or not, I don't know. Either way, I was getting more time in with Tyler.

"Remember what I told you the first time you told me about the documentary. One of the key things about a documentary that makes them engaging is the telling of a story, and with that story, you need to have a main character where a journey can be followed, an educational or revelatory one. Think back on how we executed *The Bow after the Storm.* The story followed Tyree and his stabbing death, and as we took a journey to his relatives to share his story, we expanded on that by educating the audiences about the society he lived in. So ask yourself, what is your main story and how are you building a narrative arc around that? You'll want to master that because even with your shows for the station, it'll be the same format, just to a lesser degree. Yes you are telling the news, but you are also telling a story, and the best way to stop it from dragging is to have a plot outline in place," he said.

I sat and listened to him intently. It felt like how we used to be where I sat like the student and he was the master and I would soak in his natural gift for news telling. My eyes were dreamy, and I felt my mind drifting into reminiscing on how simple times were before the degrees came. My daydream didn't last long as I was met with an interruption of my phone vibrating. It was Alec. I silenced it, Tyler noticed but didn't comment on it.

"Let's get out of here," he added. We got up from the table and walked out the door. As we walked towards our building, I began to speak, after all, I still felt like he was my best friend.

"Thank you for that, it will definitely help, and you are right. I think that's just what the documentary needs. Well, on another note, and I know not to talk to you much about Orlando, but…" We were strolling down the sidewalk, almost hand-in-hand except they were not touching. I paused what I was saying because it really felt weird talking to Tyler now like we were not lovers anymore.

"But what?" He asked

"I found out last night that he has been dating Alec for the last year and a half."

"What? Are you serious?" He asked.

"Yea, but it's not what you think though. He didn't know Alec is my best friend. He was calling himself telling me about all of his dates and as he started to describe Alec, I put two and two together."

"Damn, that's messed up. Wow-what are the odds of that huh?" He said.

"I know! I told Alec this morning. He got pissed at me for not telling him last night as soon as I found out. He called me some really bad names. I haven't talked to him since."

"Wasn't he supposed to come up here tonight?" Tyler asked.

"Yeah he was, but he's not anymore." We started to cross the street and then Tyler stopped me. I thought he was stopping me from walking out in front of a car, but no he looked me in the face.

"Look, don't you lose that friendship over a man. You know Alec has been there for you since you two were teens. Don't let that shit go down like that," Tyler said.

"That's not my plan. It happened the way it did because he was insulting me so I just told him I couldn't talk to him like this and ended the call. Orlando told me that Alec said I could have him I guess, whatever that means. I still haven't talked to Alec directly again myself though," I said.

"I'm going to tell you again, you need to make sure you fix this with Alec. You two need to talk this out. It sounds to me like a big misunderstanding and you two will need to get on the same page about it. If you didn't know and Orlando didn't know then you need to work that out. As far as I think, that shouldn't even be up for debate. You need to call him," he said.

"I did and left him a voicemail. I haven't talked to him since that," I said.

"Is that why he called you just now? Why didn't you pick up?"

"It just wasn't a good time, and I'm still hurt by all of it."

"I'm sorry to hear that then. Give him some time, but you do need to make it your business to work this out with him."

"I will. Thank you though."

"For what?"

"For just being you. I'll be forever grateful to have a friend like you in my life. I was blessed to have you as a lover as well," I said.

"There you go with that mushy shit."

Tyler and I walked back into our building together for what would be the last time together until the day we moved out. I had never lived with anyone else but him in the last 10 years of my life. It would all be new for me.

Thirty-Two

Note from the Author

Thank you for following Brandon's journey with his relationship with Tyler. I depicted this volume of The Bow to highlight some of the real struggles gay men face in relationships. HIV is usually a happenstance in every gay story to where it has become a typical trope. I wanted to tell HIV in a different way. I wanted The Bow II to depict HIV as a chronic illness that is not any different than being diabetic or having sickle cell disease. It's something that is manageable, and it's now time to decry the stigma surrounding HIV. I know a lot of HIV-positive people and all of them lead strong, productive lives. Some are married, and many of them are very well off, but we don't see this depicted a lot in black gay fiction. It's time to change that.

I also wanted to share the nuances that take place with M2M gay relationships. We shouldn't try to always follow the heteronormative playbook for how relationships work, because there are no gender roles to explore. I believe a successful M2M gay relationship calls for abandoning heteronormative gender roles and responsibilities in all areas including sex. I also believe gay men have the responsibility to deeply explore why they are with a partner before it turns into something long-term. Oftentimes, two gay men can easily get together because of the camaraderie that takes place between men naturally, which in fact makes them great partners but that doesn't always mean they are fit to be great lovers.

I wanted to also highlight how relationships reveal the issues that we have not worked on, and if we don't work on them, we will find ourselves using our partners to compensate for what we lack or we will run from the relationship. Just as Orlando says in the narrative, 'Relationships comes to show us our shit,' we should always be cognizant that a breakdown in a relationship is nothing more than a mirror on the two partners in it. Oftentimes, we only want to see the other person's issue and never our own. The success of a relationship boils down to expectations and perception.

Brandon's journey is complicated. I showed his growth from a naive boy who, in The Bow I, wanted religion to solve all of his problems to a young man who had begun to step into his own modes of exploration. I was happy to depict him sexually exploring himself or showing that although he was highly educated with a high-level job, he wasn't above getting high to take the edge off. He's you, he's also your best friend, and he's the guy you used to date. He's all of us. The point is he displays the sides of us that we want to hide from the world. He's lonely in the novel because of his upbringing. He has years of trauma that he has not fully dealt with, and as a result, he doesn't know how to show up in his relationship as a whole man. He needs Tyler to compensate for what should already be fulfilled spaces within himself. The Bow series will continue and conclude with further exploration of what drives Brandon's difficulties. Please join my mailing list to stay updated on The Bow Series.

About the Author

Jay Tripp is a contemporary LGBT new adult author. *The Bow Series* is his first fiction series. He is an advocate for equal rights for socially marginalized groups and writes to effect change in attitudes towards them.

Please follow me on social media, check out my website and join my mailing list!

Also, journey over to Apple Music and add The Bow II Forbidden Romance Playlist to your library!

You can connect with me on:

- http://jaytrippwrites.com
- https://twitter.com/iamjaytripp
- https://www.facebook.com/jaytrippwrites
- https://www.instagram.com/ jaytrippwrites
- https://music.apple.com/ us/playlist/ the-bow-ii -forbidden-romanceplaylist/pl.u-1jkVsKD5xZ9

Subscribe to my newsletter: https:// mailchi.mp/ 6f17bb61498a/ the-bow-jay-tripp- writes

Also by Jay Tripp

The Bow After the Storm

Discover how Tyler and Brandon's journey started off in the first volume of *The Bow Series.* Their journey is rich and fulfilling as they navigate their sexualities and family dynamics.